Death of a Cloudwalker

Death of a Cloudwalker

E. S. Russell

Walker and Company
New York

First published in the United States of America in 1991
by Walker Publishing Company, Inc.
Published simultaneously in Canada by Thomas Allen & Son
Canada, Limited, Markham, Ontario

Library of Congress Cataloging-in-Publication Data
Russell, E. S. (Enid S.)
Death of a cloudwalker / E. S. Russell.
     p.   cm.
ISBN 0-8027-5784-7
I. Title.
PS3568.U766D4   1991
813'.54—dc20   90-28687
                      CIP

Printed in the United States of America
2 4 6 8 10 9 7 5 3 1

The following publishers have granted
permission to use quotations from
copyrighted works: From *Joys and Sorrows*,
by Pablo Casals (as told to Albert E. Kahn).
Copyright © 1970 by Albert E. Kahn. Reprinted
by permission of Simon and Schuster. From
They Chose Honor, by Lewis Merklin, Jr. Copyright
© 1974 by Lewis Merklin, Jr. Reprinted
by permission of HarperCollins Publishers.

For Stan, of course

I want to thank Shaye Areheart for introducing me to Ivy Fischer Stone of the Fifi Oscard Agency. Their warmth and generosity opened a door that had been closed to me for a long, long time.

And special thanks to my editor, Janet Hutchings, for her support and guidance.

My mother used to say, "Every man has good and bad within him. He must make his choice. It is the choice that counts. You must hear the good in you and obey it."

Joys and Sorrows, Pablo Casals

To have a life, you have to make a choice about how you're going to behave.

—*They Chose Honor: The Problem of Conscience in Custody*, Lewis Merklin, Jr., M.D.

Prologue

THERE WERE A few moments here and there, but only in the beginning, when the pain eased just enough to let me think.

I thought: If Jean had been wearing boots instead of — stupidly! incredibly! — his own handmade moccasins. . . . If René had gone to a dentist on the way south, when his tooth began to twinge, instead of on the way north, when it practically erupted. . . . If mice hadn't shinnied down the rope to my "safe" pack suspended from the rafter, and eaten most of the food in it. . . . If I had just gone straight down to Wesser and bought something to eat and called my father. . . .

If in my excitement I had only remembered — God! so simple! — that my left foot was my dominant foot. . . .

Funny, I thought at one point, funny that I didn't have any sensation of coming down. It was more as if the air supported me for as long as it took every rock under me to rise out of the ground and smash into my various parts. . . .

I realized after a while that I was swallowing raindrops. Tastes good, I thought. Okay, time to go. You've rested enough. Still got to get to Wesser. Okay, *up* now. Dad will want to know you understand about the mountains now.

You have to tell him how you experienced the mountain not as a lump of earth but *as* a mountain. How you felt it thrusting up from its roots in the earth, pushing up to the heavens and taking you with it. How you felt no longer just *on* the earth but *of* it, your frail mortality rooted in the whole world, whose pulse beat steadily under the soles of your feet. How you became, in some wondrous way, part of a grand, glorious continuum, truly a fellow man now, one with everybody who has gone before and everyone living now and all the lives to come, for as long as the universe lasts.

And toward the end I thought, if I, a total stranger here, but in any case a man of good will, truly a fellow man, had not been made to pay for other people's crimes and other people's anguish. . . .

That was after the man and the dog left.

But before that, when I still believed I was a fellow man, a man of good will, I said, *Up* now. *Now.*

Nobody got up.

I could hear my will command me. The head obeyed, but only a little bit, maybe because it was lower than the rest of me. The right foot moved too. The rest stayed put. The left leg was oddly twisted. Arms — well, I wasn't sure where they were.

I was enraged. I was lying in the skin of an enemy that disobeyed me. I began yelling for me to help myself, my yells of rage simultaneous with assaults of pain from the enemy.

My cries got weaker. I rested, or fell asleep, or something, and then the rain beating on my face woke me up and I yelled. Scolded. Pleaded. And lay there.

After a while the enemy began to cry because I was so angry and hurt so much. Crying won't help, I said when the pain stopped a moment, and I yelled again. No response but the wild wind hurling the rain around. The pain came again and nothing else mattered. . . .

My teeth were chattering with cold, and the bruises on my bare legs burned like fire that had no power to warm me. I peed my shorts and my crotch was hot, then quickly cold again. I was colder than ever, and ashamed.

Under me was a painful thing. An arm. I began to want to get it out of there. Promising not to scream, I arched my back and rolled onto my left side. This did something unspeakable to the leg. The arm came barely out from under. Nothing about it worked.

They were scraping my face with hot wet sandpaper and blowing a piercing whistle. I opened my eyes to see what they thought they were doing.

They: A healthy young hound, wet and enthusiastic. I said hello boy and good boy and yelled, "Help! I'm down here!"

A shrill whistle, and a man's voice. "Ah *know* thet. Latchin! Latch! Git on up heah!" A light voice, slightly nasal.

The dog scrambled away up through the shrubs.

A yelp of pain. Then silence.

2

I yelled, "Don't go! Don't leave me!"

"Furriner!" The voice came floating down. "These hills ain't yer playtoy. Funnin' y'self in mah country, are yuh, whilst we'uns starve? Wal, yuh got y'self in it, so get y'self out. Die there fer all a me 'n' mine — die 'n' rot!"

He went away, the dog Latchin baying, and the only sounds left were the wind and the raindrops plopping on the leaves and a terrible kind of crying that I'd never heard before.

$\bigtriangledown$

1

I WAS EARLY, WITH time to plan my moves depending on how the luncheon went. Life being the series of malign impersonal forces I seemed to attract, I'd learned the You Never Know Principle and the In Case Principle. And their corollaries, Trust No One and Take Nothing For Granted. I was considered a pro at planning.

As a man I was a failure. Not many people knew this. I'd worked hard on my persona. I told myself not to be bitter because it wouldn't help. Sure. And if I had a nickel for every time I'd said that, at least I'd have a lot of nickels. Still, this was a perfect New England day to start a career in, a day too clear and clean for bitterness, that filthy creature that chooses to lie in its own ordure. So I locked my wild animal in its cage. My analyst couldn't say I'd learned nothing in fifteen years.

Sure. And under the layers of knowledge I'd racked up beat a vengeful heart so steeped in bitterness that sometimes I was amazed by my ability to simulate the behavior of a normal human being.

I parked in front of a coffee shop before noticing that the door was up three fan-shaped steps *sans* banister. A person could take a hell of a fall. I was a pro on falls, too. Few people knew about that, either.

Just then the door flew open and a girl rushed out, saw me, and teetered on the top step. If she hadn't stopped, she would have plunged into my arms and smashed me on the pavement. She was beautiful in a large healthy careless windblown way, with thick shoulder-length hair the color of honey. I smiled before I knew whether I could or wanted to.

She smiled back a little and came down the steps. "Hi," she said, and blushed nicely. "Look. This may sound crazy, but do you have half

5

an hour to spare? Not that it'll take as long as that. I mean, would you be willing to witness my wedding?"

"In there?"

She shrugged. "No, but it would be as good a place as any."

"All right," I said. "Lead on." It was something else to think about before that luncheon.

She nodded and went by me and across the street at a run. A car honked irritably.

"Hey!" I yelled. Running I hadn't mastered.

She looked both ways this time and came back. "Sorry." Another nice blush. "A person gets kind of caught up. I'm Pat Elliot. I'm a grad student. Sociology." A distant carillon began chiming the hour, and she made a face. "And I'm late."

"I'm Toby Frame. I'm a new associate professor. Psych. I'll be doing some work with your chairman—"

"Acting chairman!" she said with a nasty emphasis. Freckles stood out on her suddenly pale face.

"—and I'm early."

The freckles faded. She said very properly, "I'm glad to meet you, Dr. Frame. It's nice of you to help me out. A friend of mine was supposed to be here, but obviously something happened. And my, uh, Bill's waiting for me at Town Hall. Just up that hill and around—"

We drove.

The town hall, which I'd been in before, dominated the Common, its nobility and function unimpaired. No one had been allowed to smother it in plastic, stuff it with insurance agents, and stick the citizenry with an off-Common substitute in raw pink brick. Which meant that town business was a bit squeezed, but so what? To New Englanders the road to integrity, for which read continuity, is paved with discomfort of one sort or another. If we cushion it with smugness, again, so what? Anyway, some of us have little more to hang on to.

I followed Pat Elliot into the beautiful building, my fractionally arrhythmic gait sounding assured on the bare floor. We stopped at an unmarked door, which the blushing bride opened with no enthusiasm. The room was dark and smelled of dust, and it was filled by a table flanked by armchairs and littered with books. At it sat a slender girl, head propped on near fist, scribbling on a big pad. A shaft of light from the one dirty window created a nimbus around her blond curls.

Pretty theatrical, I thought sourly, then realized with my usual tardy recognition of Truth that the ceiling bulb was missing. Anyway, here's

6

the friend and I can go, I thought, suddenly depressed. Then she looked up, and I managed not to make a wrong noise.

The girl was a man of about thirty, with an epicene face that looked harried and exhausted. His eyes flicked from the girl to me and back again. He scowled faintly. "With you in a sec—had a thought—can't risk losing—"

He went on scribbling, reaching for a book even as his pencil flew across the paper. As if there were an eye in each fingertip, his left hand opened the book, flipped pages, stopped at one. Grunt of satisfaction. Place noted. Book discarded. Sigh of fatigue. More scribbling.

Pat Elliot looked at him, her lovely face impassive. I asked myself what was going on here. The affect, as we say in my racket, was false and bound to have a bad end. That someone in my position should give this marriage tacit approval was equally bad. For once my morbid curiosity about people and their motives, masked by credentials and sanctioned by society, vanished in a wave of shame.

I decided that I didn't owe these two anything. Mumbling an apology for form's sake, I reached for the doorknob. It turned in my hand and the door opened so abruptly that I lost my balance and fell against a chair.

An untidy sliver of a man in a black suit and Roman collar nodded at me cheerfully and came in. "You the witness? Good. Morning, Pat, Bill. Hell of a morning so far. Funeral at dawn, God knows why." He tugged at his collar as if it were a serious but not intolerable restraint. "Well, let's get cracking, shall we. Won't take a minute. Then we can all pop off."

He opened a small Bible that sprouted slips of paper and waited impatiently while Bill swept his things together with a practiced hand.

I timed the ceremony. A minute and twelve seconds including the Inowpronounceyou. No rings. No kisses. The priest and the groom said 'bye and darted away, Bill first.

The girl stared blindly at the doorway.

"Can I give you a ride anywhere?" I said, appalled.

"No. It isn't necessary. Thank you anyway." Her voice was a strangled whisper.

But we stood there immobilized by embarrassment. And grief, it seemed to me.

Saying something about somebody kissing the bride, I put my hands on her shoulders and bent to kiss her cheek.

She stood stiff and unyielding for a moment, and then with a little cry she came into my arms and turned her lips to mine.

$\triangledown$

2

PAT ELLIOT LIVED IN a cottage that leaned sadly in a jungle of bull brier and chokecherries. She hadn't spoken except to direct me to it, and only nodded, looking away, as she got out of the car.

I was now totally out of sync with the day and late for the lunch being given in my honor. If I hadn't made a dry run to the place earlier in the week, after meeting with the Project team, I'd have been lost and inexcusably late.

An antique house, its Historical Society plaque prominent on the mauve-pink clapboard. Shutters some shades deeper in hue. Dark-blue door. Original brass knocker, well polished. I used it approvingly. The university knew what it was doing, keeping a house like this to entertain in. A bit far from the main campus, but still, class. I'd been right to listen to my adviser and come here. "They're hot after you," he'd said, "and not without reason. But not everybody'll put up with a tight-ass like you, so for godsake loosen up and enjoy it and stop looking gift horses in the mouth. And I don't want to hear *try*. Just *do* it!"

Madge Hendron (Music), a serenely beautiful woman in worn, excellent tweeds, welcomed me in without fuss. I assumed then that the house, which complemented her so beautifully, was not the university's but hers, and the day took back its right shape. But once more things lurched out of joint as I followed her. In the pleasant surge toward me, no one, I thought, noticed.

I got my usual quick wide-angle impression of the inanimate things first. Some fine antiques, mixed with a miscellany I'd seen only in museums of modern art or ultrahigh-style magazines, things you'd expect to stand out screaming from the traditional. But a chair made of three thin bent pieces of highly polished metal, just three and no cushions, stood by a fussy Victorian love seat as comfortably as if both had been created in the same era. And that was only one example. Risky, successful, and very, very pricy. Definitely not university property, or Madge's.

She smiled, reading my thought. "This is Ault's house."

Dr. Allyn's house? Dr. Ault Allyn?

Well now. Checked again. I had assumed that I would be meeting someone old and bent, tiresomely serious, dry as dust. My doctoral dissertation, which concerned, from my point of view as a clinical psychologist with strong Freudian leanings, the hows and whys of choice-making, had garnered a letter full of gentlemanly enthusiasm from this quintessential scholar. A friend of his at Harvard had read my paper and had told him that a sociologist should develop a concept it had only alluded to, namely, that choices whether consonant or not with an individual's psychology are often at odds with his subculture as well as with the job opportunities open to him, and that the stress resulting from this collision can critically affect not only that individual but his community. Dr. Allyn asked my permission to develop this idea. I thanked him and wished him well. Several months later he wrote that his proposal to study the history, sociology, music, and perhaps the art of his university town from this perspective had been impressively and largely locally funded. He added offhandedly that Grier Mitchell, Psychology chair, was looking for an associate professor, part of whose job would be to join his, Dr. Allyn's, interdisciplinary project team.

On my adviser's urging I wrote to Grier, and was hired immediately. Then came the luncheon invitation, Ault's name not on it. I assumed not only that Grier would be the host but also that various public types would be invited, since the Project (we never called it anything else) would be delving into every aspect of their community. But only five people were in the room. It was obvious from the remains of the canapés that I'd been keeping them from the next step.

I was now ass over tea kettle with confusion. Not even Harvard or MIT housed exotics like Ault Allyn. I thought I'd learned preparedness, which included refraining from acting on an assumption until I had all the facts to make one. I had no way of knowing that by the time I learned what I had to, it would be nearly too late to profit by it.

Ault was in his late forties, tall, lean, and hard, with fine features and an open manner. His voice was light, his speech seeming to come from the bridge of his nose, like a well-bred Englishman's, and he was superbly dressed. After a few minutes I decided that all the surprises about him were congruent here and that I'd never again be rocked by anything about him. What did Pat Elliot hold against him? Probably he'd given her a low mark once.

He held out a strong slim hand to me, and my persona took over and did all the right things. Then he went into the kitchen.

Relaxed now, I said hello again to John Meiklejohn (Anthropology), Vincent James (History), and my new boss, Grier Mitchell, a gaunt weary man.

Meiklejohn, a friendly slob several years older than I, said, "Here. World's best martini. And have some cheese."

James, a dried nervous fusspot, mumbled something dismal about alcohol, salt, and cholesterol.

"Come on, Vin," Meiklejohn said. "Let up, this is a party. Have one of my specials. We only live once."

"True, but the question is *how,*" Vincent said. "And you know I gave up drinking ten years ago. Alcohol's poison."

Meiklejohn whistled silently and shook his head.

Then Ault called us to the dining table, its damask cloth gleaming with fine silver, china, and crystal, and served us a creamy mushroom soup, veal casserole, a vintage Medoc, and a hot French baguette. Salad was Belgian endive and sliced kiwi, subtly dressed. The custard tarts were exquisite, the coffee perfect. The finest French restaurant couldn't have done us any better.

What is this guy, anyway, a goddam Renaissance man? I thought sourly.

Ault was appealingly concerned that we like the casserole, which he'd been working on, he said, for some time. "The other batches—" He shrugged.

"Other batches?" Madge said.

"I threw them out," he said, and she moaned. "But not the last one to this. It was too close."

"Ault's our in-house perfectionist," Meiklejohn said jokingly. "Say, Toby, how would you analyze a perfectionist?"

I could feel Ault's eyes hit me like twin bullets. I laughed. "As a man after my own heart."

"Do me a favor, Ault," Meiklejohn said. "Next time you cook up a culinary bomb, call Madge and me. We'll force ourselves to suffer."

Vincent James looked green. He'd carefully separated the meat from the mushrooms, then pushed everything around on his plate, making a disgusting mess.

Ault appeared to notice for the first time. "Vincent seems to have done just that. What's the matter, Vin?"

"Sorry," Vincent said. "I don't eat veal. Thought I told you that, Ault." He turned to me. "Ault always asks his guests what they like to eat and don't like to eat, you see. It's one way for a perfectionist to guarantee a perfect meal. But. I Don't. Eat. Veal! Ever see pictures of the way calves are raised? Cruel. Cruel. Anyway, I'm allergic to it, it gives me diarrhea. Always did. In fact, whenever I have diarrhea after eating unidentified meat, I always know somebody served me veal."

"For godsake, Vincent," Grier said.

Ault apologized to Vincent gracefully, easily, as he did everything, saying he'd make up for it. Madge turned the conversation to the Great Artist concert series. No one made insincere offers to help in the kitchen, no one mentioned the Project, no one smoked or wanted to smoke or went out to smoke, and a good time was had by all except Vincent James, who ate bits of salad and bread as if they just might be culinary time bombs. Before we were finished with coffee, he excused himself and rushed out of the room.

"Vinnie's a health freak," Meiklejohn said. "You should see his linen closet. You've never seen anything like it except in a drugstore. A thousand years from now, some earnest bugger like me'll dig out his house and figure he was the head shaman around here."

"The poor man's so worried about living well, he hasn't enjoyed one day in all the time I've known him," Madge said. "Now, what sort of a life is that?"

"Scarcely worth living," Ault said.

"Don't feel sorry for him," I said. "He's doing what he wants to do. It's his choice."

"But, Toby, surely it's not a good choice. It isn't, is it, Grier?" Madge said in her kind way. "Wouldn't the evidence suggest otherwise?"

"Well," Grier said, "we interpret the evidence from where we sit, not where anyone else does. It's Vin's choice, as Toby said. The neurotic gratification each of us gets from a choice is what keeps us from exchanging it for another choice. So one person will overeat where another will starve — or smoke or gamble or drink or whatever. We humans do what makes us feel better, however counterproductive it may seem to an observer, or indeed be. It's that simple. This is nothing

11

whatsoever to do with justifying a choice, but only to explain why what to you is a seemingly bad choice is impossible for someone else to relinquish. One man's meat, et cetera. Sorry. I don't mean to pun."

"But what kind of gratification can Vincent possibly get from all his — all of his . . ."

Grier smiled. "A person has to be crazy to listen to music every day. Better to listen to people."

"But there's nothing better than music, Grier!" she said, half laughing, half vehement. "Oh, you irritating man, I've got you now! Tell me. In one hour can you accomplish as much change with one of your clients as I do with a Haydn sonata?"

"Two months, more likely. Guess I like to suffer more," he said, and we shouted with laughter.

"But isn't that what people call sick?" Ault said. "Toby, what would you say?"

"Well, it depends," I said. "Freud is supposed to have said that being psychologically healthy meant being able to work and to love. Able to work in one's world and able to maintain sound personal relationships. If a client comes to see that one of his choices has a demonstrably negative effect on his ability to work and/or love, but he stays with it anyhow, well, you could say he's sick. Otherwise we're talking about an eccentricity or idiosyncrasy, the sort of thing that makes us different from each other. Safely different. Not life-threateningly different. To ourselves or others." I felt uneasily like having given my first lecture, and hoped Ault approved.

"That's comforting," he said, a tinge ironically. "Now then, where will you be living, Toby? You'll be coming aboard in September. It'd be pleasant to be settled in by then."

I said I hadn't yet looked for a place.

"This is the worst time to be looking for something decent and reasonable," Vincent James said. He had come in a few minutes before, bloodless and exhausted.

"I'm afraid that's true, Toby," Madge said. "Everybody's scrambling for fall as well as summer."

Ault said, "I own a four-unit apartment house in town and there'll be a vacancy within the week. Small but attractive. Or it will be when it's emptied out. The tenant's a pack rat. He hasn't paid his rent for five months but in less than a year he's loaded the place to the ceiling with all kinds of stuff."

"What are you going to do with it — or about it?" I said. "It sounds as if you'll have more than one kind of mess."

"Legally, you mean? Oh, no problem there. And don't waste any worry on him, he's had plenty of warning. Talk about choices! If you don't find anything, drop over this day week. Here's the address." He took a notebook out of his pocket, wrote, tore out the page, handed it to me. "It should be empty by then. I'll leave a key under the mat and you can go right in. If you think you'd be comfortable there, give me a week to have the place cleaned and painted. It'll be done in any case."

As I drove back to Cambridge, I asked myself if there was any end to the bounties Ault Allyn was heaping on me. And wondered why he was bothering.

Par for the last fifteen years. I couldn't even accept a toothpick from anybody without asking myself, "Doctor, what does this mean?" I was sick, all right, though only my adviser and my analyst knew it. I could work but not love, I'd acquaintances but no friends, and years of analysis had not convinced me to dig up that basic trust I'd buried, dust it off, and put it back on like the protective cloak it actually is. I didn't even know anymore where it was. Maybe Meiklejohn could help. Digging was his bag.

3

I OWED AULT FOR my job, and that was enough. It didn't do to owe anyone too much. Creditors kept ledgers, and rubber stamps saying "Overdue."

So I put away the address Ault had given me and scoured the area for a place to rent. By the end of a week I was moving like the Tin Man, in need of a good oiling. My physical therapist in Boston gave me one, and a furious warning besides. I had no choice. A week after the luncheon I drove to Ault's apartment house near the Common.

It was a Victorian ark in perfect condition, with outsize windows, cupolas, turreted towers, deep cool encircling porches, slate roofs, a marvelous clutter of gingerbread. The clapboards were charcoal gray, the trim white, the shutters deep rose. A handsome building. But it stood far back from the sidewalk, on a hill, and I looked with dismay at the steep concrete steps leading up to it. They'd be hell in winter, even with the wrought-iron railing to cling to. Then I saw the driveway, and a path from it to the huge glassed double-front doors. Good. Parking up in back.

The driveway was blocked, and the sidewalk, and the gutter, by a noisy surging crowd. I parked across the street and limped over. Boxes, baskets, and trunks spilled out their contents along thirty feet of sidewalk, and hands pawed over the stuff, making piles, stuffing pockets, bags, and handbags, snatching, tugging, people shouting at each other, angry and greedy, crushing underfoot someone's lifetime possessions. Nothing was price-tagged. No one was collecting money.

A man staggered by carrying a towering load of books and records. Some colorful fabric hung over his arm.

I asked him what was going on.

"Damned if I know." He arched his back, hiked the load farther up on his chest. "Stuff's just here and people helping themselves. So what the hell, I did too. This here's a Jap kimono, pure silk. I paid through the nose for one in 'Nam, it came apart first washing, but this is the real thing. Books're wet, damn it. Rained last night. Records prolly warped, I bet. But what the hell, if they're no good, I'll throw 'em out, right? Or sell 'em."

He was temptingly overbalanced, but I turned away. This wasn't a yard sale but a looting resulting from the eviction Ault Allyn had hinted at last week. For me it was a housewarming of sorts. Where were the police?

I reminded myself that the evictee had made a choice and stayed with it for five months. No one had forced it on him. He'd chosen to spend his money one way rather than the other, and he'd gotten the grats he was looking for, or he would have made another choice.

So I had an apartment, and no need to feel anything but pleasure at the prospect. No need, even, to see it to know I'd like it. Not that I was about to leave without a look in. Besides, if no one in Ault's house had called the police, I would, but I'd have to bull my way up the drive by car first, to stop these bastards. On my best days the least of them could knock me over like a ninepin.

A car lurched past me to a grinding stop. I carefully stepped down off the curb, paying no attention to it or to an eruption of angry shouting. When I was almost back at my car, someone began to scream, and I did turn around, morbidly fascinated as always by the way people made horrified discoveries. Sometimes they sounded like me so many years ago, after the anaesthetic had worn off. Sometimes I almost thought they were me, and for a second or two I'd have to hold on tight. I did now.

Like an enraged or frightened bee colony, the looters were buzzing around something. I went back across the street.

No need this time to ask what was happening. Bulletins were issuing from the epicenter.

"Heart attack, betcha."

"—said this is his stuff—"

"Pick 'm up."

"Give the guy some air, move back, move back!"

"Somebody do something!"

"He ain't going nowhere now, buddy!"

"I'm a doctor," I shouted. "Move, please. I'm a doctor. Let me through. Move, please, I'm a . . ."

They'd treated themselves to someone's possessions, and now they were treating themselves to his agony, always a bracing experience. They couldn't hear anything else, the sick twisted swine. Or they didn't want to.

I got into my car, kept my thumb on the horn, and roared up the driveway. I couldn't feel sorry for the man who'd been evicted. He'd made his choice *freely* — I can't say that forcefully enough — and reached the goal implicit in it. Too bad he hadn't known enough about himself to claim the victory and celebrate it. It was not a Pyrrhic victory to *him*.

So why did I bother shouting and banging on the doors? What did it matter to me that the house stayed shut, silent, indifferent? Ault's tenants could be watching through their curtains or down on the sidewalk with the rest, but either way they were unwittingly contributing to the victory. I should have been cheering. After all, we rarely hear anyone say, "I got exactly what I wanted, and I couldn't have done it without your help."

But I could have bawled — for myself, for Ault, whose forbearance had bombed, for the man whose space I was going to occupy, for the people watching him die, for the whole human race whose enormous wealth of education only made it more blind and deaf and ignorant. But I wasn't the weeping sort. I got back into my car and drove aimlessly away.

I stopped after a while, near the coffee shop where I'd met Pat Elliot, trying to muster the energy to participate in the next human encounter, like ordering a cup of coffee and paying for it. I felt utterly alone, weary to the core. All I wanted was to go back to Cambridge.

Someone rapped briskly on the windshield. It was the priest who had joined Pat Elliot and Bill (whose surname I hadn't caught) in happy matrimony. He was dancing with impatience, waiting for me to surface. He seemed perpetually hurried and late, a White Rabbit in a dog collar, and he probably needed a ride.

I said hello and offered him one.

He opened the door and got in. "And I'll give you lunch. Fair exchange. Hang a left at the corner."

We made an intricate pattern all over the town and stopped in front of a dilapidated house that had been converted long ago into a grocery store or tailor shop, with living quarters above. There was no sign on the big store window, curtained now, but nailed above one of the recessed doors next to it was a piece of wood, deeply carved and varnished, that said HELP.

"Come on," he said and darted through the other door and out of sight. His confident directness was a tonic. I trudged laughing up the steep stairway.

Upstairs I laughed again. The apartment was like his little black Bible, its significant places marked with bits of paper. Hand-lettered filing cards were everywhere—SOAP. CLEANING SOAPS. TOWELS. COATS. DESK SUPPLIES. CANNED FOOD. LIGHT BULBS—on dresser drawers, closet shelves, and bookshelves, on doors, kitchen cabinets, hooks. Over the sink, heavily underlined in red, were two: WASH UP. EVERYTHING!!!

"They work," he said, magically throwing a lunch together as if he had six hands and a wand. "People—kids—come and go. Order's next to godliness too. Look around. Some of your students will wind up here."

The kitchen, living-room, and dining-room walls had been removed and a neat galley installed on one side. Parallel with it stood a home-made trestle table for twenty people at least. On the other side of the huge room were easy chairs, little tables, and a long couch, everything shabby but clean. A stack of books had collapsed in one of the chairs, as if personifying their owner.

The bedrooms contained bunk beds, footlockers, and rows of wall hooks. In another bedroom as big as a closet and as comfortable as a monastery cell were a cot, a hard chair, and a row of African violets blooming on a sunny windowsill.

"Flowers're necessary for mental health," he said from the kitchen. His eyes too were magical and could see through walls. "Wash up," he added.

I obeyed, then sat down at the long table, feeling that I was home. I should have clutched up at this and closed myself away, but I couldn't. That puzzled me. I summoned my bitterness and suspicion, but they were on the other side of an invisible barrier. That scared me. Then the priest bowed his head and said a simple grace, and I felt weightless and free and content.

He lit on the bench like a butterfly about to flicker away. We ate without talking—omelets and salad and toast and tea.

"Forgot," he said, and shot out his hand to me across the table. "Sam Mayo. University chaplain. Church calls me its streetwalker."

"I'm —"

"Heard. Psych. Good. What'd you think?"

Conversationally he was a mountain goat, leaping from peak to peak. This one was the wedding ceremony.

"Pretty grim," I said. "Someone had to kiss the bride, so I did. And gave her a ride home."

He was about to say something when the front door slammed and someone came bounding up the stairs. "Hey, Sam! Sam? We finally got the —"

It was the bridegroom, Bill. He stopped short, then recognized me and came over to shake hands. "Sorry about the other day, Dr. Frame," he said. "Guess I made a lousy impression, but everything was happening at once. I was trying to meet a deadline. Felt like I was spinning on my ear."

"I know the feeling," I said. "How's it going?"

"Cool, man. Pat and I finally got housing, so now I can really dig in. Sam, you're a prince. Look, if you've got something I can put that junk in, how about I take it off your hands?"

The books on the chair were his. He shoveled them into paper bags, fetched a footlocker, a pile of laundry, and assorted oddments from one of the bedrooms, and put everything down at the head of the stairs.

"Have to make a couple of trips," he said. "I'll get one of the guys to give me a hand."

"My car's downstairs," I said easily, surprising myself, and helped with the loading.

"I hear you're working on this big-deal project on the town," Bill said when we drove away. "Vincent James is my adviser, by the way. Allyn is Pat's. Small world. Bear right at the fork. How do you like the place?"

I made the usual noises. Father Mayo's effect was wearing off. I looked forward to driving back to Cambridge. I'd had enough stimulation for one day, and going up and down the stairs hadn't done me any good.

"Have you been staying with Sam?" I said.

"Had to. Couldn't get an extension on my lease, and Pat's landlady wouldn't let her stay indefinitely unless she kept to the original rental agreement. One bed, one occupant, no visitors."

He didn't seem to mind, but I said dutifully, "That must have been tough on you two."

"Not really. When we're both done here, we'll get an annulment. We're just friends, we've known each other since seventh grade. Strictly platonic is the way to go in any case, man, that's my view — Pat's got something else in mind — and married grad student housing's cheaper than anything else we could find that was even remotely affordable. QED. My name made the top of the list in the nick of time. What with the residency requirement coming up, I didn't have any choice. It was get married or watch years of work go down the drain."

"Does Sam know all this?"

"Sam knows everything. The man's weird. That Meiklejohn's another one, but even more so. That guy's specially magnetized, man, I swear. What he doesn't know isn't worth knowing. He say anything? Sam, I mean?"

"Grace."

"I mean about us."

"No."

"How'd you get tied up with this project? It's a real plum, man. My adviser — James — says I may get to do some work around the edges. Hope he's right. Old fart's coming unglued. Just let him last till I'm done, or I'm in deep trouble."

"Will Pat work on the Project too?"

"Not if she can help it. Allyn's a letch. And smooth, man? Very smooth, and very clever. Marriage is no protection against a hunk like him, not in this culture and not on this campus. She's finding that out. Here we are. The brown two-family on the corner."

He was self-centered, indiscreet, and unprofessional, his affect was inappropriate, and he probably harbored more admiration for Ault Allyn than he would allow himself to acknowledge. As for his wife, there were at least two reasons why she would manufacture slander about a discriminating, cultivated man who could have his pick of women far more suitable than she. I helped her loving husband unload my car, declined offers of a pit stop or a drink, and was glad to be rid of him. I still didn't know his last name.

I called Ault and gratefully accepted his offer of the apartment.

"You'll want to see it first, I expect?" he said. "For furnishings and so on?"

"I haven't much to bring along. It's all right. It'll be fun starting everything new. When should I come?"

We settled on a date, paint colors, and rent, and I began the long ride back to Cambridge. The best thing about it was that I was at last alone.

After supper I was too tired and full of pain to read or to do any preliminary work on the Project. Tomorrow was another day. Sufficient unto it. A bath was indicated.

While the tub was filling, I took off my shirt and tie and shoes and socks, dropped my trousers to the floor. Then I slipped off the shoulder suspension, which I found more comfortable than a belt across the pelvis. Then I removed my four-thousand-dollar left leg, which consisted of a Ready-To-Fit Above Knee Endoskeletal Modular Prosthesis, Assembled On Modular Components (Number 10-2150), which was enclosed within the Finishing Laminate Socket-Furnish and Shape (Number 10-2550), and set it aside. A plastic image of my right leg but not so beautiful.

Gingerly I removed the one-ply sock and the three-ply sock from the swollen remnant of my thigh, reached for the crutch, went back to the bathroom, eased my way down into watery bliss, and switched on the turbulence.

After a while the aches subsided along with the pain in the foot I hadn't seen in fifteen years. I finished off with aspirins and brandy, and went to bed.

$\triangledown$

4

I WAS EXHAUSTED AND depressed when I moved into Ault's house, and I got the decorating over with by filling it — assaulting it — with ticky-tacky that could be delivered immediately. The apartment fought back, demanding recognition of its irritable charm, so everything went back and I began again, feeling that I'd been challenged to a battle of wits. Ault offered to advise, but I'd begun to enjoy the war and wanted to win it on my own. So away he went on vacation, as did the rest of the Project team, and I went shopping, loaded with measurements, money, and enthusiasm. Never once in the last fifteen years had I been so excited. The one thing I couldn't spend like a drunken sailor was energy. I mapped my moves like a time-and-motion expert.

The apartment was more or less done by the time the team was back on campus, and just before the summer sessions ended they came to my housewarming.

They damn nearly came to my funeral.

In a huge closet Ault's carpenter had built wine racks and cubby-holes — freestanding and easily removable — for me, and as a result of a couple of hours with a knowledgeable liquor salesman I had four cartons of choice wines and spirits to stow away there. The day of the party, in the scented atmosphere of new paint and new wood, I happily arranged some of the best things life had to offer. Various party supplies I put up on the shelf, where everything fitted in nicely except some packages of napkins that refused to maintain the neat level stacks my obsessive nature required.

I felt under and behind them and brought down from a high recessed corner a dirty old brown accordion envelope that had lain unnoticed by mover and carpenter and me. There was a smear of paint on one corner — obviously the painter had found it and put it back when he was through. It hardly seemed worth looking into. I tossed it onto the pile of trash and went into the kitchen for a snack and a cup of tea.

Curiosity got the better of me. I had had a good look at much of the former tenant's possessions as they lay scattered and pawed over on the sidewalk. What could he once have thought worth saving — hiding? — in that old envelope on a high dark shelf? I retrieved it, opened it over the kitchen table, gave it a shake —

— and almost fell where I stood, numb with shock.

My mouth went dry. My tongue swelled up like a balloon. I couldn't swallow, I couldn't breathe. Every drop of blood drained out of my head, my whole body: poured out in a flood. I grew ice-cold and began to shudder, and my jaws clattered together like hollow bones. What lay on the table like dry leaves were photocopies of two news clippings, and as I stared at them I seemed to be strangling in terror, which is the mind's vomit. For a client in this extremity I would have done — yes, and felt — everything that was correct and necessary. For myself, when I thought about it later, I had nothing but contempt and a pitiless dislike.

Slowly, hand trembling, fingers so stiff that I could hardly bend them, I picked up the clippings as if they had the power to scorch or poison, and read them. Read, in my hometown paper, the salient parts of my history for the past fifteen years: my love of walking, my accident, my father's death, my academic and professional accomplishments, my mother's death, my university appointment. Read, in the university's faculty newsletter, my appointment and the work I was to do here.

The kettle on the stove boiled out and began to hiss as I stood sick and incredulous and filled with questions. Why had the dead man kept this information about me? Had he known either of my parents? Was there some secret about me that they or some other relative or acquaintance or teacher or friend or enemy had told him? My god! — were we in some arcane way connected that my life should be of special significance to his? Where were the original articles? Had he borrowed and returned them? To whom? And how was it that, of all the stuff that had been taken out of here and disclosed to the world with such utter disregard, a worn old envelope with two bits of paper in it should have been left behind, and in such a place?

At length I put the envelope away and filled the kettle again and forced myself to eat something. I took the trash down to the Dumpster. I soaked in a warm bath, meditated, slept, woke up feeling much better. As I got ready for my company, I put the whole business aside in the belief that there was a rational explanation for that envelope of clippings, that I would find it, that there was nothing to be alarmed about. I was determined not to spoil my own party.

I was no less determined to keep Vincent James from spoiling it as he had spoiled Ault's. Serving him what sat well on that sensitive stomach of his was not in itself what he wanted, and his bellyache, though real enough, had not caused his disgusting lapse in manners. What he was after was attention of a particular kind—why, I didn't know—and because Ault had unwittingly deprived him of it, he had treated us to a display of infantile rage masked by a genuine problem. In terms of neurotic grats, he'd made out like a bandit. I refused to connive in his trap-setting. Beyond the ordinary hellohowareyou, which requires only the ordinary finethanksandyou, I wasn't going to query him on his health, and if my menu didn't please him, I would kindly but firmly manipulate him out the door and let him be sick elsewhere. He was late, as it happened, and I hoped he wouldn't come.

Madge Hendron arrived first, with a tall, narrow-necked container of white roses. "The best place," she said, putting it on the sideboard. "Almost as good as a piano. I didn't know what colors you'd picked, Toby, and white's always safe. What a lovely room. Perfect for music. I must try it out."

She flipped through a stack of records, selected a Beethoven piano trio that my father had particularly loved, and sat listening intently, eyes closed in her beautiful face.

John Meiklejohn and Grier Mitchell, who was not a team member but who I felt should be there, came next, bearing gin and Scotch. They too made themselves at home, pouring drinks in the kitchen (Grier amicably cleaning up after Meiklejohn, who never noticed), including me in their quiet talk until the music ended, keeping out of my way as I went on with my preparations.

They too were calmly sure of themselves and each other and of me, and obviously glad to be in my home. God, I wanted this! I wanted to fit in, to make friends with these people, to do well here, to prove my adviser wrong, to be what I once had been. But even as I struggled to achieve all this, I remembered the things that Bill the Bridegroom had said, and found myself defending the places where that damned priest had subtly pierced my armor. If I spent too much time with him or people like him—Ault and Madge especially; and Meiklejohn?—my bitter resolve would leak out as through a sieve.

The pictures on my walls, the AT patches I'd sewn on a couple of my jackets, the rock samples and other oddments my father and I had collected on the Trail, the growing stack of *Appalachian Trailway News* magazines on my bookshelves, all were daily reminders, as if I needed any other than my mutilated body, that I could not let that happen. I'd put away my beloved botany and spent almost half my life studying people. I needed to understand why one particular man had just walked away from me, had chosen to walk away and leave me to die. And someday, someday, I was going to find him.

I knew this, I was sure of it. I *knew* that I was going to live long enough for it to happen, if it took a hundred years. The world was getting smaller, nothing was impossible anymore. One day that vicious bastard would cross my path, and when I recognized him, that mountain man who walked the clouds on dirty feet, I had to be pitilessly prepared to make him wish, through all his long and varied agonies, that he had never been born. And I would pray that whoever loved him, as my father had loved me, and waited in vain for his safe return, as my father had for mine, would die of grief, as my father had. For I was going to smash his bones in twenty places, with a club or a rock or my walking staff, and leave him in a cold, quiet place to die.

"Hey, Toby, lighten up," Meiklejohn said, regarding me as if I were a questionable artifact he had just uncovered.

Why was he looking at me like that? Could he have read my mind? Or—

The doorbell rang. "Just wondering when the others are coming," I said. I arranged my face appropriately and opened the door.

Vincent James, with a gift in one hand and a brown paper bag in the other.

He looked worse than he had at the luncheon. His skin was waxy gray, his eyes red and glassy. "A little something for the house," he said, handing me the gift. "And this," meaning the paper bag, "is just in case. My tum's been off lately. Thought I'd better take along something bland, you know. If you'd just put it in the fridge, Toby? Maybe I won't have to bother, but I thought just in case . . ."

In case we'd forgotten how delicate he was. How much he suffered. How much of the ordinary pleasures he was denied.

"Come after dinner next time," I said in the friendliest way possible, and opened his gift. It was a vegetarian cookbook, and would in fact be very helpful. I had more reason than most to keep my weight stable. Changes in weight (and in muscle tone) played hell with the fit of my stump.

As I made room in the refrigerator for his bag, I heard him say, "I was just telling Toby . . ."

Meiklejohn the drinkmaster came in to fetch plain seltzer for him. "Know what's the matter with his stomach, Toby? Think." He was pink and expansive from martinis, and happily raveling out at the edges. "Be right back."

"Ulcers?" I said when he returned. "Gastritis? Hyperacidity?"

"Oh, all of that. And colitis. And why? Not from genetic inheritance, which is what he claims. From booze. He's been a closet drunk since he wrapped his car around a telephone pole after a big bash three years ago. His wife died instantly. He says he started his health kick ten years ago, but that's a crock. It's also great cover, and once in a while I needle him privately and he plays it for all it's worth. I think he even believes it now. But he counts every drop we knock back and then goes home and gets bombed. He eats practically nothing, no matter where he is. And you'll notice after a while that he's always the first to leave."

"How did you find all this out?"

"I gave him a ride to a meeting before Christmas. He said his car wouldn't start, but I know a hangover when I see one — seen enough of 'em, God knows. I pushed the right button — don't even know which one — and he confessed all. Said nobody else even suspected, so why am I telling you all this? He's scared witless about his career here — our president is hell and death on drug abuse, and Grier's an old buddy of his — so keep this under your hat. Where you keep everything, I suspect. No offense meant, young Toby."

"None taken." It was the correct, the gracious thing to say, but in fact his chatter was beginning to bother me. "Where's Ault, I wonder."

"Oh, he'll come, don't you worry. Think he'd miss seeing what you've done here? And he won't just like it, Toby, he'll be grateful. He really cares about this property. You know, he may have struck you as pretty damn cool about the poor bastard he threw out, but I happen to know he held back for months — he knew the guy was sick. I did too for that matter — I know his wife. Say, don't be surprised if you find some more of his stuff under the floorboards or in odd corners." He grinned his wide mischievous grin. "I knew someone who hid diamonds as big as boulders in the newel posts and stashed negotiable stocks and bonds behind door frames. So keep your eyes peeled. I wouldn't be surprised if you found some choice little item already. There were a good few in his collection."

He downed half his drink without seeing the stunning effect of this on me, and without stopping for breath went on. "And talk about your coming man! Ault's got a knack for picking winners — you're one — who add luster to his name. A few more doctoral candidates like the ones he's grooming now, and a few more items like this project of his, which is adding luster and big bucks to the university, and he'll be right where he wants to be, in the president's office. He impresses hell out of the trustees. Me too, if it comes to that."

I managed to say calmly, "But he's not even chair of his department."

"Oh hell, that's pretty much in the bag. Jesse Thomaston's been out sick for months. The talk is he's doing well, but the money's on his resigning before Labor Day. Soon as he makes it official, Ault'll be ten more giant steps up the ladder. Ah! The great man himself!" he said as the bell chimed.

I sensed nothing snide or off-key in his gossip or manner and wanted to be glad of that but was afraid to be. Had he said what he did in order to needle me? scare me? And how in hell did he know so much, anyway?

I told myself sternly to put all of this aside and attend to my party, which right now was more important to my future than anything else was. I went out of the kitchen sweating like an interior-design student facing his final critique. I took a deep breath and opened the door.

The breath clogged my throat and I gasped.

"Sorry to be so late, Toby," Ault said, shaking hands and giving me a beautifully wrapped gift. "Madge, gentlemen, meet Pat Elliot. We've been thrashing out a thorny problem her paper's presented, and because of the time I decided to presume on your hospitality, Toby. If she's in the way, though, just toss her out the window."

"Not if I know it!" Meiklejohn said in his large, pleasant way, and I said, "Glad to meet you, Miss Elliot. Always room for one more," forgetting, in my surprise, to open Ault's gift, never mind acknowledge it.

The hand the girl held out to me was very cold, and her freckles were ugly marks on her pale cheeks. As Meiklejohn followed Ault into the living room, she held me back and whispered, "Thank you again, Dr. Frame. Can we talk later?"

There was no chance to. First, Ault insisted on a guided tour, so piece by piece I detailed the whole process I'd spent so much time and money on, and held my breath waiting for approval I'd told myself

26

aggressively I didn't need. Yet when it came, thoughtful, generous, parental, I was annoyed with myself for having wanted it so much.

Then Vincent, with a strangling grasp on his seltzer glass and a cranky rasp in his voice, got going on the virtues of wild edibles, mainly herbs and mushrooms. He was wrong on a few things, things I'd learned forever, but I let them pass. What Meiklejohn had told me about him made his performance fascinating, and I might have been detachedly taking notes behind a one-way mirror of Subject waving bit of bread around and nibbling at it while nagging Examiner.

As kindly as she could, Madge turned to Meiklejohn and began questioning him about primitive music. Pat Elliot put down her plate and went into the kitchen, perhaps expecting me to follow her. Ault did, saying, "Vincent, I give up. You simply don't know what you're talking about." And Grier added gently, "Vin, take a rest." So Vincent sat back, but with an odd little air of satisfaction, as if he'd done what he'd come to do.

And I did what I wanted to do—I kept away from the girl and actually forgot about everything threatening and frightening and began to enjoy being at my party. When it broke up at two—Vin James had gone at midnight, his brown paper bag forgotten—Pat Elliot offered to stay and help me clean up. I said I never cleaned up till morning. She said she couldn't impose on Dr. Allyn for another ride. Ault said he wouldn't allow her to walk home at that hour. So that was that.

Alone, I unwrapped his gift. It was a delicate Chinese painting, in a gilded Victorian frame, of a bird on a branch and vague mountains in the background. Judging from its provenance, which was recorded on the back, it must have cost him a fortune. The card, in his small controlled hand, read, "As we toil up the mountain of work before us, let's remember to stop now and then to hear the bird sing."

It was wonderful, and just like him. But I never did cotton to the picture. Just before the Project team met to begin planning out the work, the bird sang a dirge for Vincent James, who was, as Meiklejohn had said, always the first to leave.

27

5

P OLICE CHIEF JOSEPH BURKE came into my apartment complaining about the long humid hot spell, but he looked as if he had stepped out of a gift-wrapped box. He didn't appear to know this. I didn't believe he didn't.

In summer my orthopedist, my physical therapist, and my orthotist were the only people who knew what heat and humidity, weight loss, and changes in muscle tone did to me. In winter they were the only ones who knew what cold, weight gain, and changes in muscle tone did to me. Someday the bastard responsible would hear about it while I broke him into bits.

I brought the chief a long cold drink. He drank half of it in one gulp and plunged into the questioning like a kid letting go of the rope over a swimming hole.

"What did you do with the bag Dr. James left in your refrigerator?" he said without preamble.

"I forgot about it," I said coolly. "I finished the party food over the next few days and didn't notice the bag till the fridge was almost empty. I didn't open it. I threw it out."

"Did it smell? Was it wet or greasy?"

"No."

"How well did you know Dr. James?"

"I'd seen him at one meeting and two parties. He seemed nice enough. Able in his field."

"You didn't see him or talk to him after your party?"

"No."

"What do you think was wrong with him?"

"I'm a psychologist, not a physician, Mr. Burke. His tum was off, as he put it. I believe there was an autopsy."

"You bet. Glad I didn't have to witness it. Liver was so much jelly. Real bad cirrhosis. He drink, do you know?"

"Seltzer. Herbal tea," I said, lying unblushingly, as Meiklejohn had probably done. "He was a health nut. My grandfather died of cirrhosis. He never drank anything stronger than water."

"Sure. Like some nonsmokers die of lung cancer. But James also had all kinds of vomiting and diarrhea. The gastrointestinal tract was a real angry mess from end to end. Ulcers, gastritis, ulceritive colitis, and diverticulitis, which you wouldn't expect in a bran eater's gut. At the end, the kidneys shut down and the circulatory system collapsed. Painful way to go." He watched me expectantly over the rim of his glass.

"I'm sorry," I said. "He was a nice guy." It was the best I could do.

"Did you know anything about his private life?"

"No."

"Anything about his death occur to you?"

"I don't follow."

He shrugged his immaculate shoulders. "Well, if he took reasonable care of himself . . ."

"Mr. Burke, I'm not a mind reader or a mystic, either. Tell me what you're getting at."

"You say James was a nice guy, an able professional, a careful eater, a nondrinker with a cranky gut. But the gut looks like it went through a meat grinder. The pathologist thinks death was too sudden, too violent. Says it doesn't add up."

"What *does* he think it adds up to?" I said irritably. I'd had a bad night and wanted more than anything to dismantle myself, soak the pain away, sleep for a few hours.

He took another joyous plunge. "Poison, Dr. Frame."

"What are you suggesting? Accidental death? Suicide? Or murder?"

He seemed disappointed in me. "I was hoping you'd picked up something, sensed something out of kilter. The odd man out, so to say, often does. Fresh eye and all that."

I shook my head. "It was a compatible group. I considered myself lucky to be a part of it."

"What did Dr. James eat at your party?"

"Practically nothing. Bread. Salad. Just nibbles."

29

"And at that lunch Dr. Allyn gave for you?"

"The same. And soup. Cream of mushroom soup. I remember that, because he said it was very soothing. He asked Dr. Allyn if he gathered his own mushrooms too."

"Oh? *Too?* And does he?"

I shook my head wearily. "I didn't hear. I don't know if he does or he doesn't."

"What's it all about, anyway, this project of yours? Whose idea was it?"

"Dr. Allyn got an idea from my doctoral dissertation about examining a town in depth, seeing all the forces that created it, making some predictions and recommendations about its future. He thought this town was a good one because it began on a crossroads and all kinds of influences poured in. They still do — a fine university has that effect."

"Mmm. You had a big argument here, I heard."

"Not really. There was some talk about various kinds of diets, and Dr. James got started on healthy eating. All very important and all very boring. Then he got on to mushrooms. Said he'd been out gathering them the last few weeks."

"Kind of risky for a history teacher, wouldn't you say?"

"It's risky even for a mycologist. You can eat a mushroom or fungus for weeks or months, and suddenly develop an allergic reaction that lays you out flat. Or you might eat a certain kind that, in combination with alcohol, causes a classic antabuse reaction. Or, as Dr. Allyn pointed out, if you're using a European cookbook that recommends a certain variety, you could gather an American look-alike that's toxic. This happens. Take amanita — "

"You kidding? Amanitas are deadly."

"Amanitaceae is a big family, and some amanitas are very good. You have to know what to look for."

"Do you?"

"No."

He looked skeptical.

I said, "When I was a kid I had an idea of studying botany. I used to know a lot."

"How come you switched?"

"When I was seven, I wanted to be a fireman. What did you want to be?"

"Just what I am now, Dr. Frame. I never wanted to be anything else."

He said this as if it were a virtue.

At the door he pulled a well-known trick. "Oh, by the way. Forgot to mention this. Might interest you to know that Dr. James had enough whiskey bottles in his place to open a liquor store. So now we have to find out if he ate the wrong kind of mushrooms and who and where he got 'em from, don't we. See you."

I spent the rest of the morning in the bathtub, soothing my stump and letting my thoughts wander. Who was going to replace Vincent on the team? What had Meiklejohn and the others told Burke about him? Did Burke think I'd lied about him? What was so special about becoming at twenty-five what you'd dreamed of at seven? What would my life be like if . . .

I slept.

By midafternoon I had just begun to feel reasonably comfortable when my doorbell rang. The caller was Pat Elliot, looking tired, beautiful, and determined. I couldn't hide my annoyance, or shut the door in her face.

"What can I do for you, Miss Elliot?" I said, shifting my weight to my right leg. I was starting to hurt again.

"Call me Pat. I have to talk to you. I'm sorry to barge in like this —"

"Sure."

"All right, I'm not sorry. It's just that I thought you could help me."

"Why?"

"Because of the way you . . . behaved at my wedding. And because you're new here. You see things. And I need an advocate."

"You have a husband. And a priest."

"It might seem so, but . . ."

We were still at the door. The effects of the bath were fast disappearing. "Sit down, at least," I said sharply. I limped over to a chair and sank into it with a grunt of pain I couldn't bite back. I didn't want to discuss it. I said quickly, "Hurt my foot. No big deal." The lost left foot hurt like hell. I closed my eyes.

I could hear the little sound of jean-clad thighs brushing against each other as she came toward me. "You're in pain," she said. "What can I get you? Please let me help."

I looked up at her — at everything I could never have and had long ago convinced myself I didn't want, a rich prize beyond my reach that I eyed, snarling. "There's aspirin in the cabinet over the sink," I said, and watched her go into the kitchen, erect and graceful, and come back with a glass of water and a small bottle.

I actually dozed off, yet I felt her presence and rested in the healing warmth of it. If this was all that I could ever have from her, I didn't want

31

to be any more conscious than I was. The thought roused me like a clanging bell. "Sorry," I said. "Just the heat."

She waved my bad manners away. "You're so lucky, Dr. Frame, with these nice high ceilings, and you face north and east. Where I—where we are, it's just the opposite, and we're roasting. It'll be warmer in winter, though."

"And my heating bill will hit this nice high ceiling."

She smiled and leaned back. "A trade-off."

"Isn't everything?"

"It depends on what you're looking for."

"Or what you have to to settle for," I said bitterly. I wriggled in my chair. This conversation was going in the wrong direction. I pried myself up. "I was just going out when you came, Miss Elliot. Thanks for your help. Sorry I can't ask you to stay."

"Oh—yes. Of course. I should have called. May I have a glass of water first, please? It's a thirsty day."

I hadn't expected her to say anything except good-bye. I said stupidly, "I, uh—"

She got up immediately. "You're not very hospitable." Her eyes were as candid as a child's.

"I don't intend to be. I didn't ask you to come. I don't want to know why you did. Let me remind you that I'm a member of this faculty. Your friend Bill talks too much. Don't you. Take your complaint to the proper place."

Her hand went to her cheek as if I had slapped her. "I don't know why I came either. You don't owe me anything. But I suspect," she said slowly, assessing me, "that you haven't anything to give me anyway. Me or anybody else. I can't imagine why Sam told me to see you. Or what he saw in you. You're . . . hollow. A hollow man."

She went away quickly, leaving me ashamed and shaken. I'd been so sure my persona had been fooling all of the people all of the time, and she'd found me out in one short encounter. Had the priest done the same, and sent her not to get help but to give it? Either way, she figured that I wasn't worth it.

I couldn't accept that, and didn't stop to ask the good doctor what this meant. Hopping and skipping on my right leg, I made it to the kitchen window as she opened her car door, and yelled to her to come back. She didn't hear me, or chose not to.

I propped myself on the windowsill and stared out, seeing nothing worthwhile, not even my Jag.

An old black and yellow van I didn't recognize clawed its way up the hill like an exhausted bumblebee and parked carelessly across two spaces. The front doors opened slowly, and I suddenly knew who was going to get out.

"René! Jean! Up here!" I shouted. It was almost a year since I'd seen them.

It was more than fifteen years since I had entered the Wilderness at Bly Gap, not far from the Georgia–North Carolina border, and come upon these Québecois teachers at the Standing Indian shelter about eight miles farther on. Jean Morel was muttering unintelligibly over an infected foot. His twin, René, was massaging a jaw swollen with toothache. They were on sabbatical and had set off in February to experience the Appalachian Trail from Maine to Georgia and back again, thus enjoying a double helping of spring. They were dark, short, compact, and powerful, and their voices issued like celli – Jean's frequently sour – from their barrel chests. In the smelly fringed buckskins and hooded fur jackets they themselves had made from animals they had trapped or shot, they were living images of my boyhood heroes, the trailmakers whose footprints had laced a continent together. And they radiated more joy and contentment – of the voluble passionate Gallic kind – than I'd found in anyone except my father.

On retiring from teaching they buried the buckskins near the Trail and took to jeans and bright plaid flannel shirts. They moved in a permanent fragrance of pine needles and wood smoke, and their grizzled hair and trim beards shone. They were beautiful. In the whole world they (and my adviser) were the only people I trusted and loved.

"*Alors,* T*o*b*ee,*" Jean said. He gave me a bear hug and kissed me on both cheeks and handed me over to René, who pulverized the remains. Then we adjourned to the kitchen to create a feast. Which meant that I sat down and watched them take this and that out of the refrigerator and cabinets and perform a culinary *pas de deux*.

René rolled a sip of sherry on his tongue, closed his eyes, sniffed, swallowed. A saucepan of sliced fresh pears was thrust under his hand. He doused them with wine and they were withdrawn in the same instant. "We would 'ave come sooner but the inquest delayed us."

"What inquest?"

"You deed not know?" Jean said, sprinkling spices over the pears with both hands. It looked haphazard, but there wouldn't be a grain too much or a grain too little on those pears when he was done.

"Know what?"

"About the robbery an' murder on the Trail two weeks ago. Near 'Arpairs Ferry," Jean said impatiently. I was spoiling his concentration. "Later. It is all down in ze books."

We ate salad and crepes with spiced cottage cheese, and we talked about their retirement, the van they'd bought in Harpers Ferry, my new job, my leg. Over coffee they brought out "ze books" — replicas of the greasy well-thumbed interminably detailed little notebooks I had first seen and laughed at years ago at Standing Indian. Was I supposed to know what treasures they would prove to be?

I poured coffee and served the pears and said, "All right. Now. What about this Harpers Ferry inquest?"

Traveling north through West Virginia, they had lingered on the Loudoun Heights, enjoying the wonderful views of the Shenandoah and Potomac rivers and the way Harpers Ferry nestles so cozily between them. The town, now part of the Harpers Ferry National Historical Park, was drenched in holiday. They decided to stay a day or two, study history, visit the many restored buildings, check in at AT Conference Headquarters. Since they spoke and wrote mainly in French, they were well-known there and to the general membership for their increasingly fantastic English.

"*Alors,*" René said, "we are the hill descending. I 'ave need myself to relieve. Jean continues an' I go into the bush. I the perfect place select, an' when I am finish I turn aroun' an' see the head of a man in the fairn. He stares at me an' says nothing."

"Fairn?"

He regarded me with the dry impatient scorn of the French schoolmaster, who is like nobody else in the world. "Hef-hee-har-hen. *Fairn!*"

Fern. Of course, what else?

The fern was like a collar around the silent man's head. René called out to him but he neither answered nor moved. So René made his way over, to find a naked dead body propped against a little stump. Gently he parted the ferns, and in the cool soft sun-dappled light saw a stab wound in the back but no blood, the thrust so accurate and tidy that it might have been done by a surgeon. There was no other sign of violence on the body. The plants around it were undisturbed. It had been set down here — had the murderer been too tired to carry it farther? — like the feature display in a terrarium, thought René the science teacher. Fingertips on curled tongue, he blew a shrill blast summoning Jean.

While Jean hastened down to Harpers Ferry for the police, René examined the area. He found three clear footprints near the body and determined that the murderer was tall, heavily burdened, wore a size eleven Narrow boot, and had bushwhacked from the east, heading north.

The victim was perhaps twenty and in good health. The face even-featured and handsome. Teeth excellent. Thick blond hair, expensively cut. Fleshy pad on distal joint of left middle finger: the man was left-handed and wrote a lot. Wide band of pale skin on right pinky: ring missing. Fingernails clean and well manicured: Either he hadn't been out long on the Trail or a servant had waited on him hand and foot. Out-y belly button, uncircumcised penis, high-arched clean feet. All in all, a young man lacking nothing but eyes in the back of his head.

René took pictures, then sat down in the middle of the path and thought about the crudely written note hanging from the right wrist by a length of braided grass.

And I'll protect it now.

Thirty-six hours later the murder victim was identified as the son of a prominent lumber-company executive from Asheville, North Carolina, who had offices from Georgia to Virginia. The police dismissed the note as incomprehensible, the work of a deranged mind.

The victim's family was unavailable for comment and René and Jean did not meet them then or afterward. But a company spokesman, by way of thanks, did give them a few angry minutes of his time, more or less to this effect: "Since you didn't find Sandy's surveying instruments or anything else, it's obvious all his gear was stolen," he said. "But I don't care what the ――― social workers *or* the ――― Appalachian Trail people and others of their ilk say about that note. Sandy was not working for the company, he was just practicing, keeping his hand in till school began in the fall. We deny any interest whatsoever in timber in this part of the range, and we reject utterly any attempts by some ――― mischiefmakers to deliberately foment trouble between the logging companies and the mountain people. We get along very well with folks around here, and I hope that you gentlemen will spread that word around. We employ a lot of people throughout the range. We don't have to apologize for that."

After attending a grim inquest and a lavish funeral, René and Jean bought the van and hurried north to me.

"Ah, To*bee*. If only we could this boy 'ave saved as we you saved, *n'est-ce pas?*" René said.

Like magic I was lying there, below the Jump Up, bathed in cold gray humid mountain air, a little hound dog jumping playfully about me, his rough tongue on my cheek, a man calling "Latchin! Latchin!", a nuthatch spiraling conscientiously down a tree trunk, blackflies crawling over my face, not biting, unlike their northern cousins . . . something brushing them off my eyelids, and something hard and cold against my mouth, and sucking sounds, I sucking too, a baby, water silvery and cool, and pain from things being done to me, and voices I knew saying it marched and all was well now . . .

Unable to dissuade me from my solo walk, they examined me mercilessly on my route, my gear down to the last match — everything — as if they were going to send home a report card. My father's confidence in his beardless *bébé* Jean doused in that profound French cynicism. But their amusement at my brand-new equipment was kind. They understood that this hike was a rite of passage for which everything (except of course my boots) had to be new.

"*Alors,* the Trail will take the *haute couture* out of those ball-crushers, ay?" René remarked of my designer jeans.

Exactly what my father had said, the night of my eighteenth birthday. "More comfortable anyway," he'd added, always serious about preparations for the Trail, and, under the seriousness, powerfully grateful for whatever had given him, him personally, mountains, and next after them a son to share them with.

God! how I wished he were with me. He was, simply, everything a son wants in a father. Someone to love. To emulate. To worry about: he was in the hospital with chest pains. René and Jean seized on my mention of this and wouldn't let go. The Appalachian Trail Conference discouraged walking alone. Suppose this, ay? Suppose that? Hikers were always getting sick, always falling and breaking something. *Regardez* the foot of Jean, ay? And the tooth of René, who could now eat nothing. And had I not heard of the murder of the girl in a Tennessee shelter ten years ago? And had not there been killed a young man on the Trail *en Zhorzhah* a year before? If to me something 'appen, 'ow then would feel the dear *papa,* ay? Ay? *Alors!*

More extravagantly French than ever, they appointed themselves my guardians. I laughed. I had already begun plotting how to separate from them. Well, I'd been wrong before.

Jean's foot grew worse. Two weeks earlier a stob in the path had pierced his moccasin. (A *stob* is the stub, often lethally sharp, of a sapling or other young stem that a trail maintenance crew sometimes misses.) I offered him my walking staff, but he waved it away and limped, slid, and stumbled along in the rain, tight-lipped and irritable.

At Mooney Gap we were diverted by the arrival of eight southbound Boy Scouts and their leaders, cheerful puppies all, despite the inexplicable disappearance of one lad's pack, which had vanished from the side of the path while the boy stopped to pee.

We left their noise behind us in next morning's mist. I was increasingly depressed, and realized, finally, that I was worrying about my father. I tried to shove apprehension down into a place where I couldn't see it or feel its weight, but I always knew where it was and could have drawn a picture of it and colored it unthinkable. My enforced dependence was making positive thinking impossible, and my whole self festered with resentment, like Jean's foot and René's jaw. Since my fourth birthday, when I asked my father how a flower could grow out of the sidewalk, he had taught me botany and woodcraft, and we had walked many trails together. I didn't think I needed keepers.

My right foot gave my vaunted competence the lie by shooting out from under me. My pack lurched and I landed squarely on my left hip — a fall that clapped my jaws together and rattled my teeth. I turned a gasp of pain into a sneeze and said I was fine.

But Jean and René were not. They decided to go into Franklin for some doctoring, provided I them accompany. I flatly refused but promised to leave messages along the way and to stop right where I was at the slightest hint of trouble.

They nodded unhappily and set off for Franklin, and I put away the feeling that I should be going with them. Now at last I was free — free until Labor Day, and Harvard! — to experience the wildest, most spectacularly beautiful section of the Trail, which my father and I were going to walk together next year. My pack was featherlight, the path pleasant and well graded. It was great to be alone, to think the long thoughts of adolescence, to store up each moment to tell my father. I ambled north, alert yet dreamily at peace. Oddly, my sore hip intensified this gorgeous feeling that enclosed me as in a glowing bubble.

The bubble broke at the Cold Spring shelter. I was cold and wet, and, for all my prehike conditioning and preparation, my excellent boots had blistered my heels and my pack kept shifting. And I had only some dry cereal and a little gorp left, and I was starving.

As I wolfed the last of the gorp, I saw a shapeless figure suddenly appear out of the woods, cross the path, and disappear, quick and smooth as a snake. Bushwhacking bastard, I thought, chewing mightily, wondering if I would see him again. Probably not. He'll ruin the country cutting across to save steps with that pack of his, but he'll claim to be a through-hiker, I bet. Hope he breaks his neck.

My gorp recipe was rich in peanut butter, and I began feeling better, then got mad all over again crossing a clearing bisected by logging roads, a reminder that loggers were still raping the mountains. They'd already destroyed the culture here, courtesy of their lawyers; those stains on the profession, my lawyer father said.

A couple of miles on, I skirted the empty picnic grounds at Wayah Crest and headed hopefully for the bald. The guidebook guarantees outstanding views but never the weather to view them in. I climbed the observation tower, which looked like a medieval crenelated tower in a time warp, and stood there more than a mile above sea level and saw nothing but that ridiculous tower and the eery shifting mist. On every side, stretching from deep solid greens to faint blue shadows, were mountains. Not one long spine of them but a careless tumble resembling crumpled aluminum foil. And I couldn't see — so far hadn't seen — one. Not one.

There was nothing to do but sit right there and eat dry cereal washed down with cold water. If anyone had told me how great that most comfortless meal of my life would soon come to seem, I'd have fallen off the tower laughing.

A storm stopped me at Licklog Gap, and the next morning brought more fog and rain. My food was almost gone. I was cold and wet, my legs hurt, my hip hurt, my feet were blistered. And there was no dry wood for a fire. The level ground was the only amenity.

And I was lonesome.

The admission scared the confidence out of me. I stood off outside myself to take a good look, and for once the view was clear enough. René and Jean were right — I wasn't ready.

No. If they were right, then Dad's confidence in me was misplaced. For the first time in my life? No *way*! Confidence flooded back.

I had to put miles between me and my Frenchmen — make it look as if I'd just floated up the Trail. I tied a cheerful note — "Wesser by dusk!" — to a blazed tree and took off running. My boots felt like seven-league boots — I could walk across the sky!

And then the fog lifted, the mist shredded away, and a tentative sun peeked out. I shouted with joy.

I crossed Copper Ridge Bald, then started up the thousand feet to Tellico Bald, the Trail rocky and narrow now and continuing so across

Black Bald and Rocky Bald for about two miles. I was glad to rest at the next campsite.

The world was warming up for the first time since Bly Gap, but the sun was nowhere near full strength and my wet jeans were binding like hell around the knees. I changed to shorts, wrapped my wallet in an oiled bag, zipped it into a pocket of my pack, and finished my water. After that, the drop to Tellico Gap of almost fourteen hundred feet in little better than a mile and a half was great.

I was starving, but as I crossed the Gap under the power line, I decided not to take the gravel road to the state highway four miles away and hitch to the nearest country store. Wesser by dusk, right? Not much chance of starving to death before then. Anyway, who knew how long the sun would stay out? There was no time to lose. *Alors!*

I started up the western slope of Wesser Bald. A mile and a half on and almost a thousand feet higher, I went along a rocky ledge, heading for a special place on a blue-blazed trail. Boy, was I going to see something!

If it didn't rain. *If* the sun stayed with me. *If* I didn't drop down dead from hunger. I sounded like Jean, that sour pickle.

I couldn't have known — could I have known? — that it would be a long time before I laughed again.

The Trail had been standing on end, and my jaw was grimly set from exertion, my head light from hunger, my legs filthy and scratched. Those hobnails a mountain man had once said my father and I should wear on our backsides on the downhills would have been very welcome on my knees going up.

But when I emerged onto the bald, my voice cried Lookit! Lookit! inside my head — and I gazed openmouthed and bug-eyed at a geological spectacle all green and gray and misty blue under the anxious sun.

But, the guidebook urges, the Jump Up is even better. See it before the sun flickers out like a blown candle.

The ridge crest fell away sharply on either side of the path. It was like walking on a geological razor blade. I descended heel first, my staff a shock absorber for my bad hip, the path hurrying me downhill for another half-mile to that very special rocky outcrop.

Slipping out of my backpack, I stared north at a view such as I'd never seen before, not even from Katahdin.

And then out of nowhere a heavy black curtain advanced on the sun and an erratic wind began splattering me with rain. I was being given something and in the same moment seeing it snatched away. *"Alors!"* I shouted, as sour as Jean, and stepped up onto a rock for one last look, unthinkingly leading with my dominant foot, the left one. And sailed into space.

The last note of mine that René and Jean collected was at Tellico Gap; nothing between there and Wesser, or beyond. They went all the way to Fontana Dam before turning back to comb the mountains for me. Why? Because To*bee* would not without a word 'ave left, *n'est-ce pas*? *Alors,* something him 'ad rendered silent.

They rapidly retraced their steps, separating and coming together, separating and coming together, exploring each side trail, following whatever looked like one, excusing themselves to le Bon Dieu and the AT Conference for bushwhacking to save precious time, the forest resounding with their whistled signals. They had known something was going to happen, had been wild to get back on the Trail, but the dentist them had detained by cracking into pieces the tooth abscessed of René. *Imbécile!*

Where the blue-blazed Wesser Creek path bore downhill to the right of the Trail, heading for the Jump Up, they looked at each other, then trotted single file along the ridge crest and down to a tumble of rocks. No footprints, no belongings, nothing to mark anyone's presence there.

But, *mon frère,* is it not that there is on this steep hillside below us a path of shrubs freshly damaged?

Silent agreement again, and another descent — to something that clearly had been damaged days before and that lay filthy, unconscious, soaking wet, shuddering with chills and burning with fever, left leg swollen, dirt-filled, taut with infection, and all being destroyed by the cold rain that was keeping so fresh the broken shrubs!

They stayed with me until I was well enough to be taken home. There they read to me my father's obituary and dried my mother's tears and tried to calm my anger. They were with me during the fitting of my first prosthesis, and when I argued with them about dropping botany in favor of psychology, and when my mother died, and when I received each of my degrees . . .

The crazier their English got, the more keenly I relived the terrible ride on the litter down to Wesser and, later, the moment when I knew what had happened to me. For them this retelling was an antidote to their anger and grief over the dead boy in Harpers Ferry. He had not been dead for long. By how many minutes had René missed the killer killing?

"You'd feel worse if you knew he probably wasn't too far away," I said.

"*Oui,*" Jean said heavily. "*Mais le visage de ce garçon je le vois ici*" — bending his head and putting blunt fingertips to the strong ridge over his deep-set eyes — "an' it is bad enough I feel."

"Did you get the film developed?"

He shrugged massively. "The police the film took. *Pour l'évidence.*" He snorted at the thought of a police force unable to supply its own pictures. "It will be returned one day. For ze copies of the newspapairs we to 'Arpairs Ferry must write. For ze book, *comprends*? René all of them left in the hotel on the last day." Another snort, a bitter blast. "I will send copies."

I thought about their news. "You know," I said slowly, "robbing him of identification gave the bastard time to get away. And time to stash or sell the things he took. Say, remember that Boy Scout who couldn't find his pack? Could the same guy have taken it? And my gear too? Funny if it was."

" 'Ilarious," Jean said darkly. "Fifteen years ago!"

"Well, it's possible," I said. "And I'll tell you something else. That logging tycoon had to be lying. I think the boy met a local, a good actor, a sly ruthless con artist doing a bit of hunting or whatever, and they chatted about this and that, and the kid let a few cats out of the bag about more big changes coming in the hills. The local seems a friendly sort. The boy warns him about things to come and then turns his back — and that is that. It could have been the same man. And it *could* have been the same man who left me to die! Someone who hates all of us because he's one of the dispossessed and we're so sure of where we belong that we can afford to walk away from it just to have *fun*. We know our roots — our identity — will be there when we get back. Well, I swear to you, someday I'm going to find that bastard and — "

" 'Ow?" René said witheringly. "More likely he will fin' you! For of course it was he who your wallet stole!"

I was as shaken by his ridicule as by a wild possibility I half believed in. I only shook my head stubbornly.

"A poor mountain man like *heem* tracking you in university? A ridgerunnair who the language Eengleesh cannot speak, even? Bool*sheet*, boy," Jean said.

Their scorn could still flay me alive, and even as I bled I marveled, sometimes laughed, at their passion. But this was not the time to bring out the articles I had found in my liquor closet and argue over them. I didn't, after all, want to bleed to death.

They stayed only the one night, leaving the van for me to dispose of. After breakfast I drove them to Massachusetts Highway 23, near the entry to the Trail. My father and I had walked down that road, the Lake Buel road. There I left them.

A week later they sent me a list of accidents, illnesses, deaths, robberies, murders, acts of vandalism that had been reported on the AT, items they'd garnered during or after each trip and entered into "ze books." They apologized for not having finished grouping these data so as to show similarities and possible linkages by modus operandi, date, and/or place. The film René had taken of the dead boy, and duplicates of the newspapers he had left behind, had not yet arrived. When the day came, he would make copies and mail them. *Alors! Mon Dieu,* but was it not fortunate they 'ad retired, *n'est-ce pas?* to 'ave time for all this?

Two days later René called excitedly from Quebec.

Of the burglaries, fires, and other acts of destruction reported throughout the Appalachian range either on or near the Trail over a period of twenty-five years (mostly during the summer months), three were connected with the dead boy's father and his company. Following the cutting of a road ten years ago that displaced a mountain community of some two hundred people in Tennessee, a field office was burned. Then, after announcing the building of a mountaintop summer-home development in Georgia, the father took his family abroad for a vacation, and returned to find his home burglarized and many valuables stolen. Finally, the mountaintop guest lodge of a ski resort built and owned by him was destroyed by fire about a year and a half later.

"Any notes?" I asked.

"Notes? Ah, To*bee*, this murderer — it must be the same man, it must! — 'as the soul of a poet *véritable*!

"*Un.* 'Woodman, spare that tree!'

"*Deux.* 'Touch not a single bough!'

"*Trois* — "

"Hold on!" I scrambled through my Bartlett. Page 498.

" 'In youth it sheltered me,' " I read. "Right?"

"*Oui.* Near the ski resort."

"And the fourth line of the stanza — " I said.

Had been tied to the dead boy's wrist with strands of grass.

6

No CONNECTION WAS ESTABLISHED between Vincent James's liver and mushrooms. No one had picked mushrooms. No one had given Vin mushrooms. No one had known Vin drank. No drama came out of the inquest. No one shared Chief Burke's furious disappointment with the verdict of death from natural causes.

The day after the funeral I went looking for Pat Elliot, who had stood alone in teary silence at the graveside as if she were sole mourner. I found her at the priest's place, the place labeled HELP.

She was lying on the couch like a model for a nineteenth-century French painting, large, beautiful, totally self-involved, one hand under her tawny head, the other dangling over the floor, gazing at nothing. I sat in a facing armchair and nodded hello. Her eyes flicked over me and away, as if I were an inoffensive addition to the landscape.

The day was hot but the apartment was cool and shadowy under the big oaks. I was content to look at her and wait for a clue. If she'd blasted me down the stairs with a nasty salvo, I wouldn't have been surprised. But except for that eyeflick she might as well have been framed in gilt and hanging on the wall. I stayed awake long enough to wonder what she was thinking about, then floated peacefully away.

Time passed. I came awake, sensing that I was being watched.

"I have a strange effect on you." She wasn't smiling, but under the words laughter bubbled.

I tried to close myself in but smiled instead.

"Why did you come?" she said.

"Oh . . . to apologize, I guess. I tried before — "

"Not very hard," she said, and I knew she'd heard me call her that day from my kitchen window.

"No. Not very hard. I'm sorry. I wanted to talk to you at the funeral but you seemed more involved than — "

"Anybody else? Maybe I was. Vincent was my uncle." She went on before I could mouth platitudes. "He was good in his field. A generous teacher and adviser. Otherwise, a weak, kind, foolish man. Against certain people he never had a chance, after my aunt died. He was wonderful to me. I didn't repay him very well."

"What did you owe him?"

"Protection, maybe. I don't know. I don't know how I could've . . . It was one of the things I . . . I wanted to talk to you about."

You learn how to wait, in my racket. I watched her swing her feet to the floor.

She said, "He was my doctoral adviser. I wanted to write about history. Then one day Ault Allyn was in his office when I came in, and that's when it started." She stopped and bit her lip.

"What did?"

"Ault started . . . leaning on me. In the nicest way, of course. He's smooth. He has a way of — of enveloping you. He throws a net over you and you're . . . his property. I can't explain it. He's a — a magician. You like it at first, it's flattering. But then he asks too much, and if you can't give it or don't want to give it, he threatens you. Only it doesn't sound like that when you try to tell someone. . . ."

"What did he want?"

She looked at me and away. "He wanted me to change departments. He showed me how I could without losing any credits. I didn't want to. I had no reason to. But" — she licked her lips — "but what he really wanted was me."

"What did Vincent say?"

"That was what I couldn't understand. He urged me to make the switch. He said I'd have more job variety to choose from as a Ph.D. sociologist, which is true if that's what you're looking for. I wasn't, but he said I didn't have the talent to write the kind of history I wanted to write. He'd never said that before. Anything but! I had the feeling he was reading a script. It didn't ring true.

"Then he practically begged me. Since he'd paid for all my undergraduate work and my master's and was going to get me through my doctorate, I felt I owed him something. He was my mother's oldest brother, and my legal guardian when my parents died. He was really a father to me. So – with him at me one way and Ault another way, I – "

"You what?"

She put her head in her hands and began to cry, quietly at first, then wrenching sobs.

I had been classically trained to sit unmoving and unmoved, and had always thought I preferred it that way. I sat down next to her and took her into my arms.

"He was so good at it," she said thickly. "And I hated him for being so good at it. And I hated myself for – for liking it. I thought if I got married . . . I was a fool! Bill and I are friends. We've known each other almost all our lives. He said marriage was a stupid idea but if I thought it'd help me, then okay. He wasn't looking for anything for himself. He never has. Bill's ideal self faces all challenges alone, solves all problems without outside help, takes nothing from anybody. He has to prove his worth every day of his life. But Bill is . . . he's – "

"He's gay?"

Her head moved in a nod against my chest. "But celibate. Actually I don't think he even knows where he is, sexually. It didn't matter anyway, to Ault. I could have married a stud. Ault just laughed when I told him. He hasn't let me alone. I spend more time trying to avoid him than I do anything else. I think it just sharpens his pleasure. Bill doesn't want to hear about it. All he wants now is to get finished and get out before anything else happens. He's scared a new adviser won't approve what he's already done. He thinks the more he does, the less chance a new adviser will shoot it down. He's sick about the possibility. He's . . . changed."

She sighed, exhausted, wholly lovely. I eased away from her and went back to my chair.

I didn't think Bill had changed at all, just become less accessible to her than before, as his own problems compounded. "How is he changed?" I asked.

She rubbed her eyes. "He doesn't have anything left over anymore. He's been working at white heat since high school. No family money, never any help, just scholarships and jobs. He hasn't slept more than three hours a night since he started. If this doctorate goes down the drain, he'll never start over again – he couldn't. It represents the pinnacle for him, and if he can't reach it in this one shot he'll fall off the mountain, he'll be a failure. I think it'd kill him. Or he'd kill anyone who kept him off the top. He's brilliant, Dr. Frame. He deserves to be on top."

"Deserve suggests guarantees. There are none."

"Well, he's earned it. Everybody thinks so."

I wouldn't dispute this. It wasn't important to me anyhow, or so I thought. "Well. Back to square one. What do you want me to do for you? What *can* I do? I don't see Ault Allyn as you do. How could I?"

"Would you listen to a tape? Of us together?"

"You've taped — ?"

"No. I just thought of it. Look, why not? I could wire myself and see him in his office. Or in his car. He's always trying to give me rides. Then you could hear it — what I can't explain. You could hear how clever, how subtle he is."

"No. What I said before still holds. You should take your problem to the right person, which I am not. The dean of women, say. Or a good lawyer. Did you tell Vincent that Ault had been harassing you?"

"Yes, but he wouldn't listen, he got terribly nervous and embarrassed. He was an old woman about some things. He said Ault was the most eligible bachelor on campus. Wealthy, good looks, good taste, popular, ambitious, always got where he wanted to go. It's all true, and plenty of the women I know — and some of the men — would love to have his attentions. Vincent couldn't see why I was so upset."

"He wasn't?"

"Yes, very. But he said that sometimes we all have to do things we don't want to do. Then he said that wasn't what he meant, exactly. Then he said he wasn't feeling well and I should just do my work and have a good time and not worry about anything."

"When did you tell him about using Bill to fend Ault off?"

"Almost as soon as I thought of it. He was hurt. He said I didn't trust his judgment. Which made me feel awful. He also said what Ault said, that it was a joke, that Bill was an inadequate man. And that cheap married housing and the residency requirement, which is how Bill explains our marrying, was pure nonsense, that Bill could have gotten a room in any one of a number of houses in exchange for caretaking or minimal maintenance work or whatever.

"But I went ahead with it anyway. As you know. And then Vincent said he was saddled with another problem, getting an annulment for me because I'd told him the marriage hadn't been consummated and never would be and that he was right. I felt worse than ever. Then he got really sick and before I knew it he was dead. He was so good to me." A tear rolled down her cheek. She wiped it away with her sleeve.

"I'm his sole heir and the executrix of his estate. I've moved into his house to take care of it—"

"Bill too?"

"No." She laughed tremulously. "He said he hasn't the time to move again. I told you, he doesn't want that sort of thing. If I could buy him the degree, he wouldn't take it. He has to have it on his terms. Stubborn isn't the word for him. It isn't anything to do with that."

I let this pass. Bill wasn't important to me, but she was, along with the regret and guilt she was inclined to blame on others, notably Ault. But she hadn't been forced by any agency other than her own psychology to do anything she had not wanted to do, including allowing Ault to seduce her. As a clinical psychologist, I was glad that she was learning from her experience. As a man who wanted her, I wished I had been first.

"Pat," I said, "did you know Vincent drank?"

"Not till afterward. I'm pretty sure no one did. And now everything in his house is mine, including the bottles in his bedroom closets. Oh god!"

She bent over and cried away more grief and guilt, and I used up a lot of willpower to stay put, my arms aching to hold her again.

I mumbled something about an appointment and went down the stairs as fast as I could. When she called down to me, I looked up, inquiring and innocent, a staff member, sexless and beyond reach. A cripple, whom she wouldn't want any more than the others had, once they saw what they were getting.

"Thank you," she said, blushing nicely, as she had on her wedding day.

"You bet." I reached for the doorknob.

"Your foot's better since the last time I saw you. I'm glad."

"Thanks." I opened the door. "See you," I said, and closed it firmly behind me. I could hear her scrambling down the stairs.

Before I could get into my car, her hand was on my arm. She was pink as a rose and breathing fast, her hair like honey, richly gold. I almost kissed her then and there.

"If it wouldn't be too much trouble, Dr. Frame, would you be willing to drive me home? To Vincent's house. I was trying to walk things off. I wound up here. I generally do. And now it's late."

I drew back, feeling my face go blank as I wondered how long I could keep my hands off her.

Her cheeks went pale, then flamed with humiliation. "Oh. I didn't mean to impose. I'm sorry, please forgive me, Dr. Frame. It won't happen again." She ran inside.

I asked myself if I really wanted to accept the choice she'd made for me. Because there was a certain irony here. Sooner or later she was going to know about my leg. Then we'd see who was rejecting whom.

I went back up the stairs. She was standing at the kitchen sink running the water full force and holding a teakettle, unaware of either. I turned off the water and led her into one of the bedrooms and closed the door. She was still holding the kettle.

"I want you to see something. I don't want you to misunderstand." I undressed matter-of-factly and removed part of myself and stood it against the wall. I took the cotton socks off the remnant of thigh. Naked, I looked away, waiting for the gasp of surprise and disgust I'd heard enough times to make me opt for celibacy and the occasional jacking off which makes celibacy, if not its terrible loneliness, fractionally less unbearable.

"Oh my dear," she whispered, her hand cool and gentle on my stump. "I'm so sorry." She dropped the teakettle and put her arms around my neck and kissed me. "But there's so much more to you than that."

She was the richness in the store window. I had stood so many times outside in the cold, nose squashed yearningly against the glass. And at last the door was open.

She was the picnic, healthy and bountiful in the good sunlight. I approached incredulous, starved, cautious, then marvelously determined in my long hunger.

And she was magical. The more I took, the more she had to give.

7

THE PROJECT TEAM MET in Ault's office just after the fall semester began. Ault was bronzed and fit and, as always, at ease in his elegance, unconscious of it. Meiklejohn probably hadn't changed his clothes since the last time we'd met. Madge, serene and beautiful in ice-blue cotton, hovered over Grier, who wore his usual exhausted preoccupation like a garment.

Ault picked up a pile of manila folders and was about to pass them out when Bill the Bridegroom rushed in and fell into a chair next to Meiklejohn. "I'm sitting in for Dr. James," he said challengingly. "He didn't tell you?"

"Tell me?" Ault said blankly.

"He was going to let me help with the work – and take his place whenever he was absent. Looks like I'm a permanent fixture now, right?"

Consistent son of a brash bitch, I thought.

"As Dr. James's research assistant, naturally you'd have been welcome. But one requirement for a place on this Project is of course the doctorate. And at least three years of teaching on the university level." Ault spread his hands and smiled, the very picture of graceful regret, and Bill stamped out and slammed the outer door to the corridor, a spoiled brat in a rage.

"I thought," Ault said tranquilly, giving us each a folder, "that we should begin with the question who might fill Vincent's place."

Muffled snort from Meiklejohn.

Ault smiled faintly. "I'd be relaxed about any of these, and I know the acting History chair won't oppose me on them. One's from his department, three are from outside. Look them over while I organize the coffee. Sorry it's late. I had a telephone call—news you'll be interested in."

He left us to it and for several minutes we read silently. I knew none of the candidates. Meiklejohn said, surprised, as Ault came back, "Well, whaddyuh know! Don Holmes. I knew him in Stanford. Where'd you find him, Ault? I thought he quit this racket and went into the Peace Corps."

"He did. Just returned." Ault put down a tray loaded with coffee, cake, and doughnuts. "Two years in Central America, two in Africa. I happened to catch him on a talk show in Montréal. I'd read some of his work. He's still pretty deep in culture shock, as you can imagine, but he seems sound. Well, how do they look?"

Meiklejohn said "Mm" and reached for a doughnut, then passed the plate around.

My afternoon with Pat Elliot, wonderful as it had been (and approved, startlingly, by Father Sam Mayo, who had come back, opened the door, said, "Oh? Good," and gone away), had wrought no transformation in me or my sour view of the world. I felt better—who wouldn't?—but it hadn't grown me another leg. I thought, Candidates look good on paper, even me. So what?

Meiklejohn leaned over to me and whispered, "You know who it'll be, of course. He's got a lock on History."

Grier said, "So what's the news, Ault?"

Ault smiled and reached for a piece of cake, and Madge caught at his hand.

"Why, Ault, what a lovely ring! Much handsomer than the diamond one. Carnelian, isn't it. How different. And how interesting! Your family crest?"

Ault nodded, removed the ring, and gave it to her.

She examined it delightedly. "Lions and quarterings and all sorts of romantic things. And carved right in the stone. It must have cost a fortune. I've seen things like this in books or movies but— Look, Grier."

Grier looked at it indifferently, nodded, and passed it to me, saying, "What's up, Ault?"

"Jesse will be back for the Festival. I'm giving a party for him a week from Sunday. Hope you'll all be able to come. Make a note of it."

Meiklejohn's jaw dropped and doughnut crumbs fell onto his limp shirtfront. He said thickly, "My god, Ault, but you're very cool." He gulped the doughnut down. "Jesse was on his last legs. Puts a spoke in your wheel of fortune, doesn't it? Hitch in the ol' timetable?" He took the ring from me, glanced at it, tossed it across the table to Ault.

Grier leaned over to me. "Jesse Thomaston. Sociology chair. Had a heart attack in March."

Ault finished his bite of cake. "He's only visiting. But if he were well enough to stay, I'd be delighted."

"Well, sure," Meiklejohn said, "who wouldn't be? Jesse's a good egg. But it's odds on he won't be staying. So you won't have anything to worry about."

"I'm not," Ault said, dismissive and reproving, and picked up his cup.

There was an odd resonance in his answer. I filed it for future reference, and asked about the festival.

Ault said that the Festival—with a capital F—began as a huge outdoor meal three hundred years ago, when the town was incorporated. He laughed. "Centuries passed peacefully. Then the kids began adding refinements: games, dancing, treasure hunts, and fireworks—general hijinks—so ten years ago President Knowles volunteered the dean of students to direct the whole shebang and raise some money. We send the proceeds down to Appalachia rather than abroad, as we used to do. There's a lot of money here, after all."

Madge said, "The best part of it was Ault's idea, Toby. The students kidnap the department chairs and anybody else who's specially valuable—the registrar or the bursar—and set ransom at a dollar per pound. You wouldn't believe all the ways they've thought of to raise that kind of money!"

Grier laughed one of his rare laughs. "The music majors took Madge's thirteen-foot grand out of the recital hall last year. Had Maintenance put it in the Science Building. How much ransom did it net, Madge—a thousand bucks?"

"It began to rain," Madge said, smiling, shaking her beautiful silvery head. "I was so worried."

Ault said, "I'd been thinking it would be the perfect way to open our report, you know, and I happened to mention it to Vincent. He agreed and— Here, I'll read you his notes."

There wasn't much, a handful of pages, but Vincent's writing was not merely appropriate to the Project's high purpose, it was unexpectedly witty. Little knives of regret and shame made me wriggle in my chair.

51

Grier said, "Perfect! And Vincent did a nice job on the various town factions that managed to come together. Hope we can maintain his level."

There was a murmur of agreement and approval. "Glad you think so," Ault said. "Meanwhile . . ." and led us into other things.

By the end of the afternoon I ached from sitting so long and was glad to get home and come apart. I limped across the parking lot and was about to close the back door behind me when the other tenant on my floor, a University Hospital nurse, shouted, "Hold the door!" and came barreling in as if this were her last chance to enter. She was laden with shopping bags and I was empty-handed. So.

I was glad she was leading the way and couldn't see me leaning against the wall and sliding up it for support under my half of the load.

"Angela Tansy's me name," she said, panting. "Beer? Yuh look whacked, me boy."

I was, and surprised myself by accepting. I'd never bothered talking to her before and had missed the lilting burr in her speech.

"Yer from the university," she informed me. She took tall slender glasses from the freezer and dark green sweating bottles from the fridge. "Cheers!"

Beer gurgled down into her capacious depths. "Mother o' god, that's good! I'm tellin' yuh, I'm whacked. This weather. Dunno what I'd do without the a/c. Cool enough?"

I said it was fine, but she wasn't listening. "Yer in that poor feller's apartment. Awful shame what happened. Never a bit of luck he had from the minute he moved in here. Wife at him day 'n' night 'n' walked out on him six months ago. Wasn't surprised when he kicked the bucket, that heart a his, right out on the pavement!"

"You were there?"

"You kiddin'? I was specialin' a heart transplant. I'd've bashed their heads open, those bloody bastards that stole his things, that's what I'd've done. Kicked 'em from here t' Sunday. They'd've gotten away wid nary a bloody toothpick. He'd've been alive today— 'n' should a been too, heart or no heart."

She paused to take on beer. There was no need for me to say anything. She would ask and answer her own questions until I knew everything. I settled back, liking her. Another surprise.

"Movers put everything along the walk. Jackasses. If they'd put it in the parkin' lot, at least, but down there? I ask you! Then they left. I didn't know why till next day, 'n' oh boys! if it wasn't so hard t' find a cheaper decent place t' live, I'd tell our bloody landlord t' shove his house where it couldn't see the light a day."

I sat up, neither amused nor relaxed now, and waited.

"The bobbies left," she said, " 'cause Dr. Bloody Allyn told 'em Robert's wife was on her way. Said he'd stay till she came, that she was organizin' a removin' van, 'n' everything under control. But she never came 'n' he didn't stay—'n' Bob's yer uncle!"

The phone rang. She snatched it up, listened, said JesusMary 'n' Joseph, and slammed it down. "Gotta go back—we're short-staffed 'n' me transplant's rejectin'— 'n' me wid no time t' change! Lock up, me boy, will yuh?"

"Where is she—the wife?" I yelled down the stairs.

"Bursar's office," she yelled back, and was gone.

I had to know why Ault hadn't stayed and the wife hadn't come. A man's life had fallen through the crack there.

Call Ault? Out of the question. Wait till Angela Tansy got back, whenever that might be? I'd had enough beer. Get over to the bursar's office and see the widow? Tomorrow, when they were open. I had to get a parking sticker anyway.

In the bathtub I soaked away my now total discomfort, then ate supper and went to bed. I'd be up at the break of dawn and first on the line at the bursar's. If the widow of Robert were there and willing to talk to me, I'd *know*. At least, I'd know her truth. Then maybe I'd ask Ault his.

I was at the bursar's before eight, the new day a steamy drizzle, and paced for half an hour until a skinny undergrad in tight jeans and spike heels tottered up, gave me a pert "Hi!" and unlocked the door. I felt a little rush of cool air and followed her in gratefully. She took my car registration and application for a parking sticker and went prettily to work.

I said, "I'm looking for someone I understand works here. She lost her husband recently."

"That's Doris Williams. She comes in at nine. We plebes go over the top first. Natch. I love metaphor, don't you?" She gave the official stamp an authoritative bang. "There. You're all processed and legal now, Dr. Frame. Feel better?"

"Oh, much. It was touch and go there for a while."

This airy persiflage came to an end with the arrival of an elderly woman with a joyless face and a heavy tread. Her mouth opened enough to emit a standard greeting, no frills, then shut like a trap. She went into an inner room, leaving the door open. The girl jerked her head at it and made a face.

I rapped on the door frame. The widow looked up at me inquiringly. I went in and closed the door. For fourteen hours I'd anticipated this meeting. Pinned by those hard dark eyes, I dried up.

"Yes?" she said.

I licked my lips and told her who I was and why I'd come.

"The answer," she said, "is probably not the one you'd like to have. I wasn't arranging for a moving van. Had I been informed of what was happening, I would have."

"But Dr. Allyn—"

"Is a liar."

I gaped at her.

"I hadn't seen Robert for more than six months. Let me tell you about Robert," she said harshly, saying his name as if it had a dirty taste she couldn't get out of her mouth. "He was an Andover graduate, then *summa* in humanities from Yale. He spoke and wrote four languages. He translated five books, from German, Turkish, Italian, and French. He'd been top translator at the U.N. and in embassies all over Europe. We had a fine life, except that I had one miscarriage after another. And do you know what he was doing before he died? Driving a cab!

"And he was a pack rat like you wouldn't believe. I put up with it until I couldn't stand it any longer, until I didn't have a corner, a drawer, a tabletop to call my own. Literally! I'd go to work—as an office clerk!—and come home and find my things on the floor and more of his garbage in their place. I lived out of suitcases and cartons for months before I left, and even those he emptied and filled up with his junk.

"And he was a deadbeat, Dr. Frame. I thought if I let the bills pile up, he'd snap out of it, so I put my checks into a secret account and the bills piled sky-high. But he never even noticed, so I had to pay them, and I didn't have enough. He'd emptied our joint account as well as our savings and spent every nickel on his trash.

"I never touched his things, it made him hysterical, but I did try getting him to a doctor. I tried to make him see that something was terribly wrong, that he was sick in mind as well as body. He refused, he denied, he wouldn't discuss anything, just walked out. And came back with more junk! The only thing he ever did with it was put it down and leave it, you know. He never used any of it. I couldn't understand. I still don't.

"So I left. I'd had it. I bunked in with a friend and saved as much as

I could so as to file for divorce. I could *not* afford Robert anymore."

"Did Dr. Allyn know about his heart trouble?"

"Dr. Frame, when we moved in, Robert asked for the next vacancy on the ground floor and told Allyn why. Maybe if he'd at least paid the rent after I left, he'd have gotten the apartment downstairs from ours. We both knew that the tenants were leaving shortly."

"And Dr. Allyn never informed you of the eviction?"

"He most certainly did not. He can't say he didn't know where I'd moved to, because I'd written telling him I'd left Robert and was no longer responsible for his debts—I'd even put a notice in the paper. And he knew where I worked. Why didn't he phone me here and tell me what was going to happen? Why didn't he come in and tell me to my face? He said he sent a note in the interoffice mailbag a week before, but can you believe that? And he had to be at the house to let the police and the movers in—and of course I never came. Shouldn't he have called me from the apartment and asked me where I was? I was right here. Where else would I be? And I'd witnesses to prove it. But he didn't call. And why did the police leave, when according to law a policeman or sheriff's deputy must safeguard the possessions until removal? Because Dr. Allyn is very smooth, and the police believed him when he said I was on my way. What other explanation is there? Can you think of one?

"All I can say is, if I'd known about any eviction, either threatened or scheduled, Dr. Frame, Robert would be alive now. I loved him once. At the end I despised and pitied him. But do you believe for one minute that I wanted to see him murdered?"

"Murder's a big word, Mrs. Williams."

The widow's dead eyes stared into and through me. "Well, what would you call it? Could you call it anything else?"

8

I HAD A CUBBYHOLE in Corey Hall, which housed Psych, Anthro, History, and Sociology, and I spent the next few days there accomplishing nothing. All I could think about was the Widow Williams and the charges she could never level against Ault. Her argument might be unassailable; it was certainly unverifiable. I saw no way to brace Ault on the whole sorry business without embarrassing us both. The apartment was now spoiled for me, but how could I explain to him that I wanted to move out? I thought of the picture he'd given me, and the mountain he'd said we had to climb. It seemed higher than ever, the path hidden, the summit swathed in a miasma of doubt. I felt sick, as much from the lousy metaphor — how would the undergrad in the bursar's office rate it? — as from the box I felt myself to be in.

There were questionnaires to construct for the Project, and syllabi to write for the courses I'd be teaching in the fall. I looked at the lame beginnings I had made on a questionnaire. No soap, I told myself. I'm not in the mood.

But I knew that wouldn't wash. After all, what did the widow or her crazy dead husband have to do with me?

Well, I feel sorry for them and the rotten life they had together. What's left of hers won't be any improvement.

And whose business is it to improve it? Did she ask you to? Are you responsible for her? Did you take something you weren't entitled to? Did you guide either of them to their choices? Are you responsible for Ault's?

No. For mine.

My head cleared wonderfully. To empathize with someone is one thing. To arrogate to oneself the running of his/her life is very different. Trouble comes from getting the two mixed up. I unmixed them, submerged, and made masterful inroads on a questionnaire that would open people up like oysters.

Someone knocked on my door. I looked at my watch. Past noon. Time flies when you're having fun. "Come in," I said, and collected the work and put it into a folder.

Footsteps. Chair slammed against wall. Hard breathing.

The bridegroom, trembling with rage, and looking naked and unfinished without his usual armload of books and papers.

"You bastard—" he said.

"You seem upset."

"Don't give me any of your psychological shit!"

"Don't give me any of your bad manners. This is my office. State your business in an acceptable way, or leave."

"You owe me something, Frame, and I came to—"

"I'm not aware of owing you anything. You aren't my client, my student, or my friend."

"True. But you witnessed my marriage, you helped me move, and you screwed Mrs. Hanrahan. *My wife.*"

"Get out."

"Make me, you lousy cripple!"

His eyes glittered. Energy crackled all around him like a fiery aura. He seemed dry and brittle from the heat of his rage. I had the sense that he was disintegrating at his very core.

Some other type on the edge of a psychotic break would implode, cave in like a hole swallowing itself. This one will shatter to bits, I thought. Which meant that I was very much at risk. I didn't know how much of a fuse, if there was one, was left, or what would just detonate him.

I thought, My god, another metaphor, and said evenly, "Sit down and cool off or I call the university police." He struggled with himself, and sat down in the chair he had thrown against the wall. "What is it?"

"You can't be serious!" he sneered. His eyes were glassy and unblinking.

Feeling safe behind my rampart of a desk, I put my hand on the phone. "You have ten seconds," I said, and watched him win another struggle. Good. He still had some control left.

He licked his dry lips. "Vin James said my thesis was brilliant. He

57

said my dissertation would make my future, that I'd probably be published in hardcover. Hell, I told him that! And we were both right because that son of a bitch Allyn had tried to get me into his yard like he did Pat. And nobody who knows anything about this joint would ask why."

"So?"

"So Vincent's out, and I'm assigned another adviser, the acting chair, and *he* says my work's unacceptable — unaccept — "

His face crumbled. He put his arms over his eyes and bent over and cried sloppily, loudly, rocking back and forth. At last he pulled out a handkerchief and brought himself to a stop. Another good sign. I began to relax.

His eyes were fixed on me but his voice was unsteady. "The History Department's in Allyn's pocket. And he's got a grudge against me because of Pat. So what's he doing? Punishing me! Are you going to let him get away with it?"

"Are you kidding? I've been here two months, Bill. I don't even know where the men's room is."

"Bullshit! He's got you too. You're in his apartment. And how the hell do you think you got your job here! Who's greased the skids for you! Don't tell me you don't know!"

"I don't."

"Vincent knew. We had a rapport, man. He told me plenty about what goes on here, and about that project. How it came about. How Allyn got hold of your Harvard dissertation — "

"I know how he got hold of my paper. He knew someone who knew me. Which isn't surprising. I was there fourteen years. A lot of people know me there. And anyway, those papers aren't confidential, they aren't locked up."

"I have news for you, Frame. Allyn knows *no*body there. Never did. He told Vin once, and Vin told me. Not that he wouldn't like to be in with the Harvardians — he's a snob and a climber and to him Harvard's the cherry on top. But he set up shop here, and the presidency here is better than a Sociology chair there because he's getting closer to our more modest top. He's on his way, man. He's built an empire here and he spends lots of time grooming people who're good PR for him. But my question is, why you? I read your paper, got it from Vin, and it's not bad at all, and I can see how Allyn got the idea for the Project, but still, what's so goddam good about you that he has to get you your cushy spot here?"

His odd stress on *here* and *there, you* and *we, your* and *our*, seemed to be fueling him up again. I said carefully, "Bill, I don't know the ins and outs of the politics here or at Harvard. My adviser recommended I come here when asked, and I did. I know nothing about Allyn or anybody else — I never met any of them before, nor did my adviser. I'd be presuming to approach Dr. Allyn on your behalf. I'm not in his department or in yours."

I had said, in effect, that he was irrational. All at once he yanked me out of my chair by the shirtfront and pinned me facedown across the desk. He gave the back of my neck a sharp chop.

"Liar, liar! You did it to me, you and him! Because I'm better than you are! Better than both of you! Because you want Pat, both of you, you conniving — "

He grabbed my hair and the seat of my pants and flung me to the floor and kicked me, accompanying each kick with an obscenity, frantically gulping air that tore the linings of his throat — like an asthmatic using his last breaths in some insane dance.

He gave a guttural, triumphant "Ah!" — and the Above Knee Endoskeletal Modular Prosthesis cracked and smashed and bent under both his feet as he jumped on it. Then he began kicking the stump.

I fell screaming down down down a jagged piercing blackness into nothing.

"How is he?" Ault.

"As well as can be expected. He sleeps most of the time. Best medicine, actually." A doctor.

I floated, dizzy, in a sea of pain. Pain sat like stones on my eyelids. I was wrapped, immobilized, armored in pain, yet each voice pierced my skull like an aimed lance. Everything in the world hurt me. Everything in me hurt. Go away, I begged from inside the pain.

"He took a hell of a beating." Meiklejohn.

"A lucky young man, all things considered. Come back later. Better call first. He may be sleeping."

"Let us know if we can do anything." Grier.

Quiet shuffle of feet. They had left me at last.

"Caint he'p yuh, boy, 'n' why should Ah? Yer pleasurin' me jes *fahn*." A fifth voice. The words came just above a whisper, but clearly. The speaker patted my hand reassuringly and was gone.

For an instant the rocking dizzying sea stilled and the pain stopped and my head was crystal clear.

59

I knew that voice. I would have known it if I had died in my office and were deep in my grave now.

The realization struck me another blow, but I was too weak to scream. Down I fell into the blackness again, down down down.

$\triangledown$

9

MOSTLY I SLEPT AND the world gradually righted itself. Which allowed me to think about that fifth voice, the voice of the man who had left me broken on a mountain. Who *had* been tracking me all these years like a demented cat with the best of all possible prey. Who had stood by my bed two days ago and hinted gleefully that I'd be hearing from him. The skin on my hand crawled horribly where he had touched me, and I lacked the courage to look at it, sure that it bore his print. My blood pressure kept bouncing like a ball but was recorded without suspicion. Why should there be any? The result of trauma, the doctor said. If I told him what I had told René and Jean about the man, he would install me in a padded room and they'd pay for it.

And then I turned absolutely cold. If the man knew where I was, he might know — must know! — where René and Jean were. Had he ever done anything to them? I reached for the phone. I had to know *now*.

No phone. Nobody had thought to order one for me. No television either. No radio. No crutches. I was cut off from the world. Cut off. God. I looked down to where my stump now showed so clearly under the sheet, the doctors having decided that a sheet was no longer an agonizing weight on it and need not be raised on a frame. There were other ways of causing me pain. They should have asked me. I could have told them how wrong they were.

After lunch Pat came in with a vase of wild flowers. She put it on the night table and bent to kiss my eyelids, my bristly cheeks and cracked lips, kisses as light and fragrant as the Queen Anne's lace beside me.

"How are we this afternoon?" Behind the mocking gleam in her eyes was worry. "Didn't we have anything better to do?"

"Not that we could think of. Where's Bill?" My jaw hurt where he had kicked me.

Her hand tightened around mine. "Here. He's catatonic now. I—I saw him. Through a grill. A little grill in the door." Her voice quavered. "His father's coming to take care of things. It's like the end of a long chapter. I told you something awful would happen to him if he couldn't finish his paper. God, I'm so sorry for him."

"I'm sorrier."

"It wasn't your fault."

"No. But I triggered it. Sooner or later someone was bound to. It could have been you."

"I wish it had been me."

"No."

"He blamed Ault, you know."

"Paranoics have to blame someone, Pat."

A voice from the door. "Time yuh was leavin', young miss. There's things t' be done t' this lad. An' he's whacked, or I'm no judge."

My neighbor, Angela Tansy, brisk but not bossy, and trim in her whites, as if she spread and sweated only off duty. Her hair, like folded silver wings above her ears, was pulled back into a stylish bun.

She was right, I was exhausted, but I held on to Pat's hand. "Pat, how did I get here? What happened at my office?"

"Dr. Mitchell's secretary heard the noise and called the campus police. It took three of them to hold Bill down. They tranquilized him and put him in a straitjacket and Dr. Mitchell went with both of you in the ambulance."

"Oh? He was here, I don't know when. With Meiklejohn and Ault. I heard them. And someone else—there was someone else! Pat, who was it? Do you know who else was here?"

"No. Why? Is it important? You look so—"

Angela said, "That he does! Out wid yer now, me girl. T'morra's another day. Right now there's things I've t' do t' yer friend here."

She did them expertly and silently. Discreetly would be a better word. I decided that I could trust her.

"Angela, do you know anyone on the staff who sounds like a southerner? I mean, a mountain man?"

"A mountain man? A hillbilly, like?"

"I guess you could say that."

"Well now, I dunno. I was capped here, 'n' that's years since, but it's a big place, 'n' gettin' bigger. A mountain man from where?"

"Anywhere from Kentucky to Georgia."

"From—" Somebody else might have laughed. She only eyed me narrowly. "That's a bit of a tall order, me boy. Why d' yuh wanna know?" I didn't trust her enough, not yet. "It's a long story and I'm tired. I'll tell you some other time. But will you help me? Can you ask around? Talk to Personnel? It's not likely he'd be anything more than an orderly or a messenger, something like that. He's tall and probably slender. Age—oh, maybe about fifty. Size eleven shoe, Narrow."

She laughed richly. "Yuh know all that, so why not his address, fer the love o' god!" She gave me and the room a last look before leaving. "I'll do what I can, lad. An' I'm thinkin' ye'll be needin' a phone. That way I can be home wid me feet up when I make me reports. This could take days."

She must have had clout. Within the hour I had a phone, TV, a feast of books, magazines, and town-and-gown newspapers trundled in by a Gray Lady. I chose greedily. And fell asleep with the TV on, books and papers scattered unread all around me, and the call I had so urgently wanted to make to René and Jean clean forgotten.

Meiklejohn looked in after supper, a champagne split in his jacket pocket. "It's nice and chilled," he said, organizing the cups. "Do you good. Best thing in the world to convalesce on. I should know." He grinned like a bad boy.

He seemed genuinely anxious about me, and I was ashamed that I had ever doubted him. I sipped some of the wine through my bent glass straw, and my head immediately started spinning like a top.

"Madge sends regards," he said. "She plays for the patients sometimes. On one of those little pianos. She might be in tomorrow."

He emptied his cup as if it were medicine, then said strongly, "About your leg— I'm damn sorry, Toby. Hell of a situation. But the way you handle it, no one had any idea."

If he had said this at my party, I wouldn't have believed him. He knew too much and drank too much and talked too much, and for a chilling moment I'd wondered if he had hidden those articles in my closet. If so, there was little of importance that he didn't know about me. I decided after a while that I could trust him, but I still carried a grain of doubt around like an albatross.

Hell, *I* was my albatross.

But . . . but . . . maybe I was right, after all. Was I right? He had an offbeat sense of humor. He watched me all the time. Despite his bulk, he did plenty of walking, it was part of his work. Not only did he have a tremendous memory but he was enough older than I to have learned himself right off that mountain long before our encounter there. Could he have been playing with me all these years? Had he been playing a part all these years? Was he able to shift from the flat Midwest speech I now knew so well to the voice I could still hear as clearly as ever after fifteen years and had heard—the fifth voice—two days ago?

If you believe any of this, I told myself, then you also believe this likable slob killed that boy on the Loudoun Heights. And if you do, you know nothing about people, about behavior, about anything, and everything you've done is a mockery and a lie.

I was appalled and sickened by myself.

"I'm only technically handicapped," I said. "I've been camping and hiking for years. I've known people hike in leg casts, arm casts, neck braces, with heart conditions, multiple sclerosis, you name it. I've even done some whitewater work."

"How the hell you heroic types manage it, I'll never know. When I'm on a dig, it's all I can do to stand up on a flat surface with forty-odd pounds on my back, never mind make like a pro and do my job. Ault's come with me a few times, and I've tagged along after him. Now, there's a miracle man for you. He walks right up the side of a mountain when everybody else is crawling on their hands and knees and hanging on by their teeth. But I'm working on it. I'm actually in pretty good shape now."

I had to smile. Meiklejohn was a great pudding in his tent-size Madras shirt and chinos. Right now, with two black eyes, a broken nose and three broken ribs, damage around a kidney, and some refined surgical repair on my stump, I was in better shape than he was.

"Incidentally," he said, "Ault's going to Cambridge soon, and if you want a ride, he'll be happy to oblige."

"What for?"

"Ladies and gents, meet Toby Frame, charter member of the Close to the Chest Society. For another leg, right? The Festival's practically around the corner. You don't want to miss it."

I fell asleep smiling. It wasn't till next morning that I thought about some of the things he had said, or remembered to call René and Jean.

When the nurse finished knocking me about after breakfast, I didn't even have the strength to watch TV, never mind try sounding entirely normal to my canny Canucks. If Angela Tansy of the golden hands could special me, I'd be home in no time flat. I'd ask her. Money was no problem. As orphan and sole heir, I could buy almost anything but the *status quo ante*.

Eventually I picked up the phone.

René answered, and immediately sensed that something was wrong.

"Just a cold," I said.

"Bool*sheet*, boy."

"Have it your own way. Just answer one question. Has anything untoward happened to you two lately?"

Silence.

"René?"

"I 'eard you. We did not wish that you worry. There was in the 'ouse a fire, that is all. 'Ow it 'appen . . ."

I could *hear* the Gallic shrug. "What happened, and when?"

"Two weeks ago. Sunday. A bad wire, the firemen think. They came in time. It was not bad."

"Any sign of breaking and entering?"

"Jean says *non*."

Dark, condescending tone of disagreement, rich with the promise of a lengthy exposition. I didn't ask for one, I wasn't up for it. "Okay. I have to go to a meeting. Just thought I'd see how you were."

I'm fine, just fine, I told him silently, beaming the thought as hard as I could to that psychic Frenchman. I didn't want him or Jean worrying either. Anyway, it was too soon.

Angela Tansy said from the door, "Well, lad, I been hours at the task yuh set me, 'n' caught me one little fish, not worth the savin'. Still, thought y' oughta see 'm 'fore I throw 'm back."

I was too self-centered to notice how tired she looked.

"Well then?" she said impatiently, and in shambled a tall flat skinny object that could have served as a fence post on the farm he came from. He wore — with patent pride — orderly's greens and an ID card on his left breast pocket, and couldn't have been more than seventeen.

"Bobby Joe Jackson from Russellville, Arkansas, meet Dr. Frame," Angela said.

"Moanin', Doc," was the cheerful response. "Har yew?"

I nodded, too disappointed to speak.

Angela said, "Go," and he went. "Bloody computer couldn't come up wid any other mountain birthplace 'cept his, woudja believe? Brought yuh somethin'." She set a small radio on the night table and tuned in to something sweet and soft.

"It was a long shot." I was too depressed to say thank you. "Anyway, a person could be born in one place and grow up in another, as a foster child or adoptee, and give that residence as his place of birth. Or he could lie, if he had reason to, and didn't have to produce a birth certificate."

"Well, that's that. Fer now," she added, looking more closely at me. "Yer jaw hurts from all that talkin'. So we'll give another part a yuh somethin' to think about."

Pain was unavoidable, even under her hands. She turned on the TV, to divert me, and eventually got her chores done and let me sleep.

She may have told the doctor that I was worn out, or else nobody cared whether I was or I wasn't, because no visitors came until the next afternoon. By then I was feeling deprived and unloved and sulky.

Ault dropped by late in the day. He was, predictably, the perfect hospital visitor, with his easy conversation and the kind of treat that someone with an almost broken jaw could manage. For a little while I felt intensely well and began to think I was ready to go out and lick the world.

"Oh, I almost forgot," Ault said, taking a postcard out of his pocket. "This came to your office. Looks like it's been through the wars. Sorry." The card, forwarded from Harvard, was an invitation from Pete Flori in Virginia to join him two weeks ago for some clearing on Silers Bald, now that the Appalachian Trail Conference had approved removing the encroaching shrubs and trees that were spoiling the view. I would have gone like a shot, if not for Bill Hanrahan. I had done plenty of trail maintenance with Pete. It was in Maine that my father and I had first seen him — heard him first, fighting a loud losing battle with the fierce blackflies. A retired newspaperman, he was still active in all phases of Trail business.

"Boy, Ault, what a case study," I said, flapping the card. "When Roosevelt got the CCC going in '33, Pete was eighteen, and desperate, so he joined up, one of the first, and here's a kid doesn't know a tree from a telephone pole and he's assigned to a work detail clearing blighted chestnut trees out of Shenandoah National Park. He spent six years with the CCC. It changed his life completely—"

"The CCC changed a lot of lives in those mountains. It housed people like your friend by evicting hundreds of other people. I did a lot of fieldwork on mountain communities. Just reading about it hurts."

"But those people were relocated—"

"Sure, and then they had to pay rent. And stand around and watch the CCC boys do the work they'd always done—fight forest fires, for instance. Talk about case studies, Toby. Hundreds of poor, needy families were forced out of their homes so that other victims of the Depression could make it possible for those with time and money, or the need to *discover* themselves, to have a good time. And what they haven't taken, the lumber companies and mining companies and developers have taken. Are still taking—"

He stopped abruptly, spread his hands in apology, and smiled charmingly. "This sort of passion has no place in a sickroom. I should have known better."

"Not at all. I deal with single personalities, Ault. You deal with entire communities. So it's understandable that there has to be a geometric increase in your—"

"Affect?" he said slyly, and we both laughed.

Then Pat arrived, a disturbing intensity about her, with more flowers and something in a brown paper bag. "Oh!" she said, seeing Ault, who smiled and said hello. "I tried to catch you in your office. Guess I just missed you." Whatever she wanted to see him about, she was scared. She put the things down and took a deep breath.

I found myself doing the same. My feeling of extreme well-being had evaporated the moment she walked in. I felt apprehensive and vulnerable. And very, very curious.

"Toby," she said, "would you excuse us for a few minutes? I have something to say to Ault and I don't want to tire you."

"I'm fine," I said. But I was exhausted.

She hesitated, then plunged. "I've come to a decision, Ault. I'm going back into the History Department. Thank you for all your—your help."

"Well, I'm not surprised," he said in his spacious way. "Vincent and I talked about this just before he died."

"You—? But—"

"He didn't tell you?"

"No. He wanted me to stay in Sociology, so when I made up my mind to switch, I didn't tell him because he was so ill. I didn't want to upset him. Or you."

"Well, Pat, you couldn't go wrong in Sociology, but I agree you'll be happier with your first choice. I was wrong to persuade you otherwise, but I can't imagine why you were afraid to tell me days ago."

He slapped his thighs lightly and got up. "Well. I don't want to outstay my welcome, Toby old man, and I do have another appointment. I'll be in touch. Let me know if there's anything you need. And Pat, don't feel you have to stay away. You must know I'm entirely in your corner."

When he had gone, Pat made a production of fixing the flowers. Her hands shook. Her back was determinedly to me.

"All right," I said. "At the risk of repeating myself, what is it about him that gets you all shook? What you say and what I see —"

She whirled around, tear-streaked and furious. "I tell you he's smooth, but you don't believe me. You don't want to. Few people do. All right, show is better than tell." Her lips hardly moved, in an effort to keep from exploding.

She took a small leather-bound book with a clasp out of the paper bag and opened it. "This is Vincent's diary. I found it this morning when I was going through his things. All I've done today is read it." She flipped through the pages. "Here. Look. This entry is dated three weeks ago."

I read, " 'Confronted AA this pm supper. Said I was fed up & he cld do what he liked but noth'g m. important to me than P, & FW at S glad to have her. AA v. v. angry. Sword falls, house stands.'

"Who is FW at S?" I said.

"Franz Wilhelm at Smith. But it could be Frederick Wald at Swarthmore or Florence Wetmore at Stanford." She smiled tremulously. "Vincent knew a lot of people. Ault was aware of that."

"So that innocent act with Ault —"

"Was more for your benefit than to try to fool him. I wanted you to see that he was lying. *Now* what do you think!"

I didn't want to think, and made up my mind not to. I had enough pain as it was. Pat was a free agent and sound of wind and limb. Whatever had gone on between Vincent and Ault was irrelevant now. Pat could go where she wanted, do as she pleased. I couldn't, for two reasons, and to deal with them I had to husband all my energy. I started by closing my eyes, and when I opened them again she was gone.

The light went on sometime during the third shift, at the very moment when I woke up smiling.

"How nice to see a happy face at this hour," the nurse said, fingertips cool and firm on my wrist. "I don't often get such a welcome. You must've had a good dream."

"The best," I said.

But I hadn't been dreaming. I had only remembered that the footprints near the dead boy on the Loudoun Heights had been, René estimated, size eleven Narrow. Meiklejohn's great hoofs were shod in nothing smaller than a 14E.

10

MADGE HENDRON'S BAR PIANO was painted a shocking pink and stenciled with the names of all the great pianists from Beethoven to Bolling, and students rolled her up and down the hospital corridors singing everything from *lieder* to rock. For me she played Schumann's *Kinderscenen*, and even on that little instrument almost unstrung me, she sounded so much like my mother.

I was sorry she had come. Piercing memories were not on my agenda now, nor love, except for René and Jean. Pat was something else, the first woman to want me and enjoy me. So there would be others, when I had done what I had to do.

Right now, I had to deal with the problem of getting around. Crutches were out until my ribs knit. My stump was too tender to be fitted for a new prosthesis. And with no elevator to my apartment, a wheelchair was impossible. Hopeless.

Angela Tansy was fed up with my self-pity. "All yuh need is someone t' pick yuh up 'n' put yuh down 'n' drive yuh 'round. Wouldn't need no Hercules. Do it meself, but yer a moody sod 'n' life's too short. I'll take the matter under advisement."

The next day she was back with the orderly from Arkansas, the kid as skinny and boneless as an asparagus. My heart sank.

"Af'noon, Doc. Har yew?" Bobby Joe Jackson said affably, and by dinnertime I was home, secure and surprised. The kid was no kid, he was twenty-two, his skeleton functioned with sinew like thousand-pound-test nylon line, and he "hankered to know ever'thing about animals and aimed to know it raht." Courtesy of a prize sow he had raised and sold, he had spent a year at a small aggie school, then come north to the university's two-year program that would certify him as a veterinary assistant and put the real thing within reach. Since his sixth birthday, when a rinky-dink circus with a sick bear had set him afire, he had known where he was going to practice when he qualified as a DVM. And he wanted — had always wanted — to be called Bob.

The observable evidence seemed too good to be true, so I tested it with a few professional tricks. After all, I was a trained clinician, which is only another way of saying I had society's sanction to be the morbidly suspicious bastard I blamed force of circumstance for making me.

After two days a puzzled silent Bob was clearly ready to walk. Why? Because I was no better than that stain on *my* profession, the sadistic swine who *discovered* that infant monkeys taken from their mothers and raised in cages with the milk bottle held in a clamp and not always a carpeted post to cling to, sickened, turned vicious, even died of depression. Kids who get their jollies pulling legs off spiders to see how or if they'll walk get Ph.D.s in experimental psych when they grow up — and *they* call the antivivisectionists crazy!

I remembered just in time what the greatest clinician of all had said, that sometimes a cigar is just a cigar. The boy was nothing more or less than what I saw, that rare person who has a worthwhile goal and goes for it gracefully, patiently. As I apologized, a thought about my own career goals almost knocked me out. I put it aside to think about later, but weeks passed before I did.

Bob took a leave of absence from the hospital, and we agreed on a fetch-carry-and-cook schedule that gave him plenty of free time. He insisted on sleeping on the living-room floor in his sleeping bag, because the only noises he could stand at night were horses shifting in the hay and a cat purring in his ear.

He unfolded like a bud, petal after petal. At the end of his first week, when Angela Tansy arrived to do a little specialing on me, he greeted her with a "How are you?" that even I hadn't heard before.

"You takin' elocution?" she said, goggle-eyed.

"Nope, but Ah sure would admahr to, Angie gal. Ah jes — just keep muh ears wahd open."

She eyed them without favor. "They'll bag you more a the Queen's English than you'll know what t' do with, that's fer sure."

"Ol' Angie's okay, she just lahks to tease," he said later, helping me into bed. "Ah — *I* — open muh mouth and folks cain't see nothin' but a po' cracker. Well, Doc, I won't give 'em that pertickler handle to beat me with. So Ah practice."

A good choice, provided he wasn't ashamed of his origins and didn't try to bury them, I warned. So he spent part of his days in the Speech Department, with interns who chivvied him like a pack of Henry Higginses, and adored him.

A couple of days later he took me to Ault's party for Jesse Thomaston. Meiklejohn, whose *joie de vivre* was often childlike and ferocious, said it promised to be sticky.

Bob lifted my wheelchair up Ault's front steps and over the doorsill and told me to call him when I was ready to leave, and no rush, he had plenty to keep busy with.

Ault said, "Nonsense. Join us. It ud be raht foolish not to," and gave me the Big Joke wink.

Bob said with dignity, "Thanks very much, Dr. Allyn. I'd like that," and walked away to talk with Madge.

Ault watched him, an unreadable expression on his face. That wink of his had jolted the dickens out of me. If I hadn't been looking at him, I would have mistaken the soft nasal high-pitched voice for Bob's. Such joking mimicry did not sort with the Ault everyone knew, someone who, before anything else, was kind, gracious, thoughtful. But then, he was under a strain, what with everyone crowded around Jesse.

He admitted as much as he handed me a perfect martini and a plate of canapés. "Good heavens. I certainly didn't mean to offend the lad. But things are a little bent out of the shape I've been used to. *Sic transit* and all that? Ah well. I think you'll enjoy the Yellow Morel, Toby. It's stuffed with Eastern Cauliflower mushroom. Makes a nice combination, although morel-maniac purists like Vincent would have me hung for a rank heretic. Let me get Jesse for you."

A patient of mine once said, "I can't stand watching the wife eat a banana, it grosses me right out. It's like she's noshing on my—on my—you know what I'm saying to you?"

I knew. With me it was the morel I never could deal with. This most phallic of fruits looks, at its freshest, like a rotting penis. One bite of Ault's exquisitely sautéed creation and I would have vomited into my lap. I wrapped the thing in my cocktail napkin and Bob took it away while Ault was cutting Jesse out of the crowd.

Like a hunter exhibiting a prize specimen, Ault introduced me to Jesse Thomaston, a handsome Brahmin of the pipe and tweed persuasion with thin pale hair that suited him perfectly. But there was an air of corruption about him. His skin was waxy thick and gray, like someone already embalmed, and he shook hands as though Death too were a guest here, a guest waiting to grab him and never let go.

"Christ," Meiklejohn whispered, "no way he could stay. He's deliquescing on the hoof. All you have to do is scratch him and he'll ooze right out of that suit in a greasy puddle, right on Ault's gorgeous Persian."

I gagged behind my hand, almost vomited then and there, and Meiklejohn thought I was coughing and pounded me heartily on the back. I could have killed him.

But after that it was a nice party. The martinis flowed freely, the food was superb, and Meiklejohn urged us to keep the Festival's goal in mind and eat, drink, be merry, and *gain*. He insisted that Bob and my wheelchair be considered part of my official Festival weight, and expanded this idea so hilariously that even Jesse turned a little pink.

As for Ault, he was thoroughly relaxed and utterly charming to Bob and everybody else, and he deferred to Jesse as if the convalescent were once again back on the job.

And then all at once I'd had enough, and Bob saw my high sign and took me home.

11

AULT CALLED WHILE BOB was making breakfast and I was shaving. I mopped up and rolled out to the kitchen phone and apologized for keeping him waiting.

He laughed. "Funny you should say that. It occurred to me yesterday that a phone in the bathroom would be helpful, so I arranged to have an installer put in a jack. Also, I must get to Harvard before the end of the week and thought you might want to come along for a change of scene. To salve your conscience you can help me streamline those departmental questionnaires — there are too many dupes and overlaps in them — and I'll pitch in when I've done my errands. Then we can have dinner at the Faculty Club before driving back. Just let me know what day's best for you. Also, the Festival's only six weeks away, and your orthotist's in Cambridge, I believe. You can drop in for a fitting or whatever, and a new leg could be ready for the big day."

The surgeon was taking another look at the stump today. It was healed but still swollen, so I would have to wear an elastic stocking charmingly dubbed a stump shrinker. Only when the swelling was gone could a cast of the thigh be made. Then a fitting, adjustments, chafing, pain, another fitting, more adjustments, and a cane for a while. No, I wouldn't be ready in six weeks. But sticks on Festival Day were out of the question because they subject the body to distortion and fatigue and make you vulnerable in crowds. So, to get any pleasure out of the big day, I'd have to be in the chair, and safe. Or out of town.

I said, "I'll let you know. It'd be wonderful to be down there now, and Bob really wants to see the Square. I talk about it enough."

"He should, but some other time, I think. We've lost a lot of time, and I don't like to go much further until those questionnaires are in better shape. What do you say?"

"Yes, all right. I was only going to turn him loose, but — another time, as you said. Okay, I'll call you."

Bob's big ears twitched on hearing his name, but he only poured beaten egg into a pan and stirred it around and around, like a child absently messing with a mudpie.

"That was Dr. Allyn," I said, feeling guilty. "He's getting us a jack for the bathroom."

"That's nice."

"You don't like him, do you."

"Reckon I don't."

"Any special reason?"

"I don't rightly — I don't know what it is. Have to think on it some."

"How would you like to see Canada and meet a couple of mad Frenchmen?" I said.

"You bet. When?"

"The weekend of the Festival?"

His nice face fell. One of the speech interns was working on more than his speech during his free time.

"Never mind," I said. "I can go alone. I'll be in great shape by then. I've traveled a lot by myself."

This didn't cheer him up any, and all at once I understood that he would miss me. Strange. A few days ago he had been a paid employee with one foot out the door. Now, by a subtle process whose result I suddenly perceived, he was the younger brother I'd never had. I asked myself if I wanted one. A relationship grows on love and trust. I ate egg without tasting it.

Late in the afternoon I rolled into the doctor's office.

"What in blazes are you doing in that chair?" he said by way of greeting. "You aren't helping yourself any, sitting on your behind. Where're the sticks? Afraid you'll fall? Hmm. Drop your pants."

Dressing and undressing took some doing, because touching or looking at the stump terrified and disgusted me. My life was like a fair funhouse, full of horrible surprises, and I wandered about in it, a stranger to my own body. The doctor paced impatiently, but at last I was ready and his hands were warm, his touch gentle enough. I didn't watch.

"Well?" I said. "When can I go for a cast?"

"Too much swelling. Got a shrinker? Well, start wearing it. You might be able to have a cast made in about ten days. I wanted to see the leg you had, but it wasn't with you when you were admitted. Who made it?"

"Carlow, in Cambridge."

"Good. Okay, make yourself decent. And get on your feet and get your juices flowing and stop feeling sorry for yourself."

Something was bothering me, a phantom dancing on the edge of my eye. Home again, I rolled restlessly around the apartment, rucking up the orientals.

Bob placed my crutches across the arms of the chair. "Try another way," he said softly, the verb halfway between *trah* and *try*.

And all at once I knew what it was. I stood up and got to the phone and called Pat Elliot. I hadn't seen or spoken to her in over a week.

"Pat," I said straightaway, "what happened to my leg the day I went to the hospital?"

"Oh. I don't know. Maybe Dr. Meiklejohn does. I bumped into him the other day. He seems to know everything about everything. In the nicest possible way."

"Yes. I should have called him."

"Oh. Uh — how are you, Toby?"

"It marches."

"Have you — are you — uh — busy?"

"Now?"

"Now."

"No."

She laughed, it sounded so ridiculous, and suddenly I wanted to see her. I said, not expecting anything, and not deserving it either, "How about you come over and meet my new roommate?"

"Now?"

"Now."

She laughed and said yes and hung up.

I readjusted the crutch pads under my arms, then gave up and lowered myself gingerly to the edge of the desk and put the damned things aside. My armpits and hands were sore. No matter how much I used sticks, they always hurt.

Meiklejohn, like the rest of the educational community I had always been a part of, did not consider being called at home an intrusion on personal space. "Hey, lad! Good to hear you. Say, wasn't that a hell of a nice party the other day!"

75

"John," I said, "do you know what happened to my leg? The day I went to the hospital, I mean."

"For godsake, Toby, what's the matter?"

"Did you see it?"

"Only the medics did. Next thing we knew, you were bundled onto a stretcher and away you went, and Grier with you. What the hell's the matter, lad?"

The matter? The matter was that if no one including the doctor had seen my smashed prosthesis, how did Ault know I dealt with a Cambridge firm?

"I don't know," I said. I didn't want to talk about it.

"Well, when you do, let me in on it. I can't stand the suspense. As for that leg of yours, I bet one of the campus mutts found it and buried it in the Quad. I'll hit Ford up for some money and dig for it. Why should Ault get all the glory?"

"Why indeed." I was beginning to feel better. "What are you up to, John?"

"Right this minute? Nothing that a great scholar should be doing. I'm just not in the mood for virtue. Of any kind."

"Well, Pat Elliot—"

"That's one nice girl, Toby," he said seriously, as if it were a fact I should know.

"Yes. Well, she's coming over. And Bob's here. How'd you like to join us?"

"Laddie, I'll be there before you can uncork the Scotch!"

I told Ault's answering machine that I wouldn't be seeing my orthotist for a while but would be free on such and such days for a trip to Cambridge, he could take his pick.

Pat arrived just as I put down the phone, and Meiklejohn came soon after, breathing hard, as if he'd run all the way. Then Angela Tansy, hearing our noise when she came off shift, brought in an armload of cold beer. It was a hilarious, homogeneous party that eased away all my pain and made me ashamed of my suspicions of Meiklejohn and Ault and everybody else, and somehow, when it was over, Pat stayed and Bob went off to his speech intern.

A few days later Ault and I drove down to Cambridge in his Mercedes, a sinfully luxurious vehicle with its gorgeous leather upholstery, tiny bar, and telephone.

I was pretty brisk on my sticks now, but Ault helped settle me and a formidable pile of folders into my old carrel upstairs in the Widener before going off to pursue his errands, whatever they were. My name hadn't been erased, and I thought how good it was to be back again. Again? Had I enjoyed my student days so much, over and above the cachet of being a Harvard man following in his honored father's footsteps?

I filed this new shift in my perceptions with the others and went to work.

Ault was back in about two hours, and by late afternoon we had done a lot of solid work and were ready for a drink and dinner in the ambience he liked above all others, the faculty club of a world-class university.

"Look, Toby," he said as we packed up, "I have one more errand to run. It's just beyond the Coop, a good bit of a jaunt. Why don't you stay here or sit downstairs and relax. I won't be long. I couldn't fit in everything before, damn it."

I insisted that I felt equal to the walk, so we took the elevator down and went out into the perfected autumn dusk that was descending lovingly on one of the best parts of New England.

My appreciation couldn't last. Ault had been right again. We came through the Yard's great iron gates into a predinner fun-seeking mob that pushed me about like a live puppet, and I knew that crossing Mass. Ave. was beyond me. My crutches were padded with cement, and the pain in my armpits had spread around my chest and down my arms. My hands were frozen forever on the handholds.

My eyes clung to the Coop's imposing bulk. If only I could slide weightless and safe along my line of sight, right over the crowds and traffic. If only I still had my leg.

One thought led to another. I heard myself blurting out, "Ault, how did you know I'd be coming here for a new leg?"

He blinked, puzzled. "Oh. I looked at the old one when I locked up your office after Grier saw you to the hospital. And a useless mess it was. I put it in the closet. Why?"

For almost a week I had suspected this extraordinary man of who knows what, and he had only done another of his many thoughtful acts. I was ashamed, but all I could do now was fight to keep my balance. Another foot or two and I'd have fallen off the curbstone.

Ault pulled me back. "Good god, Toby, watch it!" he yelled in my ear. "This is terrible, and it's my fault. I was a damn fool to let you walk so far. Hang on to that lamppost while I find a cab."

He patted my shoulder and waded into the oncoming traffic to flag down a taxi. It was the worst time of day to try to get one. Resigned to a goodly wait, I turned, tucked both sticks under one arm, and reached with the other to embrace what seemed like the only stationary object in that swirling crush.

Then someone behind me grasped my stump and squeezed it. I couldn't even scream, it hurt so much. I managed to hang on to the lamppost. Then someone or something whacked me between the shoulder blades and I let go of the sticks and tumbled into the road. Brakes squealed crazily.

A fist or a knee in the small of my back was holding me down, forcing the taste and stink of the blacktop into my mouth and lungs, and people were shouting and the weight came off and someone rolled me over and Ault was reaching down a hand to me 'and saying something that sounded, in all the racket, like a foreign language.

I asked him later what it was he'd said.

He thought back, and shrugged. "Damned if I know. There was so much noise and confusion and I was so concerned about you, I didn't know who or where *I* was!"

1 2

I NEEDED TO REST after the Cambridge experience, but could only stare at the walls, write cryptic lists and tear them up, crutch irritably around the apartment, eat little, sleep less. I kept clawing my way up Ault's mountain and, all too close to my goal, tumbling down again, gladly.

After a week of this Bob said, in standard American English colored by southern sounds, "Doc, you aren't doing that stump any favors."

I was making another list, uneasiness swarming all over me like an army of ants. I opened my mouth, closed it.

"Catfish Ah landed one time looked just like that. Feel like talking?"

"Damned if I know where to start. And you have a date."

He had cleaned up the kitchen and taken out the garbage, and now he looked exactly right in his J. August slacks, pinpoint Oxford shirt, and cashmere sweater. His pale shining hair was well but not too well cut, his RocSports nicely broken in. He leaned against the wall, ankles crossed, hands in pockets, and said placidly, "Don't worry 'bout that. Just start at the beginning and go on 'til you git — get — to the end."

The beginning? The beginning was witnessing Pat Elliot's marriage, the day of Ault's luncheon for me. The end — the latest occurrence, anyway — was last Saturday afternoon in Harvard Square. In between was Vincent James's death, the looting of Robert Williams's possessions, his death from shock on the sidewalk, his wife's interpretation of it, and everything connected to Bill Hanrahan. Should René and Jean's house fire be included on the list? I had put it on another one, earlier.

A unifying theme had been struggling to take shape. I told myself there was absolutely no order other than chronological order and that significant events prior to my coming here, or in another country, were irrelevant. Why? For reasons, I told myself firmly, that I do not care to specify.

The denial did what denial usually does — brought me too near a place I wanted to avoid, a shadowy place from which someone peered out at me.

Ah yes, I said, I know who that is, it's —

And crumpled up the paper and stuffed it into my pocket.

The phone rang. Bob picked it up and said beautifully, "Good evening. Dr. Frame's residence." His face froze at the caller's response. "Yall wan' toke t' Doctah Fray-yum? He's settin' at his day-esk feelin' a maht po'ly."

"What was that all about!" I gritted the words, my hand over the speaker. Then, covering for him, I said listlessly, "Hi, Ault. What's up?"

"That's what I'd like to know. What's that — that *cracker* trying on, Toby? Sounded damned insulting to me."

"Uh, well, believe it or not, he's, uh, practicing. Some theory about sharpening the ears, feeling the speech sounds kinesthetically, that is, with all the, uh, the muscles used in speaking. He's going out for a lesson in a few minutes. Maybe the tutor'll provide further insight on this."

"I doubt if that's possible," Ault said coldly.

"Sounds weird, but it must be working. Sometimes I'm hard-pressed to tell he's from anywhere south of the Mason-Dixon Line."

"I should have thought you wouldn't be needing any help now."

"It won't be for much longer." I realized that I'd just crossed my fingers in that magical gesture that means it doesn't count. "What can I do for you?"

"Moderate your nurse/houseguest's view of me, if you can. I'm afraid I was pretty damned tactless, at that."

"You couldn't be if you tried. Hey, I almost forgot. Thanks for the questionnaires. Didn't expect you'd have them redone so fast."

"Gloria made the changes and pressed Print. Look, I called to alert you about break-ins in the neighborhood. There are plenty of bulbs near the furnace for the outside lamps, should any local louts fancy a little target practice. They have in the past. And take trash to the Dumpster during the day, if that's not too inconvenient. It's dim back there at night. All right, 'bye for now. I've some things to do — a little activity to organize," he said, and hung up.

Bob was still leaning against the wall, tight-lipped and stubborn, like a kid waiting to have his knuckles rapped.

"He really got to you," I said.

"Ah don't appreciate being treated like a stereotype, Doc. The longer Ah stay up no'th, the mo' it bugs me, folks lahk him lookin' down on me lahk Ah'm a fool—"

"Slow down."

"Ah'm not ashamed of where Ah'm from. Whah should Ah be! Ah—*I* just don't want to be cheated out of my life because I sound like a ridgerunnuh—a simple clown!"

"You're making an assumption. After all, Ault's a generous man, a real friend—"

Challenges to this claim had been popping up like evil growths on my lists. Maybe Bob could shoot it down for good, and I could get some rest.

He did, with a vicious chop of his hand. "Friend! You have to be kidding. Doc, with a friend like him you don't need enemies! He's nothing but a phony. And don't ask me how I know. I just *know*! It's like with animals, any kind of animals. All I have to do is look 'em in the eyes, and I know if I can trust 'em or I cain't."

He hadn't helped, after all. I dealt with the easiest, and for me the safest, issue. "What you think about Dr. Allyn isn't important. You aren't required to trust him or like him. You are required to be courteous. You don't have to choose to get riled. You follow?"

He separated himself from the wall. "I follow. But I'm telling you something, Doc, and this comes from what *I* know, even if I cain't produce the right kind of proof. If I were you, I'd trust the bastard only as far as I could throw him."

I sighed in relief when he went out. If having a younger brother, never mind a child of my own, was like this . . . not the worst thing in the world, actually. . . . Dad must have felt the same way sometimes. . . .

I realized that I was thinking how lucky I was, and found myself smiling. For a few moments I savored the feeling it gave me. When had I last felt even remotely like this? About a week and a half ago, at my impromptu party with Bob, Pat, Meiklejohn, and Angela. And now here I was doing it all by myself. Progress. Life's not all that bad, I thought.

The telephone rang like a tocsin. I trembled as I picked it up.

It was Jean. It was necessary, he said, that he be brief. They had spent much on the house since the fire. And on long dee*stahnce.*

What was he talking about! They'd called me only twice since early August.

Did they no calls elsewhere make?!

The question was pregnant with charges against my ability to think straight. I apologized in French and implored him to continue.

Merci! The crimes on or near the Trail, then, that they had noted in their books occurred in all the months, but mainly at Easter, Christmas, long weekends, summer *vacances*. Which told us only that people — teachers and students mostly — were free the Trail to travel during these times, *n'est-ce pas*?

"Oui," I said. "So what?"

"That is not much, To*bee*, we agree. Hi called mainly to tell you that after our fire the copies of the newspapairs of the murder we them could not fin'. The Trail Conference office in 'Arpairs Ferry we call for copies but a poor Xerox only they send of one article — but of pictures not one — which Hi you send *tout de suite* two days since. René an' Hi are eating crepes filled with brandied fresh fruit when I theenk to ask did you it get?"

As their retirement lengthened and they spent more and more time in the woods, the worse their English became. I wished my French were as good. I said no, that what with one thing and another I had forgotten all about the matter, and he snorted and hung up.

I had been busy with one of my lists when Bob brought me the mail, which in my new mania I had pushed aside. I went through it now, and interrupted the French-Canadian enjoyment of fruit-filled crepes by calling to object crankily not only to the lousy Xerox but to the fact that the reporter, not the family, had made much of the way René and Jean had changed their plans and gone to the expense of staying right through to the funeral.

"The mother was probably prostrated by grief," I said, "but the father, at least, could have taken the trouble to thank you directly. What the hell kind of man is he, anyway!"

"Ah, To*bee*, what kind indeed! The reporter mentioned talk among mountain people up and down the Appalachians about this father, that he has their hills generously sprinkled with little lumbermen, per'aps in loving exchange or apology for the trees he has stolen. But has he not their women stolen too?"

A tremendous thought struck me. "Jean. If it was common talk, was there no suggestion anywhere of revenge — revenge maybe vented on the boy?"

Jean's irritable sigh gusted down the miles of wire like an arctic wind. "To answer all your questions, *mon fils,* will a treep require—"

"A what?"

"*Mon dieu! Un* tee-har-hi-*pee*! To speak with that reporter who hus hinterviewed in 'Arpairs Ferry. And now permit me my dinner to finish. *Adieu!*"

"*Adieu* to you too," I said into a dead phone, and sat back to think of the lunatic idea that had taken hold. It might mean nothing. Or everything. Which did I prefer? I dodged the answer once again.

I watched television without seeing it, then went back to the phone and arranged two round-trip flights to West Virginia to see that reporter, and maybe the murdered boy's father, if that was where he was. It would be good to get away, despite the reason, and Pat might want to go, if Bob didn't. I'd ask him first, of course. At breakfast.

I went to bed, and summoned back with no small effort the mood I'd been in before Jean's call. Only then was I able to admit that I was a fine one to lecture Bob about choices. What about the choice that had been strangling my soul for so many years? It hadn't replaced, it could never replace, what I'd lost. You must grieve for a loss, accept it, and drop it. With practice and vigilance you do. I said aloud, "I'll drop it now!" and knew that in time I would. For the first time in days I was asleep before ten.

Before I knew it, jocund day was standing tiptoe on my windowsill and an inconsiderate bastard was pounding on my door. Why had Bob elected me hospitality chair? He slept closer to the door. I opened it.

Police Chief Burke. Behind him a younger officer, a doughy type with rubbery lips and beardless round cheeks and a roll of fat above his broad black belt. Next to him, Angela, in a shapeless flannel robe, white hair in tatters, eyes red and swollen.

"May we come in?" Burke said, and went by me, followed by the other man, who closed the door in Angela's ravaged face and stood with one hand on his pistol butt, the other behind his back.

I wasn't even minimally interested to know what fantasy he was living in. I rubbed my eyes. "What's going on, Chief? Did I miss something?"

"Sure seems that way, Dr. Frame. You don't mind if I look around?" His heels were hard and brisk on the bare floor. He came back to me. "When did you last see your nurse or attendant or whatever you call him—Bob Jackson?"

"What are you up to, Burke?" I said angrily, because I was suddenly so scared. "What did you expect to find in the broom closet, and what's Angela doing in the hall? What's happening around here!"

"Murder's what's happening. Or I should say, it's what happened."

"And you think Bob had something to do with it? You're crazy!"

"I'd appreciate you telling me when you last saw him, Dr. Frame. Then it'll be my turn to talk."

"Last night after supper."

"Did you go out too?"

I said nothing.

"All right," he said. "About half an hour ago the nurse went out with her rubbish and found Jackson with his neck broken and his pockets turned inside out. She also says your car's gone. The M.E.'s guess is that Jackson was killed last night sometime between seven and twelve. He'll know more when he does the autopsy."

I stared at him. Tears ran down my cheeks. As I turned my head to wipe my face on my sleeve, I caught the nasty smirk on the young officer's face. "You fat bastard!" I said, and lunged at his solar plexus with a crutch, pinning him hard against the door. "Get out! Get out of my house!"

Burke knocked the crutch out of my hand but put an arm about me as I staggered. "You can go, Alf," he said, and turned me around and led me to the desk. The door closed just short of a slam as I fell into the chair.

"I don't get it," I said. "We had supper. We talked awhile. He had a date with a student in the Speech Department, a nice girl he's been seeing. He was happy. Everyone liked him. He couldn't have had any enemies."

"Maybe, maybe not. How long was he going to be here?"

"Just until I got a new leg and was pretty secure on it. A couple of months, maybe. Angela found him for me. He was going to move in with her afterward—she has a second bedroom. Without help I couldn't have stayed here alone."

"Meaning?"

"A graduate student trashed my prosthesis and injured me. A paranoid type who thought I owed him something. Bob gave me a hand with the cooking and laundry and so on. He slept in a sleeping bag by the couch, except when he stayed with his girlfriend. He was free to go out when I was set for the night, and I didn't wait up for him." The tears kept leaking out. "I want to see him. Where is he?"

"On ice. I'll drive you. A couple more questions first. What exactly was the boy to you?" He handed me my crutch as if to say he knew the question wouldn't throw me.

"I don't know if you can believe this, Mr. Burke, and I don't care. But he was a combination younger brother and son and friend. Items my life hasn't been exactly blessed with."

"We live in hope, Dr. Frame," he said severely. "Who was he going to see last night?"

"A senior by the name of Mary Hubert. I met her once. Her address is in the little brown book in my desk. Help yourself."

He copied out the girl's address and phone number and put the book back. "You need help getting dressed? I'll call the nurse, if you want."

I said no and heaved myself up. That good sleep I'd had might never have happened.

"You said he was found by the trash bin," I said when we were outside. "Show me exactly where."

We went to the far end of the parking lot where a ten-yarder stood in a high palisade enclosure, the gate open. The lamp on the tall wooden post was broken, the glass in bits everywhere. Outside the enclosure two paper bags spewed trash and garbage.

"Looks like the boy was jumped as he was about to drop the stuff in before going on his date. After supper's the usual time to throw out the rubbish. So they busted the lamp and hid inside the fence and waited."

I was hardly listening. "That stuff's not our — mine. And Bob took out the garbage at least an hour before he got ready to go out."

"This stuff was right under his hands."

"I don't serve cooked cabbage or drink plonk."

"What's your theory? That he was looking for something in those bags? Or that the murderer put them there?"

"I don't feel much like theorizing. If I could just . . ."

If I could just go back to yesterday and act on the conclusion I had reached but been unable to credit, maybe Bob would be alive now.

The room Burke took me to was sterile and cold. The drawer rolled out of the wall with a horrible rumble, as if some greedy god of the dead objected to relinquishing his latest prize even for a few minutes. The stink of death crowded into my skull.

I looked down at the long thin shape under the sheet and despised myself, a modern Hamlet who had waited too long to act on a decision. Slowly I lifted the sheet away. Bob had been so shining clean. Now a bit of boiled cabbage was caught in the pale hair, and the nice plain face was dirty. His throat was badly bruised.

"Someone grabbed him around the neck and put a knee in his lumbar spine and snapped his head back," Burke said. "Someone very fast and very strong who knew exactly what he was about. But when? On the boy's way out? Or when he came back? We'll have to wait for the autopsy."

I pulled the sheet farther down, then off entirely. "Where are the rest of his clothes!"

"What rest?"

"Do you think he went out on a date in his shirtsleeves, without shoes on? On a cold night, for godsake?"

"This is how he was found. Again, what clothes?"

I took the cabbage out of the fair hair. "Pastel-blue cashmere sweater. Leather jacket, medium brown, long and boxy, unbelted. RocSport shoes, dark brown. Gold watch and stretch band. I'm not sure what money he carried. Maybe twenty dollars, in a slim leather wallet, burgundy or dark brown, I don't remember." Nor would I ever remember, for Burke's records, who had bought Bob all that stuff and where the sales slips were.

It was so cold in that terrible room. I went out without looking to see if Burke was with me.

He was. He said, "Nothing like any of that was on him or near him. And it's unlikely any of it'll turn up. His pants pockets were pulled inside out and emptied too. And your car's gone, so it's safe to say the bastard who did this took it. Jaguar XJ6, right? What's it worth, thirty-five, forty thou?"

"About."

"Some people like that kind of buggy. Me, I'll stick with a good old Ford. Come on, I'll drive you home."

Home! Home was a trap I now had another reason to want to get myself out of.

Or was I back to square one, choice-wise? Or wasn't that a good question to ask?

Go to hell, I told that inner voice of mine. And as things turned out, I damn near did.

$\triangledown$

13

I HAD A WHITE-KNUCKLE GRIP of the phone when I told Ault I had to move because of the stairs. But it wouldn't have made a nickel's worth of difference if my stump sprouted a new leg. I simply could not stay there.

"Then hire someone until the leg's ready. He can move in with Angela, if you want the place to yourself now. After all, she was going to house Bob, poor fellow. Give yourself a break, Toby, you've scarcely gotten going. If you'd seen what Williams did to the apartment, you'd appreciate what you accomplished. You wouldn't want to leave it."

"How did you manage the packing?" I said, weaseling out of another chance to tell him I'd seen the looting and heard the death.

"With difficulty. Oh, I didn't do any of it, a local firm did. And I'd be surprised if they didn't pocket a few items in the process. There were some good things here."

"How come they were put on the sidewalk? Wouldn't the parking lot have been safer?"

"Yes, and easier, but Mrs. Morrison complained about not having room to park. Any more questions? Sometimes I ask myself why I ever got into this business. Whoever said money isn't everything was dead right. But the main thing now is for you to stay nicely settled."

"Settled! For me this town's been a roller-coaster ride from day one."

"I hear you, but look at the results! Your project work's excellent, and Graham's enormously gratified by the feedback he's getting on you. Look. If you feel too close to the happening out back, I have plenty of space and all the privacy you need. Just say the word."

I actually said I'd think about it! I put the phone down and massaged my hand. I was miserable and vulnerable in the empty silence, no more the cat who walked by his lone. Bob had helped me shed my old skin, but growing a new one couldn't happen here. As hard as I'd worked on this apartment and as much as it had given me, I could walk away from it, just as it was, defenseless as I was, and keep far more than I'd left behind. A thought to conjure with, ay?

Sorry, no conjuring. It would hurt too much because it would mean reviewing all the reasons *why* it hurt, beginning with the day Angela ushered Bob into my hospital room and ending with the terrible sound of earth being dropped onto his coffin.

Back up. Bob's brief stay in my life hadn't begun or ended anything in the pain department. Signs of painful life in my bitter heart had been noted before then, and the reason for the pain was being addressed. Growth, by definition, is a painful process. But the pain wouldn't stop when I found what I was looking for. Because I sensed that when I did, I might blow myself and the Project and everything else clear out of the water. Could I hack that any better than my loneliness? Once, I would have said no. Now I thought, Maybe, just maybe, even if I die doing it.

I had to talk to someone, be with someone. Anyone but Ault. Pat was right about him. He swarmed all over you with acts of kindness and generosity, he threw a net over you and you didn't belong to yourself anymore. I rated that metaphor acceptable but dangerously incomplete, and dialed Meiklejohn and listened to ten rings and hung up. Just as well. I wasn't ready—i.e., I was still scared.

I stared moodily out of the kitchen window at my Jag, which had been returned to its usual place two days—or nights?—after Bob's murder, and cleaner than before. I had called Burke immediately.

"Is it wet?" he said.

I focused my birdwatching glasses. "Couple of drops on the roof, from the trees, I expect. Otherwise, dry as a bone."

"Interesting. The weather started clearing after midnight, so if your car's dry, it had to have been garaged somewhere. Unless whoever took it washed it for you just now to thank you for the loan. And he also took a hell of a risk both directions—going and coming back. He sure likes riding the edge, all things considered. Know anybody like that?"

"Offhand, no."

"Give it some thought; you've got the training. You're my first shrink, you know," he said with boyish candor. "I like to see the way your mind works. Now, you keep spare car keys?"

"One in my desk drawer, one in my wallet."

"Any signs of a break-in on your front door or the car? No?" He sighed gustily. "No, I wouldn't think so, not with someone as clever as our man. Looks like somehow he got a key of his own. Now, let's go through the motions, just to keep the franchise. What were you doing last night?"

"Nothing spectacular. I've been pretty tired lately, what with one thing and another. I did some work, played some records, went to bed about ten, ten-fifteen."

"I can appreciate that; you've sure had a plateful. So last night, just like two nights ago, you heard nothing and saw nothing out of the way. And if everything else was like the fatal night, the nurse was on duty again, and the people downstairs in front were watching the tube again, and the people in back were out of town again." He was correct, as it turned out. "Well. Gotta keep punching, right? Glad you got your wheels back. See you at the inquest. You're taking the body back home? Good."

It was on the flight back from the funeral that I began thinking about various happenings, making lists of them, arranging and rearranging them, my blood running hot with courage. But once back in the apartment, I flushed them down the toilet because I was scared.

I still was, more than ever. I reached for a pad and pencil and began another list. Questions, this time.

Item. How had Bill Hanrahan known about my leg? about Pat and me?

Item. Was BH as close to VJ as he had claimed?

Item. Was BH right that AA knew no one at Harvard?

Item. Was BH right that AA got me job here?

Item. How find out?

Item. More about VJ's alcoholism?

Item. Meaning of VJ's diary entry re AA?

Item. AA have some hold on VJ?

Item—

I stopped writing and examined the list. What popped out at me were relationships—Bill's to Vincent, Vincent's to Ault, Ault's to me.

I stared out of the window. A black speck far up in the sky swung like a pendulum, lazy and slow, then vanished. I glassed the area bounded by the upper window sashes. Nothing. Then I had him, a dark shape in front of a cloud. Broad wings, the primaries upcurled and spread. Short blunt tail, slightly wedge-shaped in flight. The back dark brown, the breast feathers buff with gray spots, and at the base of the tail a rusty red patch, the colors undetectable at this distance, of course, but I knew. A red-tailed hawk, nothing showy in the looks department, the elegance of him is his gorgeous competence.

I looked down at my list again but I was thinking of something else. How had Ault known Bob would be living with Angela when I was on two feet again? They had never talked to him if they could help it, and then only about superficial things, nor told him that we had become the nucleus of a family that — suddenly, wonderfully — included Meiklejohn and Pat.

Like a marble on a Chinese checkerboard — t' there t' there t' *there!* — one thought led to another. *Why* had no police officer or sheriff's deputy stood guard over the dead man's possessions until they were claimed? I hadn't asked Ault that — and wasn't going to now. I reached for the phone again.

Police Chief Burke was on another line. I waited, and another marble zigzagged across the board. Did I know anyone who, as Burke had put it, liked living on the edge? (Nice metaphor, that.) Someone addicted to adrenaline highs. Someone who reveled in acts of malevolent mischief, like committing a murder, then borrowing my Jag, and returning it dry after a rainstorm. Someone who bent time and the weather to his purpose, like the red-tail, and took his prey with an accuracy marvelous in a hawk but very dreadful in a man.

My mind's eye slid down a long list of people idiosyncratic enough to be worth remembering. I didn't expect the exercise to net me anything really new. The risk taker who had made such a swift powerful kill was too clever to leave a trail.

Take that back. What's essential to riding the edge, that edge that separates life from death? For one kind of lunatic it is by how little he can hang — usually publicly — by his teeth like a bunch of grapes tantalizingly within Death's reach, and yet survive. For another kind, who lives most authentically in the shadows, it is by how clearly he can lay a trail to his identity and yet escape detection. Both, like teasing lovers, court Death. What both want is to be recognized, applauded, then obliterated, made nothing. A rich prize. But to get it requires shortening the odds, becoming more and more audacious —

"Hello? Doc? You there?" Burke said. "Sorry to keep you waiting."

"Joe, why wasn't there a policeman at the Williams eviction?"

"What's on your mind?"

"I asked you first."

He covered a giggle with a fine harrumph. "The man on duty had the runs, and Allyn promised to stay until Mrs. Williams came. She didn't, and the collector kicked the bucket. And if you think that cop didn't get the hell of a reprimand for taking the word of a civilian instead of calling the station for a replacement, you're wrong. Okay, you're up."

This was really the beginning. I said slowly, "Mrs. Williams said she got no note from Dr. Allyn about the eviction and hadn't spoken to him for at least six months. I was at the bursar's for a parking sticker and met her there. She was pretty upset when she found out who I was."

"She has an ax to grind. And a load of guilt to work off. I think she made Dr. Allyn the heavy. If you don't mind me moving into your space."

"Be my guest. It's a tenable observation."

"But you don't buy it."

"No. Anger, regret, grief, yes. Guilt, no. I don't think so."

"Would you sign an affidavit?"

"No. Would you?"

I could sense him grinning boyishly. "Only if it had no effect on my pension, Doc. Even if everybody's a shrink these days, it's still a tricky area. Best keep the nose clean. But if she isn't lying, are you saying he is?"

Something Ault had said a little while ago slid across the front of my brain, stuck in one spot, went on again, like a tape with a glitch. My recall is good. I replayed that part, squeezing my eyes shut, listening hard, not answering. . . .

And heard again what I knew I'd hear.

I crossed my fingers. "You kidding? No, Joe, I wouldn't say that. Sorry to bother you. Thanks," and hung up.

But I made a note of what I'd heard on my tape. God, such a small thing! Had it been deliberate? I sat back to think about it and see where it led me.

After an hour I decided it wasn't leading me anygoddamwhere. Well, nowhere I cared to go. I ordered myself to be resolute, and began by trying Meiklejohn's number again.

"Sorry I wasn't here before," he said, meaning it. "How you doing?"

"Fine. What are you up to—say, for the next hour? I've got some correlations you asked for."

"I did?"

"Something we sort of circled around way back at my housewarming. Real fast, in the kitchen. I thought it looked promising."

"I don't remember— Oh yeah! Almost forgot. The correlations between— Right. If you've got any of that great brandy around, start marinating them in it, they'll go down better. Be right over."

I wrote something on a pad, and when he came I showed it to him, a warning finger to my lips. He nodded, though puzzled, and joined me in the welcoming ritual.

"Brandy's in the kitchen," I said, leading the way.

I had written: *I may be bugged. What to do?*

His black eyebrows drew together over his masterful nose. "God, this brandy's fantastic," he said, rereading the note as if it were paragraphs long and smacking his lips with gusto for the benefit of the bug. "But no more now. I came to work. What have you got?"

I really was prepared, and handed him some raw stuff on a possible correlation between demographics and ethnicity, and psychological profiles. "Don't know how sound it is. Thought I'd try it out on you first. Do we have to construct a new questionnaire or can we winkle stuff out of the ones we've got?"

"Mm, I think so. Aha! So I perfect it, you get the glory. Ah well, why not? I owe you for the brandy."

He sat down at the kitchen table, chair legs squawking on the floor as he arranged his big body, and went through the papers with genuine interest. "Mm. Mm. Mm-hm. Mm-hm. Yes, I can see where this would fit. . . . Yeah . . . Show this to Ault yet? Or Grier?"

"No. I've just been toying with it. Any suggestions?"

"Mm, mm-hm . . . I think a couple of queries here—and here. It's been done in my field—Benedict comes first to mind, though I sometimes felt she was reaching a bit. Give me a pencil and go do something and let me be a while." That too was for the bug. He waggled a beckoning hand and with the other sent the pencil slap-dashing across the pad.

Make like starting supper, he wrote. *Say you need something. I'll take over.*

"Hope I won't bother you," I said, rattling pots. "I might as well get supper going. How does quiche sound?" I did a little more rattling, dropped a knife, bowed to Meiklejohn's pantomimed applause.

"Fine. Thanks." He sounded nicely abstracted.

I took cans and boxes out of a cabinet; put them back as irritably as possible. Opened the fridge. "Damn. I don't want to renege, John, but I'm missing the crucial ingredient."

"So substitute."

"Eggs? Come on. I'm a purist."

He threw down the pencil and swished the papers into a pile. "Look. Time is passing and brandy makes me want to eat a horse. Let's kill two birds. You take me out to eat and I'll do something worthwhile to these notes of yours. Fair?"

"Fair, but you're a bloodthirsty bugger, I must say."

We left the house without undue haste, talking casually about peace and Gorbachev's visit to the White House.

Meiklejohn happily pulled the seat belt across his bulk and buckled up. "Where should we go? All this cloak-and-dagger stuff sharpens my appetite."

"I don't know about cloak-and-dagger, John. I certainly wasn't planning to present the work as mine." I sounded the least bit surprised.

He said quickly, "Sorry, Toby lad. Didn't mean it that way. Hunger does strange things to Scotsmen. How about that new place out past the dam? I hear they've got a good dinner buffet."

He kept the talk on restaurants, a subject dear to his heart, rating decor as rigorously as food, drink, service, and prices. He knew what he was talking about and I always liked listening to him, but I sighed in relief when we got out of the car and closed the doors.

Not until we were seated in a quiet corner of the dining room did he say, "You actually think even the car is bugged, don't you. Will you kindly tell me what's on your mind? Suspense does a number on my digestive processes."

I laughed. Meiklejohn's digestive processes could under any conditions dissolve a cast-iron stove.

I said, "What do you know about Ault?" and for a moment all sound and movement in the big room seemed frozen, as if the earth had stopped and was hanging in space like a dead lump.

14

MEIKLEJOHN'S BIG BLUE EYES narrowed and one bushy eye-brow shot up his forehead. "No more than anybody else does. For all his visibility he's a pretty private person. And attractive, charming, a fantastic cook and magnificent host. Superb dresser — and decorator, if you like bothering with that sort of stuff. He's got all kinds of money, and he gets more than twenty-four hours out of your standard day. And — a big *big* and — he has the most incredible memory I've ever encountered, which may account for his being clever rather than profound. An academic opportunist, you might say. As witness how he latched on to that dissertation of yours." He paused, shrugged, and drank water with less than his usual gusto.

"You were about to say something."

"Not really. Just . . . with all that perfection, I'm damned if I know what makes him tick. I sometimes think he does it by the numbers. You figure him out, that's your bag."

"Where's he from?"

"Don't know," he said almost irritably. "I'm not sure anyone else does. Try Personnel. I know one of the gals."

I laughed. "Is there any part of this place you don't have a foot in?"

"Probably not. But in this case I'd as soon pass. A brilliant student of mine had a reverse, a nine-month six-pound one named Patrick, and turned into a clerk. Pity. I go in every now and then and see how she's managing. It wouldn't take much to get Ault's date and place of birth."

A waiter hovered. Feeling that I had already eaten, I ordered a light dinner, but Meiklejohn lumbered over to the sumptuous buffet table and chose carefully. He regarded without joy what he brought back, and didn't even pick up his fork.

"What's the matter?" I said.

"You tell me. I've had about as much suspense as I can stand. What's all this bugging business? What's it got to do with Ault? I'm not sure I like this—this—"

"You think I do? Look, did you tell Ault that Bob was planning to move in with Angela after I got my leg?"

"No. Categorically no. It was a family matter, you might say."

"Well, she didn't tell him and neither did Bob—"

"Did Pat? Or Bob's girl?"

"I don't think so."

"Think isn't good enough. Eat. I'll be right back."

I had nothing else to do, so I ate, mechanically, without tasting a thing. My plate was clean when Meiklejohn came back but I felt no different from before. It was as though I'd eaten a mirage.

"I called them," he said. "Angela, Pat, and Mary. Had to track Angie down at the hospital. They didn't tell Ault anything. And wouldn't. Mary never even met him, and she hasn't had any funny phone calls or queries from anywhere about anything to do with Bob or Angela. But we probably talked about the idea during that great party. What did Ault say about it, and when?"

"I called him this morning to say I had to move out because of the stairs. He said that since Bob— He called him the fellow, the poor fellow! He referred to the murder as *the happening out back*!"

"Steady, lad."

I took a deep breath. "Yes. Well. He said that since Bob had been going to move in with Angela when I was on my feet again, why not find another gofer and park him with her now?"

"I see. Pretty thin evidence for bugging, though." He looked at me thoughtfully. "There has to be something else." I hesitated. "Look, lad. Either you don't trust me or you don't know where to begin. So just start at the beginning—"

"And go on till you come to the end." Bob had said that, his last night. I blinked hard. "You won't believe this."

I talked for a long time, Meiklejohn eating mechanically, as I had, eyebrows shooting up his forehead, eyes bulging, or eyebrows sliding down his big nose, eyes slitted, staring at his plate or into space.

When I stopped, he shook his head. "You're certifiable, you know that? Sounds like a bad movie. You're damn right I don't believe it. And yet . . ." He got up and walked twice around the table, one hand behind his back, the other clasping the nape of his neck, as if he were working out a problem. Then he darted sideways into his chair as if the music had just stopped. "Remember Ault talking about Don Holmes taking Vinnie's place? Well, I didn't tell anybody, but I went up to Montréal to see him and damn near didn't recognize him. Talk about culture shock! He'd been home for three months, but it was clear that this place would be too tough for him to take. You don't spend years in the bush anywhere and then waltz back into the twentieth century and do your old thing. Ault had to have seen that. But from what Don said, it's obvious Ault was playing with him. Enthusiastically offering him a nice berth and then telling him, Well, no, actually you're not quite ready and we really can't wait — which, to be fair, is true — and so on and so forth. It was an exercise in nasty, clothed in concern. And he was playing with us too, showing his muscle again. All that crap about knowing History would accept any candidate he gave them."

"Well, would they? Would Jesse?"

"Absolutely. History likes him and trusts him, and why not — he's a class act. Which I've long since thought is just that, an act, and I may say that this is the first time I've said it out loud. For a long time I've had the feeling he does it by the numbers. You're complicating my life, Toby, damn you. If you hadn't opened your big mouth, I could've kept on sweeping the dirt under the rug. And I just might, after all," he added. "Now. I think the only thing I can cope with right now is something concrete. No theories or wild stories, just something definite in the yes-or-no department. Bugging brought us here, so let's get cracking. To your left — over there — is the guy you want. The one waving his arms around."

I had noticed two men arguing in sign language. No one in the big room could have missed them. The large frames and thick eye-distorting lenses of the older man, and the brigandlike *mostaccios* that hid his mouth, seemed nothing more nor less than a disguise and gave the strong sense that he was untrustworthy. I watched, fascinated, as he inserted food into that black bush without its knocking anything off his fork. His companion, a handsome man with big dark eyes and chiseled, mobile features, flung down his fork and shot out of his chair. He bobbed and weaved, stamped his foot, waggled his head between his hands in mock horror. Then he sat down and shook his head forcefully during the rebuttal, eating all the while. The onlookers put the two of them into the same category with Meiklejohn and probably wondered, as I did, why deaf people didn't learn to read lips instead of thousands of gestures.

"The gymnast is Ellis Hart," Meiklejohn said. "A thirty-year-old electronics addict, computer wizard, a real nut. Give him all that weird beeping stuff to play with, puzzles, gadgets, toys, whatever, and he's in heaven. Doesn't matter that he can't hear them, as long as they have a printout or climb the walls or explode or whatever they're supposed to do. He lost his hearing when he was six, so he speaks very well, but we write. Got that pad? Okay, let's move in on them and have coffee. Norman Strong is a liar and an incompetent in Sociology. You can just ignore him. Provided you keep your back to the wall."

He hesitated, then added, "Look, lad, I can't go the distance with you on this, at least not yet. I've known Ault a long time. I need space to get this all sorted out."

He wrote on the pad, *Ellis, watch out for this guy, he's Harvard-honed,* and left abruptly, taking Norman with him.

I felt abandoned, betrayed, and all I could do was tell Ellis, on my pad, what I was after, but not why. He laughed heartily. "I like to establish moral ascendancy over people, it's such a good feeling, but I have such contempt for Norman that I'd as soon forgo it in his case. Honesty rides me hard when I've been with him any length of time. I wish I had a nickel for every time he's said 'to tell you the honest truth' or 'to be perfectly honest.' He wouldn't recognize that article if bushels of it were being given away at the door.

"All right. Bugging isn't hard to do or to find. All you need is a wireless system with a voice-activated tape that can record up to ten hours. It could take days for a tape to get filled up, if the buggee leads a quiet life, doesn't see many people or make many calls. So if you have easy access to it, you wouldn't have to check it all that often.

"Microphones are about the size of a quarter. If you open your telephone receiver where the speaker is, you'll see what they look like, more or less. You can stick mikes anywhere, but they're generally put in the room where the TV is because that's usually where people spend most of their time. The recorder can go just about anywhere, in the cellar or wherever. That's all there is to it.

"You really don't need my help finding this stuff, Dr. Frame, not that I wouldn't like to go along. Adventure's just what I need after Norman. He never learned much and he doesn't want to learn any more. Deafness becomes him. Blindness too — which he's working on!

But I've got work to do, and I have to get home. If you don't mind giving me a ride?"

I wrote, *No problem. But what about a bug on my car? Possible?*

"A homing device, not a bug. Say, this sounds really serious. Personal or professional?"

I wrote, *Personal and urgent.*

He jumped up, his eyes shining with excitement. "Then let's go. If there's anything on your car that shouldn't be there, I'll find it!"

His double garage was insulated, heated, well lighted, and half of it stuffed to the rafters with boxes and cartons. "Various transplants for my computer babies," he said. I parked in the other half, which was empty except for a collapsible table leaning against the wall. Tools covered the back wall. A dusty jumpsuit and a filthy painter's cap hung from a hook in a corner.

Ellis indicated a carton to sit on, then approached the Jag like a lover, his eyes and hands caressing it with a passionate respect. His coat and jacket flew like great bats and collapsed in a corner. He pulled on the jumpsuit and dived unbuttoned under the car as to a rendezvous, his cap coming off in his haste. Finally, regretfully, he surfaced with a small metal object in one dirty hand.

Could anything naturally dislodge it? I wrote.

"Oh, maybe a sharp impact, a really jarring bump. Want me to put it back?"

I said no, and thanks, and went back to Ault's big house, all its windows dark, and snuck down into the cellar to search for something I no more wanted to find than Meiklejohn did. I was scared and I was ashamed. My mouth was dry and I wanted a drink. My stump hurt and I had a headache and my armpits ached from the crutches and I was *hungry!* But I had opened a can of worms, and I was stuck with it. And so was Meiklejohn, like it or not.

I opened the cellar door inside the back entry and turned on the switch at the head of the stairs. Slowly, carefully, I went down the worn steps, wondering if a bug was hidden in the dim reaches below, recording every sound my crutches made and every rasping breath I drew.

There didn't have to be a bug or a recorder anywhere. I was wasting my time looking. Whoever wanted to know what I was up to, would know, sooner or later. Because Meiklejohn, who didn't have a nasty cell in that booze-loose body of his, was never able to keep his mouth shut.

$\bigtriangledown$

15

AULT MUST HAVE EMPLOYED an army to clean the cellar and keep it so. What little it contained was laid out neatly on open shelves or hung from hooks or propped against freshly whitewashed walls. The doors to old cabinets and storerooms had been removed, as if to say that here nothing was hidden. And nothing was, as far as I could tell in the dim light.

Using the flashlight from the Jag, I looked behind the furnace, under the stairs, along the joists and foundation.

Nothing. A perfectly innocent place, without a single cobwebby corner to lend credence to my mission there.

I stood in the middle of the main room, thinking. My great-grandmother's house had been like this one, and had something this one lacked, or seemed to lack. Not possible, not in a house of this vintage.

I started looking again, my flashlight beginning to die.

And then I saw what I'd missed before. About six feet in from the outside wall and the stairs, between two joists and flush against the white ceiling, was a white-painted pine door. It squeaked as it swung down. I looked up into a laundry chute whose walls were as beautifully made as the hardwood floors upstairs.

Once, domestics in ruffled caps and aprons had dropped soiled bedding and clothing down that chute into waiting tubs and baskets. On rainy days, the boldest kids of the family, kids like my father and my uncles, had landed giggling on piles of sheets and towels, voluminous petticoats and long underwear. Many a howling family cat had taken the trip too. Now a recorder about as thick as the Boston phone book but not so wide hung from a nail above the opening.

And just beyond my reach.

For some reason I always got dizzy, especially on crutches, when I stood fairly close to a building and looked up at its rooftop or steeple. Now, as I peered up into the chute's black dwindling reaches, my head spun and nausea rose in my throat, because now I had to balance on one crutch and, with the other, goose the recorder off its nail and catch it when it fell.

The right crutch tip wavered dizzyingly inches from the recorder. I swallowed part of my dinner a second time and tried again, urged on by the possibility that Ault might come at any moment. Wishing I had thought to call him and make sure that he was home, I poked too hard, teetered, and fell in a clatter of crutches, hugging the recorder to my chest. The wire connected to the microphone in my apartment lay coiled snakelike on my leg. It could have reached to the attic, there was so much of it.

I rested for a few moments, panting. When I was calmer I sat up and looked at the amount of tape piled up on the right-hand spool. Well, what do you know! I thought. I'm a star.

I pressed Pause, then Reverse. The spool hissed and began to spin. I stopped it and pressed Play. And heard myself telling Meiklejohn that the brandy was in the kitchen, heard the door closing behind us when we left, heard everything in between. Nothing significant or suspicious to the bugger (pun apt but not intended).

I reversed to the beginning of the tape, watching it pile up on the left side. Again I pressed Play.

A telephone rang and Bob said, "Good evening, Dr. Frame's residence," and then came his outrageous resumption of his old speech and my pompous lecture afterward. Just what a man needed before going out to be murdered.

I heard Burke waking me up to tell me Bob was dead. I heard my call to Burke about the return of my Jag. I heard my arrangement for a flight, never taken, to West Virginia. The arranging of a flight to Arkansas to attend Bob's funeral. My attempt to tell Ault that I was moving out. And again, the sound of fine brandy being poured into a balloon, a pencil scribbling over paper, a knife dropping, the clatter of a pot, Meiklejohn and I on our way out to eat at the new place near the dam.

Putting it back took far too long. But this time I used the aluminum stepladder I remembered seeing in one of the doorless storerooms. If I'd thought of it before, I would have saved myself a fall.

I was exhausted when I reached my apartment, but to rest there, then, was out of the question. I headed for the kitchen and gave my bug some cheerful whistling and tea-making. Obviously I had to leave the thing where it was, wherever it was, and live circumspectly, which meant, I told myself in dismay, remaining Ault's tenant, and no parties here, no Pat here or on the phone, no calls to Montréal from here, no airline reservations made from here. Ault mustn't —

Hold it! How come you're convinced he's your enemy? And if he is, pulling your horns all the way in is the same as sounding the alarm. Think again.

I leaned against the sink and thought, in relief, that I wasn't convinced and never wanted to be. I could only go by Ault's stance toward me, and never mind anybody else. If he put his foot in it now and again — his treatment of Don Holmes in Montréal, if true, was not attractive — well, he too was human and fallible. To me he'd been nothing but kind, generous, and helpful. Maybe Meiklejohn was right to bail out. Maybe I was all wrong, and not for the first time.

In the rising wind the oak tree outside the living room whispered against the window like a night spirit seeking shelter. This gave me an idea. I tiptoed to the window and meowed plaintively behind my hand. Tiptoed to the kitchen, said, "Well, I'll be — !" Tramped heavily back to the window, opened it, closed it, meowed again, louder. Back to the kitchen for milk-pouring and saucer-on-floor activity and one last meow. "There you go, little fella," I said, and thought, Now we'll see.

Making no attempt at stealth, I stuffed toothbrush, razor, clean shirt, and underwear into a supermarket plastic bag, slung it over my shoulder, and went out, temporarily leaving everything else behind.

Everything but a four-letter word I had filed that morning for future reflection. The word *here*. Ault must have called me from the Morrisons' apartment — they were away more than they were home. Some good things *here,* he had said.

If he were calling from his home or on the phone in his Mercedes, he would have said *there*.

Pat was the only person I wanted to be with, and I turned the Jag in her direction. She had driven me to the airport the day before Bob's funeral and picked me up on my return, and we'd talked on the phone a few times. But we hadn't been alone since my impromptu party three weeks ago, and I was jolted by the intensity of my need for her. It wasn't part of my plans and I didn't know what to do about it. I put this uncertainty aside with the rest, something I was getting very good at, like Hamlet, and drove a little faster. I couldn't risk, though, telling her even a part of what I'd told Meiklejohn. Anything concerning Ault had to be just fine, or at least neutral. I didn't know if I could pull it off. In her bed, in her arms, I wouldn't need to try.

I turned into one of the town's finest old streets and slowed at the driveway of an antique house smaller than Ault's but no less attractive, only one downstairs window glowing now with light. My heart beat happily. Then it stopped, and I couldn't breathe.

At the side door stood Ault's Mercedes.

16

In THE MORNING THE orthotist called to say he was free to do a cast of my stump. It was more than a month since I'd been hospitalized.

The doctor took a look and told me to forget it. "You're still losing weight and there's still inflammation. If you want more gangrene and more amputation, fine. Otherwise, eat better and exercise. Then we'll see." He didn't bother saying that depression was the real gangrene, that it was almost out of control, and that I didn't have all the time in the world to pull my socks up and get cracking.

But depression, which doesn't prevent your knowing what to do about it, prevents your mustering the energy to do it with. What energy I managed to collect I spent on my persona, my professional performance. Once home, I collapsed in a heap and stared at a wall.

Two days after I'd seen Ault's car at Pat's house, Meiklejohn stopped briefly at my office door. "Asheville, North Carolina. June 1, 1939. Satisfied?"

"I'm ... not sure. Thanks, John. You busy tonight?" He nodded and went off.

At suppertime I ignored a message on my phone tape to call Pat, had tea and stale bread, and slept from one bad dream to another, the common themes betrayal, murderous hatred, and death. In the morning I found I'd lost another pound and a half. The cotton socks on my stump were beginning to slide off.

That scared me into action. I told myself that self-pity was the most disgusting of all emotions and that learning something was the best and possibly the only antidote to depression. Interesting, if tardy. What did I want to learn? As if I didn't know. I reached for list-making paper.

I wrote for some time, then made myself my first decent breakfast in days and aggressively enjoyed every mouthful. My two classes went smoothly. My crutches seemed to hurt me less. I cooked and ate a complete dinner, watched a good movie on television, slept reasonably well.

Saturday dawned clear and brisk. With luck the weather would be this good for the Festival, two weeks from today. Since Bob's death it hadn't mattered if or with whom I went. It did now, though I wasn't in a festival mood and didn't expect to be. But I had a strong sense that it was going to be a momentous day, that something important was going to happen. Handicapped as I was, the better the weather, the more easily I would be able to keep up with events.

Meanwhile, there were other things to do. After juice, oatmeal, bacon and eggs and toast, and pastry and coffee, I went out to a phone booth to call Pat, rock-hard in my determination to say nothing about seeing Ault's car at her house Tuesday night.

"I was beginning to wonder if I'd done something wrong," she said. "When I didn't hear from you, I mean."

"I'm sorry. I haven't been the best company." Then, stupidly, rashly, unable to stop myself, I added, "Not since Tuesday night, anyway." I sounded like a stranger to myself, my voice raspy with childish, stored-up resentment.

"Tuesday night?"

"Tuesday night. Who's the innocent act for, this time? I'd be interested to know!"

"I'm sorry, Toby. I don't know what you're talking about."

"Don't you? Well now. Tuesday night I came by, saw Ault's car in your driveway—very suggestive phrase, that—and figured three's a crowd, so I kept on going."

After a pause she said coolly, "Perhaps it was just as well," and hung up, and I stood there with the receiver in my hand and rage at myself and her and Ault and the whole goddamned world roaring in my ears.

Back to the apartment to pack for an overnight. And this time I did leave town.

I spent the afternoon in my adviser's Brattle Street mansion, a drafty old place perennially imposing in its faded mustard-colored paint and dusty shrubs. I hadn't bothered calling first. He was always home on Saturdays, and I was always welcome. I arrived after lunch, when he was just settling down in his office for several hours of work.

"You've got something on your mind," he said. "I'll give you ten minutes to get it off. Then I have a client." He had stopped smoking a year ago and was now addicted to sugar-free gum, which he tongued from side to side in his mouth and occasionally cracked loudly. He was short and round and balding, and there was an endearing gap between his upper central teeth.

"The only person I've talked to about this thinks I'm crazy and dropped me like a hot potato," I said.

"He may be right. Carry on." He folded a fresh stick of gum into his mouth, leaned back, and tented his hands under his double chin.

I gave him a brief version of what I had told Meiklejohn, adding the suspicions I had had of the big man.

"Let's see if I got this straight," he said. "A poor ignorant ridgerunner with a rudimentary knowledge of the English tongue deliberately left you to die in a wilderness, is guilty of who knows how many crimes of burglary and murder, has metamorphosed into the quintessential man of the world and academe, and for fifteen years has been tracking you with evil intent, aided and abetted now if not then by an anthropologist, but you are no longer sure of that." He wrapped his gum carefully in a scrap of paper and aimed it at the wastebasket. It went wide. With an exasperated sigh he retrieved it. "You're crazy," he said, settling back again.

"The thought crossed my mind."

"It'd make a helluva best-seller. Okay, time's up."

I was halfway out the door with the faculty directory when he said, "I thought you'd learned something, Toby. Was I wrong?"

"What would you consider acceptable proof that I'm right?"

He pushed his glasses up onto his forehead and regarded me unblinkingly. He was about to answer when the front doorbell rang. "Later," he said.

I made my slow way up the wide curving stairs to "my" room, wondering if this would prove to be my last visit. I'd lived in dorms all the way to the end of my doctorate, but figuratively speaking this place had been my home since my mother's death. I wasn't sure I could bear any more losses, and made up my mind that there weren't going to be any.

I opened the directory and reached for the phone, to ask the senior staffers in History, Sociology, and Psychology, simply, if they knew Ault Allyn. I didn't know what my answer would be if they said Yes, why?

By the time the last of the fifty-minute hours downstairs was over, I had gotten exactly nowhere. I dragged down to the kitchen uncertain of myself and very tired.

My adviser was putting groceries away. Picking a route over an obstacle course of shopping bags, I headed for the dining alcove at the other side of the room.

"Betty got an emergency call about her mother just before you came," my adviser said, "so she had to take off. You look like you need a drink."

He put an excellent Scotch before me and went on unpacking the bags. It was so peaceful and ordinary there, and my tale was so bizarre. Could I find proof good enough to convince people I was right? Was there any proof? I watched my adviser stand on tiptoe to put three sane sensible boxes of spaghetti onto a high shelf, and knew myself for an utter fool.

Now wait just a damn minute! I told myself. There's the bugging, for one thing.

"Did I mention the recorder?" I said.

My adviser kicked aside one emptied bag, hoisted another onto the countertop, and impatiently tore it open. Oranges rolled like marbles. He fielded one that fell off the counter, and dropped it.

"Goddammit! What recorder?"

"In the laundry chute."

"In the laundry chute." He picked up the orange. "Of course. Where else? Who's the star turn?"

"A one-legged academic. The events of the past two weeks are all there, with plenty of space left for a lot more."

He looked at me searchingly, a modern Diogenes with a bunch of broccoli in his hand. "What did you do with it?"

"Put it back where I found it."

"And you think it's Allyn's?"

"Who else's? It's his building. He has access to it at all times. Unless it's Meiklejohn's. His knack of picking up information is legendary. Still think I'm crazy?"

He started to say something, and for the second time since I'd come was interrupted by the ring of a bell. The phone, this time. He picked it up, listened worriedly, said he'd be right there, and hung up.

"Betty," he said. "Her mother's worse. I gotta split. Stay if you want. Don't know when I'll be back."

I didn't feel like staying in that empty barn by myself but I didn't want to go home either. I booked into the Treadway, near the Square, and went across the street to eat potato pancakes at the Wursthaus. It was marvelous being back, and I didn't mind waiting for a table. I thought I might even check out the Brattle Theater afterward. Whatever was playing was worth seeing, and what I saw didn't matter anyway. It was enough just to be there.

There was a cottony, fuzzy quality to the noise that wrapped me up as in a cozy dream. I was content. The pancakes were great. I tucked in, and felt the pounds piling on healthily.

A thin voice pushed my name diffidently through the fuzz.

Reluctantly I looked up, not because I didn't like Clock the Crock but because he'd interrupted my peace.

Ken Clockedile, Sociology. Gentle, generous, capable, but not aggressive enough, because of his odd name, maybe, ever to rise above an assistantship anywhere. He must have known that he would never be tenured at Harvard, which was all he wanted of life, but he was too sensible to let this sour him. We had been in many classes together, and I had consulted him on a couple of points while writing my dissertation. I hadn't seen him since May, when he had said that the kudos Ault was getting for the Project should properly go to me. The other chair at my tiny table was empty, and he was a friend, and alone. So.

He let me buy him more coffee, and nodded sadly at the crutches propped against the wall. "I heard about your accident, Toby. Incredible, isn't it, the way students have changed. I mean, the violence these days. You never know who's going to stand up in your class and blow your brains out. Teachers ought to take out insurance against alienated youth. That fellow who attacked you—good heavens," he said mildly.

"He got the worst of it, Crock, he's still catatonic. I didn't think it was in the news, though. How did you hear about it?"

"From Ault Allyn. I bumped into him a couple of weeks ago—no, three. Over at the Brattle, waiting to go in. He was on a panel at Northeastern last June about mothers in the work force and what that portended for children in the future—and for the lucky characters like us, all that work to do, figuring things out." He smiled at his little joke. "Thought I'd go see what manner of man would be influencing your life. After the discussion I told him I knew you and asked him a few questions, and we had coffee. So he remembered me."

"Three weeks ago? On the Saturday? Crock, you sure?"

"Yes. There was a French film I wanted to see, one matinee only, and I'd always missed it before. So had he, he said. Why?"

Why indeed.

"Just wondered," I said casually, but my heart was pounding and the dinner I had enjoyed lay like so much cement in my stomach.

"Charming guy, that Allyn, you know, Toby? Very able too. Imaginative. Must be nice, working with him. But I still feel he grabbed the lion's share of your creativity. Don't let him do that again, if you can help it. Guard your output."

"Well, thanks, but I hope you didn't tell him that."

"My goodness, no. That'd be like rubbing salt in his wounds. He loves Cambridge – comes down whenever he can, though he doesn't know anybody here except for you and me. He told me he applied here, oh, about eight years ago. And you know? He never even made the short list, and still feels very bad about it. I was surprised as all getout when he said that. Right on the line at the Brattle. Can you imagine? I was a bit embarrassed. Not that he was complaining or anything. In fact, he's the most gracious man I've ever met. But – with his ability, not even to make the short list!"

My heart pounded faster. "Do you know why?"

"No. He seems the perfect type for this place. I asked Steiner about it on Monday. He wasn't department chair then, but he was on the interviewing committee. He said Allyn's paper credentials were fantastic, it wasn't that. Nothing wrong with Chapel Hill, Dartmouth, and Indiana. But the feeling was that there was something about him that was – oh, what was the word he used? Plastic. I'm not entirely sure I know what he meant. He said Allyn was exceptionally good, too much so, if that's possible. I wouldn't have said so. I mean, how can anyone be too good?

"Anyway, Toby, do yourself a favor from now on. Don't give away any more freebies. The next guy who latches on to you might not be so generous as Allyn's been."

Back home on Sunday night, I found that I had gained four pounds and that the inflammation was gone from my stump. I looked and felt better, despite the thoughts chasing each other around in my head. Again I wrote them down.

Item. Why did AA take pains to give the impression we were going to have dinner at the Harvard Faculty Club? Only faculty and their guests eat there.

Item. Was AA's important appointment in Cambridge canceled, or did he go just to see a movie?

Item. What really happened when I fell into the traffic? Did he push me? What did he say when he helped me up? It sounded — it sounded like — ???

Item. Unless the odds of my meeting KC are just too great, is AA's telling him but not me the truth an example of his riding the edge?

I felt, suddenly, as I had in my adviser's sane sensible kitchen. Like a fool. Better men than I thought I was one. René. Jean. Meiklejohn. My adviser. So would the Crock, if I had had the courage to tell him what I had told them. It wasn't bizarre, it was outrageous and unforgivable. How else could I see myself but as an absolute damn fool?

Maybe. But there's the recorder, remember. And maybe he's the one who pushed you into the traffic — and squeezed your stump besides. And he said something you half recognized, and you know it.

It could have been anybody else, I snarled. The handicapped are a treat to the bushwhacker, the sniper, the bastard who shoots from the hip. Ault isn't that sort.

I refused to discuss it further. After a long bath and a reassuring check of my stump, I ate a weight-producing snack and went to bed. It was as well to be in a healthy frame of mind, because the Project team was meeting at nine-thirty in the morning.

Despite the sticks I was in fine fettle when I arrived at Ault's big office. I looked forward to his usual coffee and cake. I felt great.

Madge gave me her usual sweet smile. Next to her was an abnormally thin middle-aged man with a bluish cast to his skin. He looked so much like Vincent exhumed that I felt chilled.

"Murray Costa, from History," Mother Madge said. "Why, Toby! I've never seen you looking better!" and Murray reached across the table to shake hands, his startlingly warm and firm.

Ault came in with a cheerful greeting and a loaded tray, the coffee steaming. Meiklejohn arrived moments later, carrying his notes and a folded jacket. He shook it out so that we could see it, then tossed it over the back of a chair. "Somebody left this in my office last week. Anybody here belong to it? Too valuable, I'd say, to be lying around." He gave me a cool nod, sat down and reached for a slice of cake from the tray, and made a production of looking into his notes.

If you are close enough to football players or ballet dancers doing their thing, you can hear their groans and grunts, you can see them wince and sweat. But when a well-schooled shrink who is also an anal type of the first water takes a sudden brutal blow to the solar plexus, you can be sitting in his lap and see not so much as the flicker of his eyelid.

My eyelid didn't flicker. I sat like a stone. Like a stone, I didn't breathe.

The jacket was dark brown, and long. It was of supple expensive leather, and beautifully tailored. I knew how much it cost because I had bought it.

For Bob.

17

"**I** PUT IT THERE, JOHN," Ault said. "It's not yours?"

The coffee's fragrance filled the room. Madge offered to pour for me. Managing a no-thank-you smile, I shook my head and shuffled my papers. The strong immaculate hands that had made that coffee had robbed Bob of his life, stripped the jacket from his body, and planted it cunningly for me to see. In Chief Burke's presence I would have signed an affidavit to that effect. There was no way that I could drink a single drop of Ault's coffee. Nausea was making my head whirl. I clenched my jaws and made meaningless notes and wanted to get away.

But I had to stay and ignore the jacket, or Ault would know he had scored. And I had to ignore the flick of Meiklejohn's eyes at me, because anything I braced him with afterward might put him permanently into Ault's camp. Another fanciful scenario? Maybe. Maybe not. He *knew* the jacket was Bob's.

On the long table under the windows were uncollated copies of the questionnaires Ault and I had worked on in Cambridge. He had already given me my packet. Whistling softly through his teeth, he began assembling others, while everyone but me drank his coffee and ate his luscious pastries. Madge began humming along with him, the way people do to supermarket music while they dream up and down the aisles. She said, "What *is* that song, Ault? I know I know it!"

"What is?" Ault turned to look at her, then continued his slow walk along the table, picking up one sheet after another. "Oh. Well, it's a ballad, actually. A love song. A pretty brisk one, at that. An old Elizabethan thing—"

"I remember now! The first phrase, anyway. 'Over the mountains and over the waves'—"

She stopped, and Ault's clear baritone took up the line. " 'Under the fountains and under the graves, under floods that are deepest, which Neptune obey—' "

Madge joined in, her voice sweet and true. " 'Over rocks that are steepest, Love will find out the way.' " She laughed merrily. "No wonder the tempo's so brisk. Love, the determined survivor—"

"Like hate. Right, Toby?" Ault said.

"Can't be any other way," I said, open-faced and pedantic, watching his unfaltering hands staple another packet and set it aside. "Everything in life and in nature has its opposite. Wet—dry, cold—hot, up—down, night—day, et cetera. Makes things interesting."

"Indeed it does. Keeps you on your toes, so to speak."

"Yes, well, perhaps," Madge said, her pleasure tainted. "Anyway, it's a marvelous song. Where did you learn it, Ault?"

"During my undergraduate fieldwork in the Appalachians." He pronounced the third syllable correctly, with a short *a*.

"Oh, really. I found it in stories about upper New York State in the early nineteenth century. Well, since it's part of the Elizabethan heritage, I expect it can be found all down the eastern coast. Probably as far as South Carolina, where the French influence comes in. Oh, there's so much richness in all the back countries! Isn't it a shame how people think ancient songs are unimportant!"

"Yes, it is. Along with the correct pronunciation of the name. A small matter to everybody but the inhabitants. As you'd expect of outsiders."

At this slightly caustic comment, I kept my head down, my face bland, my pen busy. I don't think Madge even heard. She was back in her notes, humming happily under her breath. Meiklejohn ate pastries and read the morning paper. Murray Costa, an anorexic type, stared into his lap. Finally Ault passed the collated material to them and sat down, his shadow momentarily blocking the sunlight gleaming on Bob's jacket.

We went over the revised questionnaires item by item and discussed the mechanics of distributing them to the public. Madge's terrified "Oh my god!" interrupted this essential, boring business.

A student with a horrible bloody gash on his cheek and a gaping wound showing through his torn T-shirt clung to the door frame. He sank groaning to his knees, then fell over in a heap.

Meiklejohn jumped up and went over to him. Ault stayed in his seat, his mobile lips twitching.

The lad opened one eye, winked at Meiklejohn, and got to his feet, grinning. "Pretty good, huh? Hey, I'm sorry to bust in, Dr. Allyn, but Maintenance is being real hard-nosed about access to that space we were promised. If we don't get in pretty damn quick, we just won't be ready on the big day, and I'd hate to waste any of this good stuff. Maybe you can light a fire under their—them. I sure couldn't. Here's the number. Catch you later. Gee, thanks, don't mind if I do!" He snatched up a pastry, left a slip of paper in its place, and ran off, the pastry half out of his mouth like a grotesque tongue.

Ault indulgently shook his head over the scrap of paper. "That budding sociologist evidently wants to solve people's problems by scaring them to death. He went rooting around and found some empty labs in the old Chem Building and has big plans for a house of horrors."

"Baptist Church in my town has one every Halloween. In the Sunday-school rooms," Meiklejohn said. "Oh my, the terrified girls I had to comfort down there! Every year I spent a fortune on tickets so's to keep their courage up."

Amid laughter, Madge's a little uncertain, we got back to work. I thought, Nothing sick or evil could possibly exist in this group. And then my eye fell on Bob's jacket.

Grier drifted in shortly before noon and sank into a chair, sighing. Madge immediately offered him a pastry, which he ate obediently.

"Lunch, Grier?" Ault said when the meeting was over, but Grier said he had dropped in only to collect me and talk over some department business. I went off gratefully with him, and we headed for the Faculty Club dining room.

"How's it going with the leg, Toby?"

He never really wanted clinical answers. Fine, I said.

"Pity you won't be all set for the Festival," he went on, "but I swear you're in better shape now than when you first came, in spite of everything. Best thing I ever did was get you up here. Tell me about your new idea."

"What new idea?"

"What you're working on with Meiklejohn. Ault told me."

I had had an entire morning to absorb one dreadful kick in the head, and I was getting good at it. I said calmly, "You sure it wasn't Meiklejohn who told you?"

"No, it was Ault, yesterday. Why?"

"Oh, no reason," I said. "Just wondered."

From the other end of the diagonal that split the main campus, someone hurried toward us, waving.

"Ah!" Grier said with pleasure. "That's Horace Knowles. You haven't met our president yet, Toby?"

"No, but I have an invitation to his Thanksgiving open house for new staffers."

"You'll enjoy it, it's cozier. A lot more manageable than his Christmas do." The president of the university was only a few yards away now, and Grier, livelier than usual, called out, "Horace, hello! Where are you heading? I want you to meet my latest acquisition."

Horace Knowles was even thinner than Murray Costa, and resembled a well-dressed skeleton heading back to its grave. Well, I thought, if Ault has the trustee support Meiklejohn said he does, he'll be president here even before he makes chairman of his department. But when Knowles reached us, I changed my mind. He looked like a Zen master hundreds of years old who would outlive Ault and everybody else by hundreds more.

"Precisely why I rushed after you," he said, not even breathing hard. "I recognized you from the crutches, Dr. Frame, if you'll pardon my saying so. I'm immensely impressed by everything I'm hearing about you. You have staying power, among other things. I admire that in a man."

"Thank you, sir. I'm working with a great group."

He said charmingly, "As am I. We have some conspicuously fine people here. Conspicuous for their devotion to duty and their gentlemanly acceptance of tragedy and disappointment. Very fine. Very sporting."

His charm was practiced and from another era, and he might have been addressing an honors convocation, but he meant what he said. Pleading luncheon with some trustees, he declined Grier's invitation to eat with us, shook hands, and went off at a brisk trot toward the building we had just left.

"He meant Vincent," Grier said, "for the fine way he's conducted himself all these years since his wife's death. And he meant Ault too, of course." He lowered his voice, although there was no one near us. "Ault doesn't know it yet, but Jesse will be taking over again next week. His doctor gave him a clean bill of health, and Horace wants to break the news to Ault himself. He thinks the world of him, and so do I. If for no other reason than that Ault was responsible for your coming here.

When one of my assistants left just as the Project was getting under way, Ault said we could kill two birds with one stone, as it were. But I expect he told you that."

"No," I said. "He didn't." What Ault was telling me, through Grier, was that he had a fixed purpose, a boundless patience, a sharp eye, a steady hand, a deadly aim.

But he was about to be robbed, stripped, by Jesse of what for months he had viewed as his. Cold fear gripped me. "My god!" I blurted out. "What's he going to do now!"

"Oh, I shouldn't worry about Ault, though it does you credit," Grier said placidly. "He's a resourceful type."

18

THAT AFTERNOON THE DOCTOR, irritable with surprise, pronounced me ready for a cast. This was done on Saturday. Progress. About six weeks and one or two fittings later, I would be walking again.

After the cast-making I drove to my adviser's house to bring him up to date, get his feedback this time on my general health and stability, and use his phone. He was on his way to a meeting and rushed by, telling me to stay put. Par.

Betty gave me lunch in the big kitchen. We talked about her mother and senility and grateful death, and she began to weep. I kissed her cheek and went into the study to call Pete Flori in Virginia.

"Sorry I couldn't get back to you sooner, Pete, but — "

"Yeah, I heard. Too bad about the leg, Toby. One of your colleagues filled me in. Nice of him to call."

"He *what*? *Who* called?" But I knew. Ault had acquired another messenger.

"Allyn with a y. Ault Allyn. Good old southern name. Said he reads all my columns. Very flattering, I must say. He's been following the Grassy Ridge Bald dispute in particular. I expect you've talked about that, the two of you. Okay, so what's on your mind?"

"You'll think I'm nuts, Pete."

"Are you?"

"No. But everybody else — "

"Everybody else hasn't led the life I've led. Okay, I'm switching to listening mode. Try me."

I tried him with the bare bones, no names.

"Could be," he said calmly, but I knew the old newshound's nostrils were quivering. "I've heard wilder ones, most of 'em true. So?"

"I want to talk to the father of the kid René and Jean found on the Loudoun Heights."

"Why? Think your mysterious persecutor's involved?"

"Maybe. Listen, Pete, what do you know about him—the father? What's he like?"

"Randal Shelton? Well, businesswise he's rough, tough, and imaginative. His ancestors're English nobility who came over in the sixteen hundreds, and the family's been plundering the mountains, the people, and the state and federal governments ever since. So he inherited plenty and made and married plenty more, but he's never been conspicuously generous to Appalachia. Like J. P. Morgan, he feels he owes the public nothing. In short, a ruthless son of a bitch. Has a lifelong rep all over the area as a cocksman, which might count as generosity of a kind. Handsome. Very fit. In his late sixties but seems ten, fifteen years younger. They say the boy's death doesn't seem to have slowed him down any. Hard to believe—his only son."

"Any paternity suits or claims against him?"

"Oh, people talk. You know. Small towns. Villages. But such botheration he could settle handily out of court, and probably has. His personal property and the company's have been burglarized and vandalized over the years, but the common view is that it's retaliation by the locals for his despoiling their mountains, not their women. Never seems to stop him, though. He just builds more and buys more, and the company grows too. Put him in a novel of the mid-nineteenth century, when men were brawling and boisterous and women were lusty and loyal, and he'd fit right in." He sighed heavily. "Some men just don't seem to fit their times, you know?"

He wasn't looking for an answer. Some favored fantasy had claimed him. Were he able to live it, it would render him unrecognizable—if not to himself, to everyone who knew him.

I waited.

"So," he said briskly, the attack over. "You want to meet this character, eh? You proposing to shrink him? He's nobody to mess with, boy."

"I only want to know what's been stolen from him."

"What makes you think he'd tell you?"

"It's worth a shot. Any idea where I can reach him?"

"Ask those crazy Frenchmen I read about. They've probably got his jockstrap size in those books of theirs, along with his address and everything else."

"I'd rather keep them out of it for now, Pete."

"Oh? Well, okay, hold on a minute."

I could hear him whistling through his teeth as he opened drawers and doors and slammed them shut. "Okay," he said at last. "Best thing is to contact his Asheville office. He lives nearby."

I wrote down the number he gave me, and promised to keep in touch.

Now, should I write, call, or just appear? And would that modern pirate talk to me when I did?

I shelved the problem and went back into the kitchen. It was empty. Betty might be upstairs crying or sleeping, or out somewhere, and god knew when my adviser would be back. I was too restless to wait around, and too tired to cope with my adviser's examination of my state of mind, motives, et al. I scribbled a note on the chalkboard by the phone and drove home — home, god save the mark! — for a long soak and a rest. My stump had been uncovered and scrutinized and arranged and measured like a lump of meat connected to the rest of me by merest accident, and I was newly revolted by my deformity. To have to undress again for bath and bed seemed almost too great a price to pay for the easing of my soreness and exhaustion. But I paid it, and survived.

In the morning, over a gigantic breakfast, I scanned the professional journals and found exactly what I wanted — the announcement of an APA conference in Chapel Hill a couple of weeks before Thanksgiving. A members-only do, which meant that Ault would not be able to attend even as a guest. It would be nice though not essential to have my leg by then. I reached for the phone and made flight reservations to Chapel Hill and back by way of Asheville, and hotel accommodations in both cities.

If I was wrong about Ault, then I really was paranoid and had better go back to the shop for repairs. After all, there was no proof that the tape recorder in the laundry chute was his, and his actions so far, even leaving Bob's jacket in Meiklejohn's office or telling Grier about the new work, could be rationally explained away. If I was right, he would go down to the cellar during a safe quiet time and listen to my long phone chore and then plan a move on me that might take him out of the darkness in which he lurked into the full daylight of disclosure. Which in his case was, as I have said, synonymous with death.

And he would take me with him.

Yuh do what yuh hafta, a client always told me, implying a clear-sighted recognition of Truth and Duty. Nonsense. All of us make choices consonant with and implicit in our psychology, choices so clothed in rationalization's golden glow that no matter how rotten, even catastrophic, their outcomes, we see ourselves as conscious, dispassionate, and wise.

Can we ever catch on, and learn? Yes, if we want to. Most people don't believe this or don't want to, but it's that simple. No matter how long it takes, no matter how hard it is to acquire self-knowledge, the bottom line is, simply, *wanting* to know, and then doing what's necessary to know it, and then practicing new and better behaviors.

At the moment I didn't want to. A tremendous magnet was pulling me right over that edge along with Ault. I had to let it. I had to.

Sure.

Grier phoned while I was washing the dishes. "Thought you'd like to know what the students are saying about you, Toby, since your first evaluation's about to be written up. They think you're competent, thorough, fair, knowledgeable, interesting, and sexy, and will fetch a king's ransom at the Festival. Which puts you in the same category with Ault and a few others. He's very proud of you, as am I. I'll keep the report clean for the president, but I thought you'd like the unexpurgated version." He laughed softly and hung up.

I spent the middle of the day on coursework, then had dinner at the restaurant Meiklejohn had taken me to. I saw him only in passing and at Project meetings now, and he'd made it clear that he preferred it that way. I hadn't seen Pat or heard from her either, though this was as much my choice as hers. Even Angie next door was invisible these days. For all my reputed popularity, I was as lonely as I'd ever been. Lonelier, maybe, given all I'd had, even for such a short time, and lost.

On Monday morning on my way to class I met Angie, who was struggling to arrange her bulk under the steering wheel of her car. "Where the divil yuh been?" she shouted. "Haven't seen yuh in a month a Sundays. Or anybody else. We had a family, seems like, 'n' then all of a sudden, poof! What happened?"

I leaned in and kissed her pink smooth cheek and said I didn't know.

She gave me one of her shrewd looks, but said only, "Well, gotta be off or I'll be late, f' once in me life. Say. I'm sorry 'bout yer cat."

"My – ?"

"Yuh didn't see?" She heaved herself out of the car, a generous gesture, and went toward the Dumpster. I followed her, suddenly cold with apprehension as she pointed to a small plastic trash bag that lay inside the gate. A note was pinned to it.

It read: "Sorry about your cat. Expect it was hit by one of the cars here. By the way, pets are excluded from terms of lease." It was signed "AA."

I bent to open the bag. Angie's strong freckled hand on my arm stopped me. "Don't, lad. Left hind leg's gone. Cut off by some vicious sod 'round here rather than any car, I'd say. Must a suffered somethin' terrible. Pretty thing it was. D'you want it cremated at the vet's, or should I—"

Like a blow to the gut, nausea struck me and I swayed dizzily. "That's where you found Bob, where he—"

I turned away and vomited up my breakfast, and with it my hopes that I was wrong, my doubts that I was right. All that was left in me now was anger for the rank acid in my soul to feed on.

$\triangledown$

1 9

I LOOKED AULT IN the eye and said I'd gotten his note *re* cat, and he looked me in the eye and said he was sorry.

Murray Costa and Madge said what cat.

"An orphan of the storm adopted me briefly," I said, turning to them, and Ault's note crackled in my pocket. By now the cat he had mutilated was a heap of gray ash and bits of bone. How had he taken off the little leg—with a carving knife? a scissors? Had he torn it off? bitten it off? The taste of vomit was still strong in my mouth. "His name, though not for very long," I added, "was Latchin."

Out of the corner of my eye I caught the complicated expression on Ault's face—shocked surprise, and then a flash of joyous triumph. It thrilled me, I wasn't sure why.

"I'll have that oak limb trimmed, Toby." Ault's fine gray eyes gleamed wickedly in his lean face. "Your predecessor found it annoying in windy weather."

Murray and Madge said what oak limb, and then Meiklejohn arrived, uncharacteristically irritable as well as late. He flung himself into a chair with a grunt that passed for "Sorry."

Ault hefted a familiar-looking stack of papers and dropped it dramatically onto the table. "Toby, it looks as if your questionnaires will have to be modified. It means dumping more work on your shoulders and putting off the official launching of the Project from Monday week until just before Thanksgiving. To certain townspeople questions about mental retardation, illiteracy, alcoholism, incest, et cetera in their families are intolerable invasions of privacy, as well as an absolute guarantee of more hard feeling between town and gown."

"First I've heard of it," Meiklejohn said aggressively. "Come on, Ault, no questionnaires have been distributed yet, so what hard feeling are these bullshitters talking about, and who are they, anyway? I probably know them. I'll straighten them out."

"Anyway," Murray said, "nobody has to sign anything or answer questions they don't want to answer. Everyone must know that by now. It's been in all the announcements."

Madge said, "I don't see how we can justify the waste involved, just to pacify a few paranoid types."

Ault looked amused. "Insurrection in the ranks? Well now. Next June first is our absolute deadline, and next July Fourth is the official celebration of the town's tricentennial. We can't offend the biggest contributors to our grant who are among the town's most prominent families. They help pay the pipers so they get to call at least some of the tunes. If we ignore a major string to their generosity, which happens to be that deadline, it will be a long day before they're so forthcoming again."

His charming QED shrug said that committing me to hours of unnecessary work was a settled thing, and the questionnaires on which he and I had worked so hard he now shoved aside like so much garbage.

"What changes did you have in mind, exactly?" I said.

He took the top packet off one tall pile and skated it across the table to me. "The starred items. All too many of them, I'm afraid, but there it is."

I looked, and shook my head. "Sorry, Ault. Even if I could come up with new ways to ask the same things, I couldn't be ready before or even by Thanksgiving. I didn't have a chance to tell you, but I'll be away from the ninth through the fifteenth—"

"Oh boy, that's one conference I'd sure like to go to," Meiklejohn said glumly. My breath caught in my throat, and his eyes went from me to Ault, slicing the air like a knife. He reddened but went on, with a false enthusiasm. "Always wanted to hear Ernest Becker in the flesh. I've been thinking of doing a comparative study on death—you know, the way every known culture handles it or has handled it. Starting with the Neanderthals."

"The Neanderthals?" Murray Costa said. "Come on. Those animals? You have to be kidding."

"No I'm not. All I can say is, Toby, if Becker speaks as well as he writes, you're in for a double treat."

I couldn't look at him.

"Attending that conference isn't part of your contract, you know, Toby," Ault said.

The terms of my contract, which were between Grier and me, were not the issue, and we both knew it. Then once again someone unwittingly put an end to our charade.

Madge said, "Ault, just tape a media statement explaining what the questionnaires are all about and how people should handle them, and I know—I know!—you'll settle any fears they may have. They'll be so intrigued, they'll be champing at the bit to fill them out."

Ault gave in immediately, of course. He had delivered a direct message to me this time via a concoction containing enough validity to shake everybody up. Was he also saying that I could expect to see him in Chapel Hill? If so, it was all right with me. I wanted my life settled. Whatever the risk, I wanted closure. I'd waited fifteen years for it. I would welcome it no matter if it finished me.

Ault asked Murray how he'd been following up Vincent's elegant introduction to the Project, and Murray began reading incomparably dull notes. I tuned out, distracted by Meiklejohn who was pursing his lips and shaking his head disgustedly. What was making him so cranky? and did it have anything to do with me? and would he tell me if I asked? He just might, because he caught my eye and grinned mischievously, grinned as if nothing had changed between us, and jabbed his thumb downward at the tabletop.

Ault's face closed up, at Murray for his poor contribution, and at Meiklejohn for his childish display. Then Madge yawned noisily. I couldn't help it, I giggled. Murray looked up and said, blinking, "Wha? Wha?" and Meiklejohn exploded into his irresistible wall-shaking laughter. Ault's lips began to twitch. Then he put his head back and laughed too, as uncomplicated and likable for those few moments as the best of people.

"Let's go over this later, Murray, when you're—" he began, and was interrupted by a bloodcurdling groan at the door, the sound of a body crashing to the floor, and a shriek from Madge.

The body—the same student who had come in once before for help with the Festival's house of horrors—righted itself.

"Was that strictly necessary, Clark?" Ault said, not laughing now.

The lad looked as if he was missing half his face. "Yes, sir, it was."

Tentatively he pressed down the edges of the rubber makeup, then peeled it off. "*Yecch!* Had to make sure this'd deliver the hell of a wallop—sorry, Dr. Hendron, won't happen again—or else I'd have to do some more work on it, and I'm running out of time. Thing is, can you lend me twenty bucks, Dr. Allyn? I got to get to the hardware, and I don't have time to go home for my stash."

An indulgent uncle now, Ault reached for his wallet. He was always in his element with kids. Even Madge smiled, shakily.

Grier's secretary came in a few minutes later. "A call for you, Dr. Frame. From a Pete Flori in Virginia? He sounds kind of urgent, so I thought I'd better—"

Ault's eyes burned into me, and I was suddenly sure that he must have bugged my office and probably Grier's. "Say I'll call back later today, will you, Jackie? I've a class soon."

Ault said casually, putting away his wallet, "Toby, when you talk to Pete, tell him I'd be glad to help. I always have, projects like those. Been planning to get away then, as a matter of fact. Okay, folks, there's this other matter of scheduling Madge's program."

Help with what? Get away when? I wasn't going to ask him, and I knew he didn't care. He didn't have to.

When my class was over there was only one place from which I felt I could safely call Pete Flori. I made sure that no one followed me there. Late in the afternoon I trudged up the steep stairs into Father Sam Mayo's big room.

Someone was sitting at the long table, back to me, in the midst of a mess of books. Bill Hanrahan! I thought, and knew it was impossible, seeing the long rich hair. Tentatively I said hi. Pat turned, looked at me for a long moment, nodded.

I crutched across the islands of scatter rugs on the bare floor and sat down beside her. "I was looking for Sam but I'm glad it's you," I said. "I want to apologize."

"You don't have to. You don't owe me anything." Her eyes were direct, her voice without anger. She even smiled. A bad sign. She had finished with me.

"I owe you an apology, Pat. I was angry. I was stupid and childish. Then it seemed . . . best to leave things as they were."

"Why? Because you saw Ault's car at my house one night? Well, I don't owe you anything either, but an explanation probably won't compromise my integrity. My car died in front of the library. I went back in to call road service and Ault saw me—he was coming out of the stacks—and insisted I take his car because he was only walking across the Quad to the president's house for dinner. He said someone could drive him home and I could pick him up in the morning before first class, if I was willing. He was perfectly ordinary, and I was tired, so I accepted and that was that. I didn't think it would matter anymore. He's been leaving me alone lately."

"Pat, with him it always matters. Always. Look. I wanted to misunderstand. I chose to, I guess because I thought it would make my life easier. That was wrong too."

"Why?"

I couldn't tell her why. Meiklejohn in his loose careless way had betrayed me, but he appeared to be solidly in Ault's camp now, so he was safe. If I told Pat my story, she would fight for me, that was certain, and what Ault would do to her then did not bear thinking about. There was no way I could tell her.

The silence between us deepened. Presently, in much the way Bill had, she swept her things together and said good-bye.

The next few moments were as miserable as any I had ever known. At last I looked at my watch. Pete Flori was waiting for me to call.

He answered on the first ring. "About time," he said.

"Sorry, Pete. By the way, Ault Allyn says to tell you he'll be glad to help on that project of yours. What project?"

"Work on Grassy Ridge Bald. The owners damaged it badly just before the feds took it over last year. Didn't you read the March/April *Trailway News*? Grassy Ridge isn't my project, I just did some articles on it for the papers. I'm not sure when the next work party goes up there, though.

"Anyway, now to the matter at hand. Why shouldn't a hiking academic frequent, crimewise, the Groves of Academe? It happens there's a number of colleges and universities along Interstate 81 paralleling the Trail—Sweet Briar, Mary Baldwin, Washington and Lee, Virginia Military, Emory and Henry Call. I called the state and local cops first, then all the campus police. Usual rash of crimes in and out of the schools. Some car thefts, lots of B & Es. Money, jewelry, various small articles, credit cards. Nothing of real significance.

"Then I called the libraries. And it is a move such as this, my lad, that illustrates true reporting genius and creative journalism."

He stopped for dramatic effect and to make me ask why.

"Why?" I said, and grinned, he was so boyishly pleased with himself.

"A Washington and Lee librarian—a Miss Peach, can you believe it? — remembered one man in particular," he went on, gratified. "Not just because over the last few years he's asked for information on a wide variety of subjects, which most students do not do, certainly not at single sittings, but because he didn't look or sound like the type who could even write his name."

"Plenty of students don't even know theirs."

"No irony now, lad, it's been a long hard day. To press on, this man always carried a knapsack — "

"Most students do."

"Not like this one — it represented serious walking. Camping."

"Did she describe him?"

"Sure. Mid-forties, maybe. Weathered. Clean enough but somewhat trail-scruffy. Tall and lean. Spoke in an upcountry accent, not local, that she couldn't place and that didn't match his reading menu by half. And yet, an indefinable air of class, which surprised the hell out of her. She sounded more than a little taken with him. Ring any bells?"

I wasn't ready to answer that. I said, "Did she remember what he read?"

"Just about everything from antiques to zithers. Architecture, jewelry, clothing, furniture, heraldry, precious stones. He'd sit for hours, not moving except to turn pages. Must have a photographic memory, because he never took notes. What librarian wouldn't remember a customer like that! I called the others again and asked them if he sounded familiar, but none of them was sure."

"Did she ever ask to see his ID? I take it she knew he wasn't a student there."

"God. I never thought to ask. Guess I'm not all that much of a hotshot after all."

He wasn't, or he would have done one more very obvious thing. Something I would have to do on my trip south next month. I made all the necessary changes and arrangements to include that stop on my itinerary. Then, stomach clutching up and lips suddenly paper dry, I picked up the phone a third time and dialed Quebec. René answered.

We chatted for a few minutes, and then I asked him to send me the original articles on the Loudoun Heights murder.

Gallic suspicion corroded the wire. *"Pourquoi?"*

"Just curious," I said coolly.

"Bool*sheet*, boy. But I shall do as you ask."

I was making out a check for the calls plus some extra when Father Sam Mayo came bounding up the stairs. He was glad to see me and my check, and invited me to stay for supper. "Business has been slow up here, and maybe it's as well. We're a bit short on funds. I just bumped into Pat Elliot. She seems to think you've got a problem. Feel like talking?"

He brought out bread and honey and milk, and over that ancient simple meal I found myself telling him my story, holding back nothing, not even Ault's name. He said, when I'd finished, "Drop it, Toby."

"Why? For the good of my immortal soul?"

"What better reason?"

"Doing unto others is reason enough."

"Don't joke, it isn't seemly."

"Sam, I've never been more serious in my life."

"Or more wrong."

Going home was out of the question. There wouldn't have been enough room in the apartment for me and Sam's concern for me, which I couldn't shuck. The coffee shop on Main Street where I had first met Pat Elliot was brightly lighted. I made my careful way up its treacherous steps for what at this hour would be bitter coffee and a stale doughnut.

Meiklejohn, at a crowded table in the rear, saw me immediately but did not signal me to join him. I thought, Now's as good a time as any for a confrontation, and approached him like a walking fortress, armored in caution; a mobile bomb, ready to detonate. His tablemates took one look at me and scattered, and he half rose to follow. If he could have moved his big body faster, he would have gone too.

I ordered coffee and a doughnut I didn't want. I said, "What was bugging you this morning, John? Your buddy Ault wasn't too pleased."

"So I noticed," he said, not meeting my eyes.

"How did you know I was going to Chapel Hill?"

"What? Look, I don't know what you're talking about. And what is this anyway, laddie? What are you getting at?"

"Yesterday after breakfast I decided to go to Chapel Hill. Then," I said pointedly, "I picked up the phone in my apartment in Ault's house and made reservations. And you knew."

The waitress slapped coffee and a tired doughnut down in front of me and pasted a limp check to the dirty tabletop. I asked her if she wouldn't mind giving the table a wipe. She minded. She smeared the mess around with a dirty towel and stalked off.

This interruption gave Meiklejohn the opportunity to hoist himself up. "I'm really looking forward to the Festival," he said, falsely jovial. "Hope the weather's good. How about making the rounds together? We ought to have a blast." He looked carefully at his watch. "Hey, listen, I'd really like to stay and chat but someone's waiting for me. See you later, laddie." He almost ran out.

I had accomplished nothing, with Pat, with Sam Mayo, with Meiklejohn, with myself. I couldn't even drink the coffee. I left money on the table and went home.

The apartment was a haven no longer. What I was frightened of now was my renewed isolation and despair.

I'll give Meiklejohn the benefit of the doubt, I thought. I'll tell him what's really on my mind. I wasn't fair to him.

I put my hand on the phone. And took it off.

Ault would know, I told myself. I couldn't risk it.

What the hell, I couldn't risk trying to talk to Meiklejohn anywhere about anything. He lied about recognizing Bob's jacket. He didn't want to know anything about the bugging of my apartment. He couldn't and wouldn't think badly of Ault. He didn't want to know whether Ellis Hart had helped me. He ducked out of that whole business. And he lied about Chapel Hill. Not once but twice. I couldn't trust him anymore. Couldn't trust him any farther than I could throw him. That great friendship was over.

Well, so what? I wasn't much worse off than when I first came to this place. I'd manage. Hadn't I always?

What the hell, I thought, I'll go to the Festival with Angela. We always have a good time together.

I sank into a chair, telling myself that it was going to be all right.

What a hope.

$\triangledown$

20

THE NEXT FOUR DAYS didn't allow time for hope, or for other big emotions like vengeful anger. The campus was frantic with last-minute Festival business and midsemester exams, and one of my two, among others, had been unalterably scheduled for Saturday morning. It was like living through a disaster, when everyone behaves supernormally and everything gets done. Once again — and for the last time, though I did not know it as I gave out blue books and sat down to proctor — once again I began to think I'd been wrong about Ault, Pat, Meiklejohn, and myself, myself most of all, and that I was now seeing things as they really were.

Sure.

That Saturday was a flawless New England October, blue and red and orange and gold, crisp and scented and crystal clear after a midnight rain. At noon, after exams, Horace Knowles stood on the library's broad steps and opened the Festival with a graceful speech about being our brothers' keepers. Ault, whom he introduced as the heart and soul of the Festival, spoke with charming intensity about its purpose, and I leaned against a marble column and cheered him along with everyone else in that vast throng. He caught my eye and waved happily. The student president ceremoniously tied ribbons around Knowles's arm, then Ault's, and instantly the university turned into an ant colony that has been stimulated to fever pitch and exposed for observation.

Students erupted from the buildings and ran all around. Booths offering food, toys, dopey games, seemed to grow out of the ground.

Trash was picked up by platoons of obsessive-compulsives who had paid into the Festival fund for the privilege. The air began to ring with triumphant shouts as captures were made and borne off to be recorded. Every half hour, signs bearing the running total of ransom pledges bobbed above the throngs. By three-thirty the grand total had reached a respectable figure. The air buzzed happily.

In the midst of all this merrymaking I felt abandoned, angry, and disgustingly sorry for myself. I had expected to be with Bob, Pat, Angela Tansy, and Meiklejohn. But Bob had been murdered, Pat had dropped me, Angela was on shift, and I had given up all thoughts of somehow, who knows how, straightening things out with Meiklejohn. I had made that impossible. And not one of the students who Grier said were hot after my sexy one-legged body had claimed it. Alone and on sticks, I was frighteningly vulnerable and tired. Time to go home, and send the Festival fund a check.

I tore the ribbon off my arm and flung it down. A voice at my shoulder said, "Hey, lad, take it easy."

Meiklejohn. Holding the ribbon out to me like a peace offering, doing what I couldn't do, letting the past go.

"John, I — " Shame shriveled me up. I bent to tie the ribbon on again; to hide my face.

"Forget it. Let's go have a good time. This week's been bloody. God, I'm starving. There's a great food stand over by R.L., and I could use a dozen of everything they've got. How about you?"

Suddenly the sun was bright and beneficent, and all six feet six inches of Meiklejohn my bulwark against the crowds. At the food stand by the Romance Languages Building he unblushingly downed a "first course" of four hot dogs to my one. We shied tennis balls at pop bottles, ate ice cream, guessed the number of beans in a jar, ate candy and popcorn and potato chips, traded fierce insults with other contestants, ate hamburgers and fries, were thoroughly, infectiously ridiculous.

"I don't know about you," Meiklejohn said after two hours of this, "but I'm whacked."

I ached all over, the lost foot most of all. Our building was close by. We went up to the staff lounge near Grier's office and found him chatting with Madge and Jesse over coffee, Jesse looking like a well-prepared corpse ready for burial, his gold watch chain gleaming across his portly waist.

"Seen the sights?" Grier said in his preoccupied, tired way, not really interested, dampening even Meiklejohn's enthusiasm.

Then Ault looked in, carrying a hideous mask by its edge, and Meiklejohn said, "Who'd you scalp, Ault, anybody I know? C'mon, folks, let's go to Ault's horror show and catch the beautiful damsels when they faint."

Madge said, "After that dreadful preview we were treated to Monday, Ault, it'd take a herd of elephants to drag me there. I still haven't gotten over the shock."

"Well, that is the idea, after all," Jesse said. He pulled out his pocket watch and opened the gold case. A familiar phrase of music sounded; Mozart, I thought. "It's still plenty early, Madge. How about it?"

"Oh, Jesse, really!"

"Really what? It's just a deliberate concoction of nonsense. We couldn't possibly fall for it. So why not show the kids our support and have a good time into the bargain. Besides, some of my students are involved, and they'd be vastly disappointed if I didn't show my face."

Ault said, "Madge is right, Jesse. It's not for the faint of heart, literally or physically. Just look at this. Those rascals said it wasn't scary enough and gave it to me as a memento! You can't begin to imagine what they've cooked up. I was scared silly." He laughed and shook his handsome head. "I don't know whether to be impressed or have them arrested. Look."

The mask he pulled down over his head was a revolting creation of green slime and running sores. In this and his hand-tailored suit and Gucci tie, he looked like the picture of Dorian Grey come horribly alive at the height of his depravity. He stood very still, menacingly still, eyes gleaming in the mask's eyeholes.

Jesse shrank gasping into his chair.

"That's what I mean, Jesse," Ault said, his voice muffled behind the latex. He took it off and smoothed his hair. "I'd take it as a personal favor if you'd pass. You too, Toby. It's not a place for crutches. Neither of you should feel you have anything to prove."

He looked at his watch, said he was supposed to meet someone ten minutes ago, and took off at a run.

"There's nothing wrong with my heart!" Jesse said angrily, jumping up. "I'm completely recovered!" He trotted out briskly. I didn't want to think what the effort cost him. Mother Madge rushed after him. Reluctantly Meiklejohn heaved himself up saying something about backup, and followed.

I left Grier to his peaceful coffee and went after them, but stopped first in the little staff lav to check my stump. It was swollen and hurt like hell, so I locked the door, dropped my pants, and spent a few minutes bathing the remnant in warm water. I had been on my feet, so to speak, too long. Almost half an hour later Grier was still sitting alone in the lounge when I took off for the old Chem Building.

It was not far away, but the closer I got to it the harder I had to work to keep from being swept back again by a tide of students flowing determinedly in the other direction. If anything was wrong, no one stopped to tell me so.

Why, I asked myself, aching and sweating as I crutched along, Why am I bothering to catch up? The obvious answer was that I wanted to see what happened to Jesse.

A shiver thrilled down my spine. Shut up, I told myself.

Hey, listen, said that inner voice I hated, If you don't like the answer, don't ask the question.

Now that the new Physical Sciences Building was open, this oldest of the university buildings, a ramshackle brick pile, was soon to be torn down. It stood on a knoll that fell away toward the back, so that much of the basement was at ground level. In the bowels of the earth below it were the furnaces, gas and water mains, and so on. Maintenance was stripping the building, and only for Ault had it grudgingly opened up two basement labs for the Festival and given him a key to the door.

The building looked deserted. A boy and girl running hand in hand up the driveway said breathlessly that everyone had had to leave and that they were the last. I said I was only looking for someone, and they nodded and kept running. The areaway down in back was empty, and the only posted notice I saw told me to hook my index finger into the left eye socket of a skull hanging from a nail, and rap three times. I saw no reason not to. The door creaked open. A sepulchral voice invited me to enter. I walked into a velvety blackness filled with invisible animals that hooted, scratched, screeched, chittered, the racket reaching a swift crescendo, then stopping abruptly as the door closed behind me.

Instantly a skeleton glowing phosphorescently rattled down to dangle inches from my face. I staggered backward. Something – a hand? – in the small of my back stopped my fall and was withdrawn. The skeleton danced away upward and vanished.

Balancing on my sticks, I put out my hands to either side and touched rough material that moved in the slight draft like some live but boneless thing. No light showed over, under, or through this cloth tunnel, as if every last gleam had been sucked out of the air. How in hell had those kids done it?

As I moved along, thunder began, a bare whisper that grew slowly into a full-throated roar and as slowly died away, punctuated with shrieks of insane laughter.

My heart bounced around my chest and up into my throat. I managed to take another step. All at once blue and red and white bits scattered everywhere — strobes — and before me stood a tall apparition, holding its head under one arm. It raised its other hand to stop me, then opened a door in the blackness and waved me by, into a greenish smoky writhing mist. Again a door closed behind me.

Out of the smoke, which smelled faintly of gas, loomed a tall ladder. I tried going around it but both sides were blocked by unidentifiable objects I couldn't step over. I stood helpless, then turned to go back. The headless figure sprang out of the smoke, its head falling with a dreadful thump and rolling away as it raised both arms to stop me. It snickered maliciously as I stumbled in fright. My cheeks burned with humiliation.

"Hell awaits at the bottom, you pitiful fool. There is no escape, no-o-o esca-a-a-ape," a voice whispered, and laughed nastily. "No esca-a-a-ape thi-i-i-is ti-i-i-ime."

There was nothing for it but to climb the ladder. Somehow, somehow, I got to the top, recognizing that I was on the tallest playground slide I had ever seen. I managed the necessary arrangements, crutches over shoulder like ski poles, and slid down while cymbals crashed deafeningly. The brittle rattling sounds I added to the din when I hit bottom told me I had fallen into a pile of real bones.

I moved on, hearing nothing, wondering why it was so quiet, wondering where Jesse, Madge, and Meiklejohn were. Either they had gone through while I was in the lavatory or they hadn't come. I shouldn't have; I didn't owe Jesse anything. And the smell of gas was giving me a headache. Ault's warning should have been more explicit. Again, but briefly, I was angry with Meiklejohn for not staying with me. Jesse didn't need the big man, not with Madge at his side.

The thunder began again, low and menacing. Shafts of lightning split the smoky dimness. I came to a huge wooden tub that gurgled and splashed water. Out of it rose a monster that made up in hideousness what it lacked in size. In the ghostly light that fell on it, it twisted in agony on the end of a fishing line, streaming water and seaweed, then fell back into the tub with a horrible *plop!* and the light went out.

My mouth was absolutely dry, my lungs straining. Just a put-on, I reminded myself, and relaxed momentarily. With the next step I walked into a huge sticky spiderweb. At its center clung a spider as meaty and hairy as Meiklejohn's hand. Its eyes stared fixedly at me and it began to move.

Forgetting my one-leggedness and my crutches, I leaped backward and fell in a clattering heap, gasping for air, groaning in pain. I couldn't help it.

A voice said, "Thass jes the beginnin', boy. Hit's gonna git a whole lot wuss'n that."

That voice! The voice I'd first heard more than fifteen years ago. And again in the hospital. And again — I acknowledged it now — in Harvard Square, the day Ault and I went to Cambridge, when someone — Ault? — shoved me into the road. When he reached out a hand to help me up and said something I didn't understand, didn't want to understand. Something very much like this.

The voice gave a low short laugh of purest enjoyment.

Then, silence.

I sat collecting myself, then got up and went on, the greenish smoke or mist or whatever it was swirling about me, the floor invisible.

A weird distorted figure lit by a pale-yellow glow came toward me, wiggling and shaking. My reflection in a trick mirror. I poked angrily at it with a crutch, resisting the urge to give it a good whack. It would have made a lovely racket, shattering all over.

Why was the place so quiet? Where was everyone?

The greenish smoke ended at another narrow black tunnel of the same soft swaying material, and I realized that I was no longer frightened. I was too tired and too full of pain, from my head to the foot I didn't have. All I wanted was to get out and go home. There can't be much more of this, I thought hopefully, moving along a little faster.

And tripped over something that had evidently been wired to switch on a distant light on impact. In a pale-blue glow I fell headlong, hitting my forehead on the edge of god knew what as I went down. I let out a bellow of pain.

Once again I lay on cement floor, prone this time, trying to assess the damage and wondering why no one had come to help me. I'd certainly made enough noise. My forehead was wet and sticky. Real blood. Eventually I got up, balancing on knee and crutch, and put out a trembling hand to the object that had wounded me. It was an old wooden coffin, the kind that vampires commonly sleep in.

I reached in. And fearfully, tentatively, felt cloth and buttons and a metal chain. A Dracula dummy, what else? I smiled a little despite the pain in my head.

But what yielded under my exploring fingertips was not the softness of a homemade Halloween doll stuffed with hay or rags and tied at the neck with a silken stock and flowing ribbon bow. It was the softness of a human body in tweeds and narrow woolen tie, its bulk still springy, the face warm.

I touched the metal chain again. Pulled one end free. Heard the watch ticking like a heartbeat in the black silence. Pressed the spring and heard the cover snap open. Heard the tiny music box inside playing its tinkly tune.

Jesse.

And then a tremendous noise came from somewhere below and I flew through the air into that long, welcoming blackness I had known many times before.

21

THEY FOUND ME IN a heap against a far wall, clutching Jesse Thomaston's watch chain, and wound up in black sheeting as in a shroud. I found myself in the hospital again, shocked, bruised, miraculously unbroken. In the dim nightlight above my bed, my eyes focused on someone sitting near me in an armchair, head sagging to one side, rich hair spilling down over one shoulder onto her breast; asleep.

Pat.

I stirred, and she woke up and almost smiled at me. My various parts were loosely and painfully connected. It took a long time to stretch out a hand to her. She glanced at it but did not move.

Time passed.

Eventually I said hello, and, a little later, "What happened?"

"You don't remember?"

Shook my head. Closed my eyes.

Remembered.

Shuddered violently.

She took my hand and stroked it; held it in her warm one. "It's all right. It's all right, take it easy. I'm here."

I remembered more. I said urgently, "I really don't need you here. You'll have to go. Thanks anyway." But my hand tightened on hers and drew her to me.

She got up and gave me a visitor's kiss on the cheek.

I wanted her to go but for some unknown reason moved my head, trying to reach her lips.

"No," she said. "I have to know why, Toby."

"I — I can't."

"Why? Tell me, Toby. Why do I have to go? Tell me the reason."

"Reason? Why should I have to have a reason? I don't need you and that's that."

I was the cool cat, crippled and unlovable, unloving and isolated, that chose to walk by itself, free to define itself in its own way to itself and to nobody else. Why must it have any other reason for its choice, or be made to justify its need? I had fought hard, and never more than now, to believe this. But I had a better reason, and it hit me with the force of a second explosion, knocking down more walls. I stared at Pat, weak and appalled in the rubble of my old defenses.

"My god," I said slowly. "I love you. Pat, I love you. I didn't know I did. Then I didn't want to. Almost convinced myself I didn't. But right from the beginning . . ."

"Yes?"

"And he knows, and he'll hurt you. I couldn't bear it. That's the truth, Pat, and that's why I want you to go. So please go!"

"No. You can't make choices for other people, Toby, only for yourself, isn't that right? Isn't that what you believe and teach? Well, my choice is to stay. I talked to Father Sam. I heard the whole incredible story from him, and I'm staying, because I love you too, whether I can talk sense into you or not, and that's that."

I reached for her but she moved easily away.

"Pat!"

"No. Sorry. It wouldn't do your condition any good to kiss you, that's clear. Some other time, maybe. We'll see."

"Damn it, Pat!"

She sat laughing at me. Then she lay down beside me on the narrow bed, and generously and without reservation helped me to mend forever the rift between us, and some of the rifts within myself. Amazing, to accomplish so much without interruption, on third or any other shift. We might have been home.

If we had been, Police Chief Burke would have rung the bell and waited to be asked in. Here, the instant the shift changed, he entered briskly along with Angela Tansy, a thermometer, a blood-pressure cuff, breakfast, and a manila envelope.

Angela handed me the envelope. "I had to sign for it. Seemed urgent, sent like that, so I thought yuh'd want it right away."

The Loudoun Heights murder articles Jean had promised me. I

couldn't have said why, but it was important to hide the envelope under the covers so that not even Pat could see it.

"Five minutes, that's it," Angela told Burke crankily, and stalked out.

"Well, Dr. Frame. Glad to see you're feeling better than when I first looked in," Burke said dryly, pulling his little notebook out of his neat breast pocket. "Now. What happened yesterday?"

"I don't really know."

"You went over to the old Chem Building when?"

"At about four or a little later—"

"Alone?"

"Yes. Jesse Thomaston, John Meiklejohn, and Madge Hendron had gone on ahead of me, or so I thought, but the place looked deserted when I got there. Everybody seemed to be going the other way. One student said something about being the last ones, but I didn't know what she meant and nobody seemed upset, so I kept going and—went in."

"And?"

I had disclosed plenty of myself in the last few hours and would be the better for it. But old habits die hard: I didn't feel up to admitting even to Pat how scared I had been in that house of horrors.

"And," I said lightly, "the fun began. I couldn't have been there more than six or seven minutes when I tripped and hit my head on something. Just as I realized what it was and what—who—was in it, everything went to pieces."

"To coin a phrase. Yes, well, it was Dr. Thomaston. Medics had to pry that watch chain of his out of your fist. Watch was still ticking, can you believe it?"

"What—what happened to him?"

"Massive coronary. Happened before all the whoop-de-doo, the M.E. said. Did you know he was dead?"

"I sensed it. Even though—"

"Even though what?"

The memory was a horrible lump in my throat that I couldn't swallow. "He—his face, his cheek, seemed warm. I don't know if that proves anything. I mean, it was cool but not all that cold down there. He might have . . . only just died."

"And fell neatly into that coffin as he croaked? Or he felt sick and got in it to lie down awhile? Or maybe he was a vampire and checked that watch of his and knew it was time to take a nap? Funny. He was still in the goddam thing and the lid was down when we found him. You're right, he had probably died within minutes, more or less, and we know he had a coronary. The question is, what caused it?"

I couldn't say anything. My jaws were busy clamping down on nausea. I wished he would change the subject, and he did.

"When you went in," he said, "what did you see and hear?"

"I didn't see anything, it was too dark, but there were a lot of recorded sound effects, the kind of thing you'd expect. Animals. Crazy laughter. It was well done. For what that's worth."

"Maybe quite a lot. What else?"

"Well . . . when you entered, you had to walk through a kind of narrow corridor of black sheeting or scrim or something . . ."

"You ever go in there, Ms. Elliot?" Burke said. She shook her head, and he told me to go on.

"Well, it was absolutely black in there. I kept wondering how they'd done it. Then a skeleton painted with some glow paint came rattling down in front of my face and was yanked up again. Then a weird light went on and there was a headless figure holding its head under its arm. It said something predictably weird, about hell awaiting me and no escape. That sort of thing."

"Did you recognize the voice?"

"No." Nor had I. But when I couldn't get around that slide and tried to turn back, then I knew. And had told Pat, not too long ago.

She gasped. I managed not to look at her.

Burke noticed, but only said, "And then?"

"Then I had to get up a ladder and go down a slide. That was when I stumbled and hit my head. I felt around and realized what I'd—what it was. And then there was this terrific noise and I seemed to be flying through the air. Then I woke up—here."

"Did you at any time smell gas?"

"Yes. It gave me a headache."

"I'm surprised you went. Alone. On crutches."

"I hadn't expected to be alone. Meiklejohn and I had been having a good time. We went up to the staff lounge in Corey Hall to rest, and Grier Mitchell was there talking with Madge and Jesse. Ault Allyn dropped in for a minute, and left. Then Jesse took off, and Madge and Meiklejohn went after him. I left too, but stopped off in the lav first. When I finally went out, I thought I'd be right behind them. That there'd be a crowd at the Chem Building, I mean, and I'd catch up. But I didn't see anybody."

"Meiklejohn and Dr. Hendron were captured for ransom the minute they left Corey Hall to go after Thomaston. He resisted capture and took off like a bat out of hell, but they went along with the fun and forgot about him. Now. You said the old building seemed empty. And you detected gas. And the students who were leaving sounded like they were warning you off but you weren't sure. And there was no keep-out notice on the back door. And you saw one person only, that headless creature, before finding Thomaston."

"So?"

"So the fire marshal hasn't made his statement yet, but I'll tell you what he's gonna say. First, that somebody'd uncapped the gas main in the subbasement, and gas was pouring out for half an hour or more by the time you got there. Second, the timer on the temperature-control thermostat upstairs near the labs was set back from eight P.M., where Maintenance has been keeping it, to four-thirty. Reset by accident, given all the people milling around in there earlier? Or by the person or persons unknown who tampered with the gas main?

"So here's the gas pouring out, and the furnace with its electrical ignition is near it and makes its big fat spark when four-thirty comes along—and *kerplooey!*

"The oil tank being outside, that wasn't a problem. 'Course, the gas was still flowing when the troops arrived, and it had to be recapped again, but things could've been a lot worse, all in all.

"You could've been barbecued or busted into a million pieces, or both, you realize that? But you were goddam lucky, because that explosion was like all explosions—unpredictable. So it did what they sometimes do without any help—put out its own fire. Plus, some of the force went out through a couple of doors and windows that happen to be nearer to the furnace than you were upstairs. So the building's still more or less intact, for what that's worth, what with the plan to tear it down one of these days. Too bad, too. Nice old pile. Picturesque, I always thought.

"Now. The Horrors Committee say Maintenance called sometime after three-thirty and told them to get everybody out because of a gas leak and said someone would be over to post warnings on all doors and cordon off the area. So don't it seem strange to you that absolutely nobody from Maintenance made any calls to any students about any gas leak there? And that no warnings and cordons were in evidence when first Thomaston and then you showed up? And that after the explosion there were still no cordons, but warnings were found pasted on the doors—including the back door, which was blown right off its hinges? Real strange, right?"

I blinked at him and said nothing.

"Is it beyond the bounds of possibility that, after the alleged call from Maintenance, whoever went into that building wasn't meant to leave it in one piece?"

What could I say? Nothing.

"You and Dr. Thomaston," Burke said, "weren't in great shape one way and another. So how come nobody but you two get stuck in that building when she blows? Didn't anyone warn you—someone who knew what those crazy kids had done in there? Isn't it strange that no one warned you? Dr. Allyn, for instance. He said he'd been helping with that horror show."

"He did warn us," I said. Or rather, challenged us, and so cleverly that our going was anything but strange, it was a certainty. But I could not say that either.

"So why go?"

"Just curious, I guess," I said weakly.

"Curiosity killed the cat, remember? I tell you, I find this whole thing very strange. So strange that we're left with a very nasty thought."

He did what he had done after Bob's body was found—invited me to join his club and do a bit of theorizing. I wasn't in the mood so I let him say it, and he did, without noticeable pleasure. "Murder One is what I'm thinking, Doc. The question is, who and why? Someone who stood to gain by two particular deaths, Thomaston's and yours, right? Any candidates?"

I could feel Pat's taut and total stillness. Could he? I mentally crossed my fingers and shook my head. The envelope from Quebec lay like a ton of bricks on my chest under the light blanket.

"Come on," he said. "Give it a shot."

"Don't think I have the ammunition. I didn't know Jesse at all, and we weren't going to have much of a connection because Ault would still be heading up the Project when Jesse resumed the chair. Maybe my being there was just a miscalculation on the murderer's part. After all, I haven't been here very long."

The miscalculation on the murderer's part lay in making no allowance for the possibility of plain dumb luck. I could hardly complain of his error. But then, neither could he, not when my survival filled him—as it must; if I knew anything, I knew this—with a perverse, a terrible joy.

"Yeah. I guess," Burke said. "But it could have been the other way around, you know. You the target and Thomaston the miscalculation. I'll have to look into that."

"And the coffin?" I said thickly, almost too jolted to talk.

"Yes, there's that. We can't get away from that, no matter what you may or may not have meant to the murderer. And you do agree there was a murderer."

God! my mouth was dry. "Yes, I think it's obvious — the coffin, the alleged call from Maintenance, the warnings found posted after the explosion. Jesse was to be scared to death or blown to kingdom come. But who would benefit?"

"Amazing how fast we can establish some things. His heart attack in March ate up his savings, medical insurance or no medical insurance. He had no life insurance, so his wife would be a lot better fixed if he'd've gone on living and working. Also, we're pretty sure he had no enemies outside the school. So that leaves inside the school, and the fact is that with him gone for good, Allyn will head up the department and go who knows how far up from there. Right?"

My head moved in assent on my neck, astonishingly, considering that I had turned to stone. Yet the envelope burned my skin like fire.

"Wrong. Allyn's completely broken up. And do you know what he's doing now? Organizing the funeral, making all the arrangements, paying for everything! So — murder for personal gain? I mean, a lousy chairmanship — something he could get anywhere he wanted? Come on! I'll tell you something. The bastard who says a man like Allyn could do a thing like that — well, I'll arrest him myself. Because anyone who could suggest such a thing would have to be a dangerous lunatic."

I'd be safer in North Carolina than around Burke, I knew that, because I couldn't have been more certain whose hand was clearly upon that gas pipe and that thermostat timer than if I had seen it there myself.

The inquest on Jesse Thomaston — astoundingly, and to Burke's utter fury, I heard later — returned a verdict of death from natural causes. Jesse was buried the following day. I sent flowers to Mrs. Thomaston, whom I hadn't even met, and stayed away from the services.

Burke called later to ask why.

Because, I said, although the hospital had discharged me three days before, I was bushed.

He could hardly argue this, and didn't, but said he wanted to talk with me again when I was feeling up to it.

So Ault, riding the edge again, had fallen off. Onto the safe side. Into the shadows. Which meant that the mad mix of disappointment and exhilaration he must be feeling would produce an even gaudier challenge, yes, and plea, to Death to take him — and me — if He could.

The farther I could get from Ault and Burke, the better. I could hardly wait to go. The next couple of weeks I avoided them, and even Pat, worked not too hard, rested, maintained my weight, lucked out on cast, first fitting, and second fitting, and then tied on my brand-new leg and went.

In my wallet were two photographs I had cut out of the newspapers Jean had sent. One was of the boy found murdered on the Loudoun Heights above Harpers Ferry. The other was of his father.

Two photos, one face.

A face I knew well. A face I had loved.

22

I FLEW FROM BOSTON to Baltimore to Virginia's Shenandoah Valley Airport in less than three hours. Some thirty-five miles away was Miss Peach, the Washington and Lee University librarian who remembered a trail-scruffy hiker who read for hours and never took notes. I didn't bother calling for an appointment with her for the morning. She would be on duty because that was her job, and because the hiker might come again.

For the fourth time that day I folded myself into a vehicle and an hour later climbed out again, this time to sign the register at the Alexander-Withrow House in the center of Old Lexington. The house was long on authentic charm and short on food, served no meals at all, in fact, but the day had been such a brute that I had no eye for my surroundings and didn't care if I never ate again. Even my cane, which I had taken after all, seemed to wilt where it leaned against the wall. But on behalf of my stump in its new leg – and in gratitude for the joy my beautiful Seattle foot with its natural springiness was giving me, albeit requiring more time to get used to, hence the cane – I rested, then asked the manager to recommend a restaurant. A Virginia guidebook instructed me while I ate and thought about my future. By nine, filled with good food and only pleasantly weary, my stump not too sore and red, I was sound asleep.

Next morning I was ready to appreciate the antiques and fine reproductions in my bedroom, sitting room, living room, *and* two bathrooms. Outside, breakfast-bound, I looked with pleasure at the handsome 1789 building, at its glazed brick headers set in marvelous diamond patterns around the upper stories, at its four corner chimneys that seemed to support the bright sky. Pat will love all this, I thought.

The town, like the house, was drenched in neo-Classical charm, all red brick and white pillars, all peace and order, grace and rootedness and elegant logic. A New Englander could feel perfectly at home here, I thought, swinging my cane jauntily, looking up and around, noting that there were no utility poles to spoil the view. Pat will love this, I thought, and tripped on the brick walk, as happened now and then on Beacon Hill. A passerby helped me up without fuss, assured me that I was by no means the first, handed me my cane, and went on his way.

After breakfast and a consultation with the guidebook, I headed for the library of Washington and Lee University, a fine complex of neo-Classical buildings not far from my lodging. I went along more carefully, but now I was not interested in architecture and atmosphere. My jacket pocket sagged with the weight of two newspaper pictures of a murdered college student and his father.

What would Miss Peach think of them? What would she be like? What would I say to her? What would she say to me?

Sweating from nervousness, I approached the library's main desk and asked the student sitting behind it with his face in a tome if he knew where I could find Miss Cristina Peach.

He pointed. "Ovuh they-uh," he said in a soft southern voice as nearly like a down-easter's as made no difference.

I knocked on the door, which was partly open, and a woman's voice invited me, without conviction, to come in.

"Miss Peach?" I said.

She blushed and cleared her throat. "Yes? What can I do for you?"

She was in her mid-forties, and stout, her eyes pain-filled and shyly hopeful that at last the man who would want her had arrived. Her hair was straight as a wall, her eyebrows shaggy, her arms furry. Her dress was patterned in floppy roses and might once have been a tablecloth.

This woman had been handling books all her life and gotten nothing valuable from them. She was the kind who tried too hard in all the wrong ways, and let you see, thus share, her failure. Who stuck you with it, and would be appalled to know that she had. Another kind of user.

If Pete Flori had finished the sleuthing job he'd congratulated himself on, I thought angrily, I would not have had to stop down here and do it. I wasn't into empathy now, except on my own behalf.

I introduced myself as a friend of the journalist who had called her about—

"Oh, I remember!" she said. "Mr. Flori. Yes. He asked me about a man who— Oh dear, is something wrong?"

"No no, not at all. But as I happened to be in your neighborhood, I wondered if you might be able to do something for me. I've been trying to locate someone. I, uh, have something he wants, and I wondered"— taking out the pictures—"I wondered if this might be the man you described to Mr. Flori."

I had copied the articles and sent the copies back, with apologies, to René. The original pictures of father and son I had cut out because they were clearer, though hardly of portrait quality. I lay them on her desk, the son's under the father's, and waited, my breath caught in my throat.

"Oh yes," she said happily and without hesitation. A stubby fingertip, nail bitten to the quick, moved in a slow caress over Randal Shelton's eyes, his aristocratic jaw. She picked up the photograph. "I wouldn't have said he was as old as this, but when people dress up . . . A handsome man . . . Oh yes, that's my reader. My mountain man, I call him . . .

"Oh dear! We really shouldn't think we can tell a book by its cover—if you'll forgive a perfectly dreadful professional joke—although I suspect everyone does it far too often. Judges without knowing, I mean." Reluctantly she put down the picture. "You know, we have over half a million volumes here, and I sometimes think he's aiming to read them all." She touched the picture of the murdered boy. "I expect this is he when he was younger? A nice boy."

"That's his brother. I didn't mean to bother you with that one," I lied. I put the pictures back into my pocket, under her greedy eye. "Miss Peach, can you remember when he comes here? I ask because I always seem to miss him. We've been trying to connect, but . . ." I shrugged ruefully. And realized, with that artful touch, that I had stopped sweating. It was getting easier and easier to lie, evade, equivocate, and tell the truth all in twenty-five words or less.

Well, it would be cruel to blast her fantasy to bits, I told myself, and self said nastily that it sure would.

"He was last here at the end of July," she said promptly. "He'd almost the whole place to himself that day, and I . . ." She blushed furiously at what she hadn't finished saying. "He often comes when most of the students are away on weekends or holidays. Which is why

I remember him, I guess. And of course I do a lot of fetching and carrying for him, more than for most students, I expect because he needs it more."

René had found the murdered youth on the Loudoun Heights at the end of July.

"Of course," I said, not quite knowing what I meant.

I wanted to ask her how many times he had come, and what he had said initially to gain use of the facilities, and what he had subsequently talked about, as he must have done to an adoring old maid. She would be able to quote his every word verbatim, and no matter what part he was playing for her benefit, he would inevitably have said something as characteristic of him as his fingerprints, and I wanted to know what it was. But I had to leave. It would be imprudent to do anything else.

"Well," I said, "sooner or later we'll get together, I'm sure. It's of no particular consequence, really. Put it out of your mind." And I knew that the next time she saw Ault, she would tell him, because it was something else to talk about, to share, that another of his friends, the one with the limp and the cane, was looking for him.

She struggled up out of her chair like a creature emerging from a hole. She really was immense. "Do you have a particular reason for being here, Mr. – uh – ?"

"Frame. Yes. I'm making a tour of gardens. I'll be seeing the Coker Arboretum in Chapel Hill tomorrow, and the Botanical Garden in Asheville on Friday or Saturday. I'm really very excited about this trip. I guess you could call me a lapsed botanist. Lapsed but about to reapply." I was illogically glad to end the interview with three true statements.

"Isn't it a bit late in the year?" She walked with me to the door. "I mean, how much is growing now?"

"Enough," I said happily. I thanked her, not making too much of it, and left, eager to be alone, to ask how one – *I* – could at once drop the past and return to it. By magic? Not really. By fulfilling my present contract and then beginning graduate work in botany. Simple. It was something to be happy about. For a little while I didn't even wonder if I would live long enough to go forward by going back.

There was time before my flight back to Baltimore to admire, with due regard for the brick walks, the main academic buildings clustering gracefully, seriously, on a mall under the autumn trees. I passed Robert E. Lee on his low plinth, and saluted inwardly. He looked as impressive in civilian clothes as in uniform, and stared intently beyond me, into the past or the future, maybe both. Going by the chapel in which he and his family lay buried, I wondered how it feels to plan and build your own tomb, knowing that you have made a lasting mark on your world. I wanted to see more but it was time to pack, check out, be driven those thirty-five miles to the airport. Back to Baltimore and on to Chapel Hill via the Raleigh-Durham Airport twenty miles away.

Four hours later I checked into the Carolina Inn, whose southern Colonial style, red brick, and white pillars gave it a quiet permanent confident air, like Lexington's. I knew from the North Carolina guide-book, however, that it was only sixty-five years old, with a recent addition that blended in beautifully. Professors, parents, and alums filled the couches and chairs in the great lobby and talked the kind of talk I'd been hearing all my life. Meeting rooms all around the big space buzzed like hives. I felt instantly at home and looked forward to my stay, forgetting for that instant what my real errand was.

The desk clerk greeted me happily. "Glad you're here, Dr. Frame. Good trip? Fine, fine. If you'll just sign here, please. And oh yes, we've corrected our error and made your room reservation as Dr. Allyn instructed — for both of you, instead of a single for you. And may we suggest that in view of the time you might want to make a dinner reservation in the Hill Room. It's staffed by students and the service is superb, as is the food, so any number of townspeople come, not just university folks. I'm sure you'll like it, and the lunches too. The cafeteria's more than adequate, especially for breakfast, but no one sleeps in, these days, everybody seems to be breakfasting at the crack of dawn. We're always crowded, of course, but this — ! You people have a big draw in Dr. Becker, Dr. Frame," he said severely.

He produced a room key, waggled it gently at someone behind me, and handed me a slip of paper. "A telephone message for you. We were specifically asked to say that the matter was urgent."

He royally nodded a bellboy away with my room key and bag, but I stood rooted to the spot. I managed to say, "Is Dr. Allyn here now?"

"No, not yet, Dr. Frame. He called to say he'd been delayed."

When — *when* had he called? And from where? What was he up to? The gall of the man, to change my reservation, and teetering on that edge and laughing while he did it. I wanted to turn tail and run, but could hardly make myself ridiculous playing hide-and-seek with a colleague who would know within minutes, probably already did know, that I was there. And besides, where would I hide?

Dully I looked at the telephone message. It said, "Call me soonest," and was signed Meiklejohn.

Meiklejohn.

So he was with Ault, after all.

And they were closing in on me.

$$\triangledown$$

23

M̲y GOD. AT THE Festival, and after, we'd been friends again, Meiklejohn and I. He told me in the hospital that he hoped I'd still be able to go down and hear Becker, that he wished he could go with me and to please take notes. But he had been lying to me again. It had all been a lie. He was Ault's creature — Ault, who had only sent a card this time, and fruit (which I didn't eat).

The bellboy said, "Sir?" at my elbow.

I said sorry, and asked him to take me to the APA registration desk first. There, at the end of a long line, I took back my bag, tipped the boy lavishly, and dismissed him, saying that I would find my way to my room later. If Ault was indeed somewhere around, I was going elsewhere, fast. I would only stop long enough to see what that bastard Meiklejohn was up to.

The clerk, pale with excitement, at length made a check against my name, gave me an ID card I didn't intend using now, said no, Dr. Allyn hadn't yet registered but would be attending the conference on someone else's card — "A practice we dislike, but . . ." — and turned distractedly to someone else.

Clammy with fear, I found a public phone and dialed the number on the little pink slip. I didn't know where Meiklejohn was, and I almost didn't want him to answer. But he did.

"God," he said fervently. "Am I glad to hear your voice, laddie! I've been spending money for over an hour in a great little food and drinks shop, waiting for the phone to ring. But better than waiting in that damned great lobby. Piedmont was kind enough to tell me," — he chuckled — "you were on the 1:36 from Baltimore. Sit tight, I'll be right along with all the makings. Better than any bloody bar. We'll go to your room."

To corner me, get me in a little box, put me out of action? I had to be sure.

Meiklejohn arrived, jacket pockets stuffed with newspapers and magazines, arms full of brown paper bags, and I laughed despite my horrible alarm, watching him breast the human sea like a tugboat moving purposefully through a deranged flotilla of cockleshells.

He would say nothing until we were in the big double room with hefty Scotches and all manner of treats from the paper bags to hand. I made sure that the door was not only unlocked but slightly ajar in case I had to get out fast, even though I was making it easy for Ault to come right in and lock the door behind him. If he came, it wouldn't make any difference anyway. I sat down next to the telephone. That might help, in a pinch.

"I don't want food and drink, John," I said coldly. "I want the truth. For once tell me the truth. How did you get here, and where is Ault?"

"In a temper, and I don't know. He said he was going to this conference on Grier's card, so I thought I'd better tag along."

"Why?" I shivered. Even my new foot felt cold.

"Because he woke me up at six this morning — six, can you believe it? — to tell me that, and it smelled fishy. Then he said why not come too, and to meet him at Logan — God knows why! Something told me you might be going to need help. And don't ask me what I mean because I don't know that either. All of a sudden there were just too many things that didn't jive. Jesse's death. That damned Festival that fizzles out with an explosion. Too many things.

"It all comes down to wanting to level with you, and apologize." His eyes were steady on mine. "You asked me in the coffee shop how I knew you were coming down here. Well, I had dinner with Ault the night before, and he told me. I didn't think anything much about it until Grier stopped me about something just before the meeting, which is why I was late, and I asked him if he was going with you. After all. Becker. Big stuff. He said no and that you hadn't said anything about it but it was good for your professional growth and all that. I said any chance I could go on his membership card — I really am working up a major paper on death, maybe a book, as I think I said — even the Neanderthals dealt with death ceremoniously, to a degree, just like real people — and he said it was something he never did and he'd already turned Ault down. So this morning when Ault called, it hit me – he was *not* going down on Grier's card but one way or another he was going. So I just got scared. For you. This may sound farfetched, but he asked me to go trail-clearing with him down in the Smokies during semester break, said it was great down there then and he was going to invite you and maybe a couple of others along and –

"Toby, would you go if asked?"

"Would he make the telling move on me if I did? And suppose he did?" I said cruelly. "When he started turning the screw, would you identify with the aggressor again?"

His nice friendly flabby face wilted like a flower in an icy blast, but still his eyes held mine. "Guess I deserved that, but the answer to your question is no, laddie, never again. Not that I wouldn't be scared shitless and have to work my way up to proving I was a man."

I took my hand away from the telephone and got up and closed the door and sat down again.

He didn't notice. He said, "It was the way Ault went after you and the way you reacted when I put my foot in my mouth when I mentioned wanting to hear Becker. I knew everything you told me about him was true. I was so totally shook, I almost got up and left. Funny, though. I had the distinct impression he wanted you to know he knew."

I felt warmer now. I said, "Did you ever tell him I knew I was being bugged?"

He hung his head like a small boy. "Guess I did, once. I run my mouth a lot when I'm high, and he's so clever, so quick. I've always been a little afraid of him. You got it right about identifying with the aggressor. That's me all over. And denial's my middle name. I even denied recognizing Bob's jacket – you remember – when Ault left it in my office and I brought it in and played dumb – and knew you knew I did. And why did I? Because the kid had been murdered and I was afraid to get involved, afraid to start thinking about who and why and the other things I didn't want to think about. Ault, mainly, I guess. I'm not proud of it, but I've always dodged trouble and fuss. Life's too short, and anyway I heard enough of it when I was growing up. Living in the past, with the past – hell of a lot easier than dealing with the present."

He was giving me all the truth he was capable of giving. More, I was certain, than he had given anyone else. He was more honest and courageous than I had ever been, even with Pat in the hospital in the middle of the night during third shift. It couldn't be too late to apologize. I held out my hand and did, with all my heart.

"It wasn't easy but it was worth it. We've both learned, laddie," he said generously. "God, but I'm whacked. I hate these feeder flights that bounce you up and down like a ball, an hour here, an hour there. Worse than eleven hours nonstop, which I've been known to do." He heaved a tremendous sigh and shook his big shaggy head. "Well anyway, to finish the story, when I got to Logan, Ault had left word that he'd been delayed! Why? What the hell's he up to! I just don't like this. You haven't seen him, of course? Good, because I want to be with you when you do. And don't ask me why about that either. We Celts have the sight, is all. I'm getting bad vibes, one of which is — "

His big blue eyes had darkened with worry. "Christ!" he exploded. "This expensive plastic glass is filthy!" He jumped up and went into the bathroom and ran the water fast and irritably.

I saw, as I picked up one of his wrinkled newspapers, that my hand was shaking. Meiklejohn was an ally now, someone I would love and trust for the rest of my life, but how long was my life going to last? I was actually afraid that any minute Ault would walk right through the door and, in the most charming way, do something dreadful. And then I saw a familiar photograph on the front page and read the lead article that went with it.

Randal Shelton, grief-stricken since the murder of his only son four months ago, was gifting the University of North Carolina with a few of his mountains, along with millions of dollars to study them with, and, following appropriate changes in his will, he would make a formal presentation in his son's name to the University Board of Trustees.

The paper slipped out of my hand.

Meiklejohn came out of the bathroom drying his glass on a crumple of toilet paper. "Would it be an imposition if I ask to bunk in with you, Toby? I couldn't find a spot for love or money. Too late in the day, damn that Ault."

"What?"

"I said — What's the matter, Toby? You're white as a sheet."

"Oh. No, I'm okay. Sorry—what did you say?"

"Would you mind my taking one bed? The way Ault talked, I assumed he and I would be staying together."

"John, I booked a single, days ago. He knew it because he listened to that tape in the cellar. I'd told no one about it, no one. Not Pat or anybody else. When I got here the desk said Ault had corrected that 'error,' their error, and they had a double for us."

He stared at me. "Jesus. Toby, if I were you, I'd get on the phone — "

"Too late for that." I picked up the paper, Randal Shelton's picture prominent, and gave it to him. "You see this, John?"

"Glanced at it. Heard some chatter in the store about that gift. Wish somebody'd give my department a few modest picks and shovels, not that I'd wish 'em to come out of pain and sorrow." He filled his glass again, sat down with another sigh, and looked more carefully at the article. "Randal Shelton. A very rich sad man, it says here. Well, I don't know about anybody else, but I've always held that it's easier to be sad when you're loaded—

"Uh-oh! How did I miss it? My god. One face."

"Remember that story I told you, John?"

"The saga of the lost leg? Think I'd forget? No chance. Or fail to note that something was conspicuously absent from one part of it but not from the rest. Your mythical malefactor's name. Ault, right? I want to tell you, Toby, that insane story cost me a lot of sleep. So what's your theory now? How does it tie up with this rich miserable lumber executive whom Ault closely resembles?"

"The talk in the mountains is that practically the only thing Shelton gave the families there was extra babies. I think Ault was the first of them—and possibly the only one to survive. And, if not the only one to find out who his real father was, probably the only one who acted on the knowledge. I think his mother and some if not all of his sibs died young of overwork and deprivation and heartbreak, when the rapacity of the lumber and mining companies threw them and other families off the mountains and into the towns.

"Ault must have been spotted as an extraordinary kid, and schooled. Like Bob he wanted to better himself, but unlike Bob he ruthlessly hid his origins and became what we know. With a memory like his it would be easy for him to learn anything he wanted to. And he did. It's happened before.

"But I think anger long ago rotted his soul, his moral fiber. His enemies are the people who have or seem to have what he was robbed of—his name, his birthright, his *place*. I think he braced Shelton many times over the years to recognize him publicly and legally, and when Shelton refused—although he may have given Ault money from time to time—he answered every refusal with an act of increasing hostility. Arson, murder, endless B and Es, Vincent's murder, Bill Hanrahan's collapse, Bob's murder, Jesse's, even the man who lived in the apartment before me."

"That guy had an infarct right out on the street, laddie."

154

"Yes. I was there. I never told Ault, though. But if that wasn't an act of murder — I'll tell you the details some other time — I don't know what is. God knows how many Ault committed. Even that little cat — "

Meiklejohn choked on his Scotch. "Wait a minute! I mean — *Vinnie*?"

"Yes, Vinnie. Ault wanted Pat — had her for a while — and he knew her uncle Vincent drank. He forced her to change her doctoral field — more of his power-wielding. When she balked, and then when she met me, he threatened to tell Knowles about Vin's drinking unless Vin helped keep her in line. Vin really was afraid the news would end his career."

"It would have, for sure. So?"

"She appealed to Vin one last time, and he advised her to do what she wanted to do. He wrote in his diary, which she showed me, that her happiness was more important to him than anything else, that Ault could do what he liked but he, Vin, wasn't playing anymore, even though all he'd have left would be the equity in the house to support her through her doctorate. He referred to someone who wanted her, presumably as a doctoral candidate, so I infer that he was planning to send her elsewhere and to hell with Ault. Then he and Ault had supper together, and an argument, and a week later he was dead."

"Jesus. How do you think it happened?"

"I'm virtually certain that Ault either poisoned him with a deadly look-alike morel, the *Gyromitra esculenta* — I won't bother describing morels, they're a kind of cult issue among serious mycologists, and Ault and Vin loved them — or else kept him — Vin — supplied with what are called Inky Caps — "

"Which make a dangerous combo with booze, right?"

"Right. So does the Black Morel, and the Wrinkled Thimblecap — and that toothsome morsel can cause your muscle coordination to go if you eat a lot of it at once or over several days. The Veined Cup is also poisonous unless you cook it. I bet, though, from what I remember, that the severity of the symptoms Burke was so graphic about got a boost from the Gabled False Morel — diarrhea, vomiting, severe headaches. That beauty can even give you blood poisoning if it delivers the full wallop, though I don't remember that any fatalities have been noted. I'd have to check all this out to be sure, but it's near enough, and I don't want to bore you with the rest. Morels are a big family, as I said."

"I gather you're good at your trade, but I never saw you talk about it with anything I'd call enthusiasm. Sure you didn't miss your calling?"

I grinned. "I've been considering the possibility. Tell you about that later too. Anyway, whatever Vin ate, and with all he kept drinking, he must have been in agony, John, those last hours. And all alone, without complaining, dealing with what amounted to a classic antabuse reaction. That's gallantry, but a straight-arrow like Knowles wouldn't think so."

"That's for damn sure. And Bob? What about Bob?"

"He didn't hide the fact that he'd sensed that Ault was a phony, and I didn't want to believe him any more than you did me. I talked to him about courtesy, for godsake! when it's clear that Ault has a paranoic's response to criticism. Anyway, Ault called to warn us to keep clear of the Dumpster at night, said there were malefactors about! And then he waited in the dark—he'd smashed the light bulb out back—and broke Bob's neck when he was going out to see his girl. As a final lily-gilder he stole the Jag for two days. I keep a spare key in my desk and he's the landlord, right?"

"I didn't know about the wheels. But I recognized that swell jacket—the kid was wearing it when he went to see his girl after that little party you organized. I didn't know it was Ault who put it in my office until he came out with it at the meeting. Christ! And Bill Hanrahan?"

"Bill was a bonus. I think Ault simply enjoyed smashing him in the process of removing Vinnie. Pat must inadvertently have told him that what was supremely important to Bill was his dissertation, so he simply leaned on Bill's new adviser—"

"Murray, I'll bet."

"Probably. Who said, sorry, what Vin approved was unacceptable to him, so Bill must start his work all over again. And who could argue about that? Nobody! And Bill knew from Vin about my leg and also that Ault was responsible for getting me my job, something else I didn't think about till later."

"Ault's whole Project grew out of your dissertation, so what's so sinister in his having touted your talents to Grier?"

"Nothing, unless you put it with other things. Look. He said a Harvard sociologist friend of his told him about my dissertation and the terrific concept in it that we now know and love so well, but, John, he *never* knew anyone at Harvard—he told someone who told me—and my paper was good but it wasn't an academic best-seller, it wasn't published in hardcover and featured in stores. So how did Ault know where I was? Someday I'll show you the articles from my local paper about my accident when I was eighteen, and my academic career. I

156

found them on the shelf in my liquor closet when I moved in. Who do you think put them there for me to find? And told Vinnie, who told his protégé, Bill Hanrahan, about me? He enjoyed knowing that sooner or later, through one or both of them, I'd get the word he'd been tracking me all these years, that eventually I'd catch on to who he was. And I did. Remember, no one here, not even Grier, knew about my leg when I was hired. Oh, it's in my personnel file, sure, but it's obvious that Grier, if he noticed at all, forgot it immediately. But when Bill came to me for help and got furious because I said I couldn't give the kind he wanted, he said he knew all about me, taunted me with it, and then jumped me. *Now* do you see?"

"Well, yeah. It's all circumstantial but it fits. Bill was like Ault's killer dog. You know? Well. Jesse's death is easy to figure, but Ault was a fool there. He wouldn't have had to wait very long to go from acting to permanent chair."

"Oh, he's patient enough. But Jesse's stubbornness was a replay of his father and all father figures who gave him a no-you-can't. It infuriated him. In retrospect I think I saw through his control, and very good it was too, at that luncheon he gave for me. So he used all the resources the Festival offered to get rid of Jesse—and me too. I think he was enraged and also pleased that he failed to bag me."

"Yes. I'm beginning to understand why. And what about Sandy, his probable half brother. How do you think Ault got to him?"

"He may have been tracking the kid. He may have come on him by accident. The boy probably didn't recognize him, but I'm sure he knew the boy and tried making a connection with him, pleading, offering proof, citing the sacredness of blood ties, family ties, and Sandy, the spoiled only son of a family going back hundreds of years and with royal or semiroyal blood, had to have laughed in his face, probably said something like, 'You kidding, you ridgerunning old bastard? Get lost,' and turned his back, and Ault stabbed him in a rage. And there's that signet ring—you saw it at one of the meetings—"

"Yes, I saw it. 'To my beloved son on his eighteenth birthday.' All that heraldry and stuff fits Ault like a glove. He's one elegant sonofabitch."

"But that inscription was too clear to have been done thirty-five years ago when he was eighteen, unless he never wore it, which is just not possible. No, he took it off the boy's finger after killing him, John, and that only-son phrase in the papers must be corroding the last shreds of whatever's holding him together. I think he's now quite mad. Certifiably insane. Even if he never commits another crime."

"Fat chance. Know why? Because Randal Shelton, whatever else he is, has got to be in big trouble now. What the hell was he thinking of, to make such a public statement, a veiled screw-you challenge he knew Ault would see! He has to have seen it, he spends a lot of time away from school, you notice? I think he travels far and very fast. I bet he's down here a lot, and why not? It takes barely half a day, and with that memory of his he doesn't have to spend time on preparation like everybody else does. I've known him simply read students' papers and criticize them succinctly—pro and con—as he gives them back. It takes me hours to correct mine. He's a damn good teacher, he's brilliant, for godsake! and he really loves his students."

"Yes. I know." I stood up and went for my cane and bag. "Stay if you want to, John. You'll have the room to yourself, if I know anything about anything, and you can have my card and my ID to pin on. Who's going to challenge you? I'll settle the bill. But I have to go."

"You kidding? I know what you've got in mind—going to Asheville, right? To warn Shelton. Well, I'm going too, laddie. My bag's right downstairs. One of the APA registration clerks is looking after it. I didn't really expect Ault to be here, not after the way he's engineered this trip and jerked me around, never mind everything else. We can leave right now. I'm ready."

I stood still. "Everything else what, John? That's the second time you started to say something and didn't. Everything else what?"

He stopped putting the treats into the shopping bags and turned around to me. "I didn't want to tell you, but I have this strong sense that Pat is with him. And I'm at least as concerned about her as about Ault's putative daddy. So let's get cracking!"

We left the inn by a side door. A taxi driver just settling with his last passenger took us to a Hertz office, and we shot out of Chapel Hill as from a cannon, heading west in a brand-new Thunderbird.

By the time we stopped for more gas and a coke at Asheville's outer limits, we were firm friends, a result of my burgeoning maturity, and his. And cementing the relationship also kept us from worrying too much about Pat and Shelton. But we could have gone slower and safer, because there never was a hope of telling Randal Shelton that he stood in greatest jeopardy.

I was paying for the gas when Meiklejohn, reading the evening headlines through the newpaper dispenser's dirty glass, knew without having to spend fifty cents that Randal Shelton had learned the hard way about jeopardy.

Early that morning he and his wife had been sideswiped by a hit-and-run driver on a mountain road and killed instantly. And since the legalities *re* his announced gift to the university of land and money had not been completed, his estate, or the bulk of it, would pass to the next of kin — if any.

▽

24

A GENIUS HAD BUILT Randal Shelton a house that seemed as native to the mountain as the trees and shrubs around it, possibly because Shelton's love for his mountain was so clearly stated everywhere. Against his will my father would have liked Randal Shelton.

A familiar Mercedes stood proud and confident in the driveway. By now, I was sure, Ault believed that he had never lived anywhere else. "He's *here!*" I said.

"Looks like it. And are we really surprised?"

Behind the Mercedes was an old, well-cared-for Chevy.

"Looks like Grier's," Meiklejohn said, turning to look as I drove past both. "My god. Can you imagine what he'd make of this caper!"

"He wouldn't have the energy. What's the matter with him, anyway? I've never had the nerve to ask him."

"Nothing but boredom, would you believe? Madge thinks he's sick, but all it is is that he wants to quit so bad he can taste it. Talk about burnout. He'd be no help here. Glad we won't be alone, though. But on the other hand, whoever else is here might be in his pocket. One thing's certain, that Merc's simon-pure. Had to be some other vehicle drove the Sheltons off the road. Wonder where he hid it. Oh boy. Notice how I'm taking things for granted?"

"Me too." My foot slipped nervously on the brake pedal and we came to a jerky stop. "But let's keep cool and play it as agreed. And hope it doesn't blow up in our faces. Got the flowers — and the brandy? Okay, over the top!"

My hands were cold, my stomach in knots, the brandy safe in Meiklejohn's sacklike pocket, the flowers behind his back, shyly.

Well, here goes! I thought. I fixed my face in some semblance of a smile and reached for the doorbell. Before I had a chance to press it, the door swung open.

"I knew you'd come!" Ault said, and for a split second I loved him as I once had, for the authentic warmth with which he ushered us in.

"We came as soon as we heard," Meiklejohn said, producing the flowers and brandy.

"I'm damned sorry, Ault," I said, and steeled myself not to shrink away when he put an arm around each of us and hugged us to him.

He let go of Meiklejohn to accept the gifts, but walked me into the living room, his arm a vise around my shoulders. "Yes, we both know what it is to lose a father, don't we, Toby, and under dreadful circumstances." He patted my back consolingly and let go of me: a pet on the end of a string. "Come meet my other guests," he said expansively. Whenever he wanted to, he could jerk me back again.

One of the guests was Pat, her big gracious body folded small in the corner of a couch, chin to chest, elbows held in a white-knuckled grasp. Her eyes were red and puffy, and she was so plainly terrified and exhausted that even her hair had lost its sunny glow. There were bruises on her cheeks and neck.

Ault introduced us to her as if we had never seen her before, and asked us to excuse her because she was feeling a bit under the weather. I gave her a casual nod and said, "Nice to meet you," as did Meiklejohn, and comprehension leaped like a little flame in her tired eyes. Ault missed it as he led us past her to a man seated across the room.

"Bill, I want you to meet my friends and colleagues," he said, and to us, "William Ross. My father's attorney. And now mine. Obviously," he added cheerfully.

Ross, a tough little man with an underslung jaw and an unbecoming suit, made no effort to shake hands. He gave us the kind of nod we had given Pat, and waited.

No point in waiting. I said, "A really marvelous place, Ault," and pushed a little harder. "It suits you." I gave him an open smile.

He smiled back and sat down in a chair made of three pieces of shining metal, a twin to the one in his house. Hands dangling relaxed and assured over the flat arms, legs elegantly crossed, the murdered half brother's carnelian ring with the Shelton escutcheon gleaming on his left hand, he couldn't have looked more regal with a rightful crown resting on his head.

He kept smiling slightly, inclining his head as to a courtier, and in that moment the picture went absolutely askew. Without any doubt we were in for big trouble.

"And I love that chair." This I aimed at Ross. We had to know whose side he was on, or at least what he was thinking about. "It's doubly unusual for looking correct in any setting. A mark of perfect taste, don't you think so, John?"

"I do indeed, laddie. Struck me immediately. Your father gave you the one back home, Ault, right?"

Ault's fingertips stroked and smoothed the metal sides. He looked beyond us at some distant spot, eyes glittering. "Yes. And now I've got them—both!" His hand thrust out and clenched into a fist, as if he had caught a fly. "I wonder," he said dreamily, "should I leave the other one there or bring it back here?" Then his eyes swung flashing to Meiklejohn. "This *is* my home! Remember that."

"But of course, Ault," Meiklejohn said.

William Ross said easily, "Dr. Allyn is under a serious misapprehension, gentlemen. And you as well, I'm afraid."

"Oh? What's that?" I said.

"That he has a claim on the Shelton estate. And the Shelton name."

"Please don't talk nonsense, Bill," Ault said. "After all I've been through, I haven't the patience for it."

"It's anything but nonsense." Ross spoke slowly, grinding up his words with gusto before letting the remains out of his mouth, and his jaws came together with a snap on the last particularly delicious morsel. "Herndon versus Robinson, 1982. Let me cite North Carolina General Statute 29-19. An illegitimate child—"

"There are no illegitimate children, Bill," Ault said reprovingly.

"Correct," I said, and got a sharp nod from Ault.

"The sociologist's point of view, no doubt," Ross said, "and the psychologist's. All very well in their way. Even laudable. But I'm talking law, gentlemen, which is how Dr. Allyn's claim must be examined." He held up a stubby hand as Ault stirred restlessly. "If I may continue without interruption? An illegitimate child may inherit from a parent only—repeat only—if paternity is officially, that is to say formally, acknowledged in writing and duly notarized.

"Moreover, the name and identification of the putative father must be furnished. A mere personal letter from one individual to another, whether claiming, hinting, or charging paternity—in this case a hinting letter Dr. Allyn says his mother received years ago from Mr. Shelton—proves nothing."

"You haven't seen it yet," Ault said.

"True. But it wouldn't matter if I had. The law requires a document reading as I've outlined, which must be voluntarily and knowingly signed and executed. Regardless of your personal feelings or mine—"

"And your personal feelings, Mr. Ross?" I said.

"Have no bearing on Dr. Allyn's claim, Dr. Frame," he said calmly. "I've told you what's relevant. With such a document as I've described, Dr. Allyn could challenge Randal Shelton's will, possibly have it set aside. In court. Of some advantage might be the fact that with Sandy's—the Shelton son's death last summer, there are no other heirs. He was unfortunately the last of the line. Of record," he added composedly, seeing Ault bridle.

"What about a blood test?" Meiklejohn said.

"When the putative father is deceased? Impossible. In any event a blood test can at best only eliminate a paternity claim, in fact any number of paternity claims against the same individual. It cannot prove any. But . . ." He shook his head as though cautioning himself against indiscretion.

"Yes?" I said. "But what?"

"I was only going to say," Ross said, clearly not wanting to, "that a strong physical resemblance is often better evidence in paternity cases than a blood test. No matter what people like to think, a baby doesn't look like its mother or father or much of anyone else when it's born, nor much like itself when fully grown. But! With age the physical resemblance to a parent increases, whether or not it includes inheritable characteristics like flapping ears or frizzy hair or what have you.

"And I will go so far as to say—off the record at this juncture, naturally—that Dr. Allyn does bear a very strong resemblance to Randal Shelton."

Ault said, "There you are! You see?"

"In itself it proves nothing. Please bear in mind that many public figures—politicians, for instance, or actors—have doubles for one purpose or another. People who have no connection of any kind with their principals."

But Ault didn't bother listening to this. He jumped up and walked around straightening pictures, moving things from one position to another, looking with intense satisfaction at the richness of the room.

"Did you ever meet Ault before, Mr. Ross?" I said.

"Oh, I've seen him on and off for years," was the astonishing reply. "In point of fact, I met him here thirty-odd years ago. A bright boy, sure enough. Mr. Shelton helped him through college."

"Well, that must mean something, anyway," I said, knowing that it did not.

"Not really." Seeing Ault stiffen at this seemingly careless discarding of himself, Ross added hastily, "What I should have said was that Mr. Shelton helped several mountain children. He believed in sharing his wealth."

"Mr. Ross," I said, "a minute ago you said Ault could challenge Mr. Shelton's will and possibly have it set aside. What do you mean by possibly? What would the impediments be?"

Ault came back to us. "I'd like to meet the man who says there are any, Bill. Or could be any." His voice was tight with menace.

"Look, Ault. If there are any impediments, we really ought to know. So as to know what to do," I said.

"I will not hear any more of your legal rot," Ault said. "It's nothing to do with me, so just drop it, it's upsetting me. I've got a brute of a headache, which I didn't have before you came!"

"Well, but Toby's right, Ault," Meiklejohn said. "Knowledge is the best defense, you know. We know you're whacked, this is very trying for you, and that's why we came. To help. But let's listen to Mr. Ross. Tell us what you meant, sir. Undue influence on the testator, right? Or forgery, maybe, of the will or of a signature on it? How about threats against other heirs to try forcing them out? Or maybe leaning on the attorney so as to get him to lean on the testator?"

"Speaking generally, yes," Ross said, and for the first time stirred uneasily in his chair. "But only generally."

"But I suppose," Meiklejohn went on, "I suppose that really the biggest bar to property rights is the failure to prove paternity, Mr. Ross?" His big blue eyes were guileless as a child's, and I wondered if he was as scared as I of what had to be the lawyer's response, and Ault's reaction to it.

There was no reason why Ross should have suspected Ault of anything, and I don't think he did, but our prodding had made him uneasy. He waffled, as I would in his place, and repeated what he had said about insufficient evidence of paternity being the biggest bar to property rights.

"No, it isn't, Bill," Ault said, sitting down in the metal chair and crossing his legs calmly, all suggestion of tension gone. "It's murder. You couldn't have forgotten that. Murder is the gravest bar of all. A slayer cannot profit by his wrongdoing, you see." He spread his hands, waiting for our assent, the way he always did, then slapped his thighs lightly and stood up.

"What we all need is a good drink and dinner," he said. Meiklejohn and I, and probably Pat, had heard him say it so many times. "And I've scouted the kitchen. I'm going to give you a marvelous meal and then I'll tell you the rest of my plans. I hope you're all very fit. As for me, I'm starving!"

Ross stood up too. "Impossible, Dr. Allyn. I can't allow you to make free with this house. As Mr. Shelton's executor I have the responsibility to protect the assets of the estate, and until the estate is settled, anyone in here except myself is a trespasser. So rather than asking you all baldly to leave, let me take you as my guests to the Biltmore House. It's the most popular place in the whole western part of the state. I'll just use the phone in the study and call for a reservation. I'll join you outside in a few minutes." He took a handkerchief out of his back pocket and mopped his forehead as he disappeared. I wondered if he was going to call the police as well as, possibly instead of, the hotel, because Ault was looking thunderous.

"He's right, Ault," I said, standing up and stretching. "I'm a lawyer's son, remember? I mean, technically Ross has no choice. Come on, let's drink and dine in Asheville and go over all this tomorrow. We may even get back to Chapel Hill for Becker, remember?"

"Hey, Ault," Meiklejohn said, "I've read about that Biltmore. What a place! French Renaissance chateau on eleven thousand acres. Seventy-two-foot banquet hall, with a ceiling that arches up to seventy-five feet. And Gothic thrones, for godsake, and rare Flemish tapestries. And fantastic food. Plus, there's a four-acre walled garden the guidebook says is the finest English garden in the You Ess of Ay. Just your cup of tea, right, Toby? So why don't we stay the night, see the sights, and then head back to the conference?"

"I know the Biltmore very well," Ault said. His eyes were glittering wildly again, and he looked from Meiklejohn to me without seeing us, the color high in his cheeks. "Go on out, and take her with you. I'll only be a minute. I left my coat in my father's study."

He watched Meiklejohn reach the front door and open it. He waited for Pat and me to follow, Pat dragging herself up off the couch like a broken thing. Only then did he leave the room, snatching up the brandy bottle, holding it like a club.

"He hurt me, Toby," Pat whispered. "When I wouldn't – I wouldn't – he raped me. Help me, Toby, please. He's crazy, he's out of his head."

I put a warning finger to her lips, and the three of us stood stock still, the door halfway open.

From the room into which Ault had followed Ross came first one voice then the other uttering animal sounds of fear and rage. Then glass shattered. There was a heavy thud. Then a triumphant laugh.

The three of us were frozen in place.

Ault appeared, brushing off his jacket. When he saw us he said happily, "Bill won't be coming, after all."

He reached inside his jacket, took out a small flat gun, released its safety catch, pointed it at me. "I'll have your cane, I think, Toby."

I gave it to him.

He smiled, amused. "Good. Sit down. On the couch. You too, John, Pat."

We sat.

Gun dangling on the middle finger of his right hand, he broke the cane across his thigh, and at once a deafening noise filled the room, a black hole appeared in the fine carpet, and acrid smoke stung our eyes and nostrils.

He bent down and looked regretfully at the hole.

"It can be mended," Meiklejohn said. "Don't worry."

Ault stood up; looked contemptuously at him. "You didn't fool me, not for a minute. Either of you. Don't try again. Now. This is what we're going to do."

Again there was that instant mood shift. He smiled as before, happily. "I've been planning this for a long time. Something I've wanted to share with you three since Toby came aboard. First we're going to eat. In my kitchen. In my house. My home. And then we're going out for a walk. In my mountains. All we have to do is pack the car and go."

And that was what we did.

By dawn the Merc was smoothly through Waynesville, Dillsboro, Bryson City, little Lauada, and other places I scarcely saw for fatigue and pain. At length Ault left Route 19 for Route 28, heading west and north to Fontana Village, the three of us tied up and rigid as mannequins in the big back seat.

$\triangledown$

25

AULT HAD PACKED BRILLIANTLY. Out of the Merc, which he left safely in Fontana Village, came four perfect packs, along with sweaters, woolen caps, down parkas, and rain gear. But one thing, other than trail fitness, even he could not provide — footwear. He would not let us stop to look for any, though it was unlikely anyway that even at the height of the season this little resort town, torpid now, could accommodate Meiklejohn's enormous feet.

By the time we reached the overlook at Fontana Dam some three miles away, we were exhausted and stale, having slept in our clothes in the Shelton living room until Ault took us away at four in the morning. Meiklejohn scuffed along in his shapeless loafers. My stump, unbathed and unchanged since I had left Virginia, was a fiery shrinking lump in its brand-new container. Pat was limping barefoot. Ault told her to put her shoes back on. Then, surprisingly, he bent and brushed away her fumbling hands and tied the laces.

At his command we gazed dully at the sparkling lake far below, and at the high blazing mountains.

"Magnificent achievement, this dam," he said. We said obediently that it was.

"Before the TVA built it in '46, this was the poorest major river basin in the whole country."

We said we didn't know that.

"Know what the TVA made possible? Industry and flood control and recreation and power service. Prosperity, folks. For people whose annual income didn't average much more than three hundred dollars. Impressive!"

Very, we said.

"Sure, and do you know how many homes drowned under all that water? how many farms and roads and meadows and little burying grounds and broken precious toys? Do you know what accomplished all that progress? Strip mining, that's what! Have you the least idea what that's done to these mountains?"

My father and I had pored over photographs of the violated mountains. I could still hear him curse the miners and lumbermen and developers, the lawyers and judges who had raped them, stolen their riches, dispossessed their people. Ault's passion was waxing, but I ventured to say yes, I had some idea.

"You know nothing, Harvard man," Ault said with a bitter look that almost knocked me down. Coldly he told us to get moving.

We were on the hard-surfaced foot-punishing road that runs along the lake. Presently Ault herded us away and into the woods, and I knew, if the others didn't, that we were heading for the Great Smokies.

"Easier on the feet, this path," Meiklejohn said. I said it wouldn't help much. Ault told us to shut up.

"For godsake!" Meiklejohn exploded, whirling around to face him. "What the hell's the matter with you, Ault? And what's this caper all about? Can't we even—" He gasped down the barrel of Ault's gun.

"No," Ault said. "You can't." He had fitted a silencer to the gun. "And don't ever speak in that tone to me again. Apologize."

"I thought we were friends, Ault," Meiklejohn said.

"I'm waiting."

"Sure, if you tell me—"

Dust exploded not half an inch from his foot, the sound of the bullet nothing like so great as the surprise of it. He staggered backward and fell, untidily.

Ault laughed. "Get up, you fat fool."

I moved to help.

"No," Ault said. "No help. Go on, John, get up. If you can."

I looked away and saw Pat crying, and eventually Meiklejohn got up and Ault put away his gun and we went on.

Warm fingers of sunlight touched us, but the air, six or seven hundred feet up now, was cool. At two, three, four, five thousand feet and more, if Ault could manage to get us up that far, it would be cold, dark, and damp. And when the rain began, which, here, could happen at any moment . . .

Think about something else, I thought, limping along caneless in front of Ault and his madness and his gun, and despite everything I began to look around. There wasn't much to see along this mid-November path but summer's dregs, like faded goldenrod quivering in the breeze, or a waist-high snakeroot, its white flowers spent but its large-toothed leaves still bright green and their poison still potent. If I see any more, I'll pick it, I thought, and wondered how much of it would kill him and how I could prepare a lethal dose and how I could get it into him—

I spotted a dead sturdy branch with a V on one end, and picked it up.

"Drop that," Ault said.

Not looking at him, I measured the branch against my length and broke it smartly off.

"Drop it. I will not tell you a third time."

"Come on, Ault," I said, calmly neatening up the branch, wishing I could brain him with it, "you need me and I need this." I set the V under my armpit and went on, knowing that my crossing him, and my reason for doing so, had intensified his dark, dreadful happiness. The climax would be a while yet. Before then I would have found—I had to find!— some way to foil him. God! I thought, if only René and Jean could come galloping down the trail right now like a couple of Royal Mounties!

Two nights ago I had told them everything, and they no longer ridiculed my mountain-man theory. Jean was now convinced that my "treep" would settle everything, not in Harpers Ferry or Chapel Hill or Asheville but at the Jump Up in the Nantahalas, where Ault had left me to die, or on Grassy Ridge Bald, which he had pointedly mentioned to Pete Flori. René had disagreed. The Roan massif was too public for someone like Ault. " 'E is secretive an' wild like the boar, greedy like the bear. An' like both, stubborn to the death. The end weel be, I theenk, een the Smokies. Ah, eef thees one time we could to Knoxville fly, per'aps to Gatlinburg, an' the Trail from Davenport Gap take sout' an' meet you coming up!"

Simple? Not even if the air force dropped them from a 'copter. Not even if they knew we'd at least be on one of the blue-blazed trails. Unless we stood on a bald that really was bald, they'd never see us. Ault wouldn't stay on the blue-blazed trails anyway. He'd whip us up into some mountain fastness where few if any men have gone, where even René and Jean could never find us, pitting his enormous competence and unquenchable anger against mountains, bears, boars, weather, and not caring, in the end, if even he survived. Not wanting to.

Hey, listen, I told myself, that's just the worst-case scenario. Keep a good thought. But for all the fire in my stump I was cold and wished more than anything that Ault would let us stop and make cocoa, the hiker's comfort. I wished I had my trail guide with me, although he probably would not allow me to look at it. I wished I'd never thought to flush him once and for all out of the shadows by coming south. I wished I'd stayed at Harvard.

And knew, as I had known for a long time, that I didn't have a thing to say about any of it.

We dragged ourselves up a ridge, from which a fire tower was visible — Shuckstack, Ault said — and collapsed at a gap a few miles on. The day was still clear and the fine view to the south was one of the few we might get to see at this or any time of year, but the three of us slipped out of our packs and lay on the ground. We could not have mustered among us one weak blow to Ault's power. He spent several unselfconscious minutes enjoying the view, then allowed us two swallows of water from our canteens and told us to get up. We couldn't.

"Just a mile and a half to the shelter, a good hot meal, and bed. Come on, guys, you can do it." He sounded like the kind of Boy Scout leader kids genuinely love, and we believed him and gathered ourselves up and went on. But it was a good thing that the shelter, when we reached it after a punishing climb, was down a little slope. If Paradise itself had awaited us up a slope however gentle, we wouldn't have had the strength to say the hell with it, but fallen where we stood.

Meiklejohn collapsed sick and gray-faced onto one of the dozen wire bunks, wiped out less by weight and poor condition than by totally inadequate shoes, which do a number on the entire skeletal system and geometrically increase fatigue. Pat fell onto another bunk and turned to the wall, rocking herself gently until she fell asleep. Ault was already gathering firewood. I stood my crutch against a wall and set about unpacking food for supper. A man has his pride, I told myself. Which goeth before a fall, my inner voice said, and shut down, at last, out of exhaustion.

The low ground in the shelter area was muddy and littered. "A poor view," Ault said apologetically, halfway into the meal.

"But a damn good supper," I said. "And we can do a cleanup in the morning."

Meiklejohn and Pat would not eat, and maybe it was just as well; food might give them diarrhea or vomiting or both. But the evening was cold and getting colder. Tenderly Ault brought them sweetened tea. They drank a little, and fell asleep again, and we sat in an astoundingly companionable, utterly natural silence and listened to the deepening night.

Ault said, "I want to show you something," and took from his breast pocket a little oilskin pouch. He handed it to me and switched on his flashlight.

Inside the oilskin was a letter, brown with age, and stained. I opened it carefully, my hands trembling in the unwavering circle of light.

It was dated December 6, 1941, and said, "Dear Liddy, Reverend Jonas just brought me the great news. We'll call him Ault after my father, and Allyn after yours. I'll be with you soon. Your Randal."

The handwriting was large and clear, as if written by or for a child.

"She couldn't read, my poor mother," Ault said. "She learned on that. She could read pretty well when she died. She was so proud of herself."

"He didn't come?"

"Pearl Harbor came. He enlisted the next day. Maybe he had to, maybe he wanted to. He never wrote again. She died in '44. Of grief, they said. But she was always sick. I remember the day she died. It rained. God, how it rained. The coffin was just a wooden box. They wrapped her in blue calico. It was pretty. She'd never had a dress that pretty. The box was wrapped in black. The dye ran."

"And then?"

"Then? Then I grew up. Some social workers studied the whole area and said our community was the neediest in the southern mountains. They did what they could to help. They taught sanitation and child care and about Christmas and how to earn a living. They helped us start a little school and let me go to it when I was four because my grandparents had no one to leave me with when they went out to work. Some of my classmates" — he laughed sourly — "were men in their twenties. We sat on the floor. I learned even then. Then the developers tricked us off our mountains and I wound up in the city. I was bright. I knew by then who my father was. So just before my grandfather died, he took me to see him. Bill Ross was there, so my father agreed to help. He might not have, otherwise. Medical care, clothes, that sort of thing. He even paid for my grandfather's funeral."

"But this?" Meaning the letter, which lay between us. "Didn't this help?"

Ault picked it up, gave it a careless flick of his fingernails, reached out, and tossed it into the fireplace.

"Ault!"

He smiled wryly. "That's how much it helped. I only kept it this long because I wanted you to see it."

"But — but what did he say?"

171

"Something memorable. He said that if he claimed every brat he'd gotten on the mountain girls, he could have his own army."

"That many?"

"God knows. I only knew six or seven. All dead now." He began gathering up the remains of supper. "I stood while I ate, you know, Toby. The grown-ups used the chairs. We ate off the covers of the lard pails. My father ate off the finest china. I saw it once, after I read the society columns in the Asheville papers about his coming wedding and the settlement he was making on her and all the rest of it. He was forty-two and it was his first. I went to see him, though I'd seen him many times before, as Bill Ross said. But this time I showed him the letter and demanded my rights."

"And?"

"And he laughed. Said it was as much proof of paternity as you could stick in your eye. That the most he'd do was put me through university, but only if I kept shut about it. The wife-to-be had everything he had — family, money, connections, education, looks — and he wanted all of that too. But she was Snow White, the Virgin Queen, and she could overlook his reputation but not his bastard. He'd have been out on his ear. So he wouldn't even bother asking her to let him recognize me. I was only five years younger than she was anyway, he said, and surely I could understand the many ramifications."

"Did you ever ask him again?"

"Several times. He didn't like being asked, and I didn't like being turned down. He was sorrier than I was, in the event." He slapped his thighs lightly, as he always did, and got up. "Well. Let's bear-proof this place and get to bed."

We cleaned up, hung the packs from trees, relieved ourselves, and settled into our bunks, Ault last because he had to secure the chain link across the front of the shelter.

"Toby—" he said, and stopped, and I could hear him lying down.

"Yes, Ault?"

". . . Nothing. Thanks for the talk. Sleep well."

"You too," I said, falling deliciously into sleep. The long difficult impossible unbelievable day was done, all that had happened in it a wild misunderstanding. Some grotesque jokester had inserted a chunk of another time into ours, that was it. But tomorrow would be normal, Ault as normal as he'd been all evening, and we would get back to Fontana Village and go home—

Piercing screams of terror and pain woke me.

26

THE SPACE ENCLOSED BY floor, roof, and three stone walls held a rancid stink. Bear. From my bed on the back wall I could see its mass against the dimness of the night as it bent snorting and grunting over the bunk nearest the shelter's open side. Since our arrival Pat had lain there motionless and beyond hunger. Now she struggled, screaming, to free herself from the mummy bag that Ault and I had zipped her into. It was a trap, a soft clinging prison that even Ault could not open in such a situation. Had he deliberately chosen it for her instead of a rectangular, Velcro-fastened bag?

The bear grasped its prize in its powerful jaws and dragged it off the bunk. As it backed out of the shelter, the screams stopped. There was no sound from Meiklejohn. I wasn't even sure he was still there.

I ripped open my sleeping bag and swung my one leg to the floor. Hopeless to try putting on the prosthesis—I would have had to take off my slacks first, and that would have been only the beginning. There was nothing else for it. I reached for the crutch, set it under my arm, and launched a hopping bellowing rush on the bear.

It must have been old or sick or starved, because it would not open its jaws and either fight or run. An easy target. With the crutch end I stabbed again and again at its eyes and nose, balancing as best I could, shouting, staggering, falling on Pat as momentum carried me onto my one knee. I rolled over and away, tangling myself up in the empty pant leg. In a panic I almost stopped to tear it off, but I managed to get up, still yelling for all I was worth. I raised the crutch for another strike and hit the bear solidly between the eyes.

Frightened and confused at last, it let go of Pat and stood up on its hind legs with a roar like a human cry. I balanced as on a high wire, expecting an attack, since we were approximately the same height and I was menacingly close, an enemy who could and must be taken. Instead, the bear rubbed its face where I had hurt it and lumbered off into the woods crying like a child.

I collapsed panting and sweating in the chill air and bent over the sleeping bag. It was torn now and smelled of bacon as well as bear. I noticed too that there were bits of food on the ground under my hand.

That bastard, that lunatic. That utter swine. He had smeared bacon grease on the sleeping bag, opened the chain-link, scattered food in the clearing, and hidden somewhere in the night, up a tree, probably, to wait and see what would happen. I wanted to kill him, that charming psychopath who had fooled me so many times. Choking rage rose in me; rage and helplessness. I couldn't see, I was so stifled and blinded with it.

Pat stirred and whimpered. Unable to slide out of the bag, she had managed to get deeper in and hold on. I pulled the zipper down a little and gathered her into my arms, rocking her, saying her name, kissing her forehead and telling her it was all right and I loved her and it was all right now. She trembled and clung, sobbing deep shuddering sobs, gasping my name. Presently she quieted. And then, amazingly, she was asleep.

We couldn't stay there, it was too cold and there were other aggressive animals about. But I couldn't pick her up and carry her in, or shell her like a nutmeat and get her standing. I began bellowing again, for Meiklejohn, angry at him now for being another dead weight, my anger cold fire against this brisk night.

A voice said in my ear, confidentially, "I didn't want to shoot the poor creature. I might have hit you. Besides, he'd more right than you to be here. Come on, let me help. You did well, boy."

I hadn't heard him come, the bastard. And doubly bastard for making me so grateful for his approval, so proud to have it. I felt my cheeks burn with waves of rage and pride. *Felt*. It *felt* perfectly natural to take this murderer's hand and let him pull me up. Rational thought was beyond me.

Still no sound from Meiklejohn. But now I didn't care. The matter of the bear had been a test, and only I had passed it. Everything was going to be all right at last. I closed my eyes.

Something shook me awake, the voice harsh and loud. The bear, back to wreak his vengeance, and too close to fight off again. I had nothing left to fight with. I covered my face and waited, whimpering, for his paws to tear my hands away and smash my head to pulp.

But it was Ault, derisively ordering me to "git up." My surprise was as total as my terror. I fumbled my way out of both, dizzy and ashamed.

Cold rain was drumming on the metal roof, and Ault had made no fire. He woke the others and gave us cold water and crackers, watchful and silent as we ate. Then we cleaned up the place, relieved ourselves in shame like children committing an unspeakable act, packed our gear, and stumbled away in a heavy fog that blanketed everything in the world but a few feet of slippery trail before us.

Meiklejohn and Pat could hardly walk on their swollen feet and legs, and Pat's sleeve, I saw now, was torn from bear teeth, and bloody. Ault commanded her to go ahead of me, and she nodded dully to me as she passed, as if she didn't remember what had happened in the night. Meiklejohn did, because he reddened and didn't meet my eyes. I despised him for his cowardice. And saw in it a reflection of my own.

Full consciousness flooded back at last. Mentally I apologized to Meiklejohn, and began to conserve my strength and sharpen my awareness. Even if it made no difference in the end, and it couldn't, at least all the garbage in my head would have been burned away and I'd die, as it were, clean. I can go with that, I told myself, and thought that in the circumstances a bad pun was something to be *getting on* with. I almost laughed out loud.

We hadn't gone much more than a mile up the narrow path, from which the ground fell away to the left, when Meiklejohn groaned behind me. I turned and saw him sink to his knees and bend over, hitting his forehead on a stone. For a few seconds he balanced thus, as in submission, then slowly slipped one arm out of his pack strap and rolled onto his side, his back against the rising ground on the right. Ault came up from behind and kicked his buttocks and ordered him to get up. His eyelids fluttered. He moved his lips but no sound came.

"Gawd damn yuh, git up!" Ault shouted. "Git on yuh feet, Ah said!" He took out his gun, the silencer still on it, and fired. Stone chips and sand burst up in a little geiser, and blood dotted Meiklejohn's gray sagging face.

He had been lying doggo for hours, even forgoing food, awaiting the chance to fight back. Almost in one movement he got halfway to his feet, freed his other arm, and hurled his pack at Ault, who ducked and shot wide. Meiklejohn rushed him but lost his balance and slipped and fell off the path. Ault fired two more bullets after him as he crashed and tumbled down the hill, scaring the birds out of the trees. He disappeared into underbrush and heavy fog, and the birds quieted and everything was silent.

I took off my pack and started down the hill. Another shot, un-silenced this time, resounded through the forest. Again the birds erupted, squawking frantically, and Pat screamed my name.

"Git up heah or Ah kill yuh," Ault said quietly, his voice carrying easily.

"Go ahead and kill me," I said over my shoulder, and kept going, knowing he wasn't going to kill me, not yet.

Another tremendous roar sent me flying into the underbrush. I lay there wondering what had happened and where I had been shot. Nothing hurt except the bruises one collects from falling down a hill. Ault had only been bluffing.

My crutch was somewhere around, and I would have to find it, so as to get to Meiklejohn. I held on to a tree, got up on my right leg, took a step, and fell immediately, driving my stump into a tangle of plastic and steel. It was my turn to scream.

Ault's delighted laugh floated down to me. He hadn't been bluffing, just accomplishing my destruction in deliciously slow stages by smash-ing my wonderful new leg.

27

I<small>N</small> THE COLD RAIN Ault sat smiling on his haunches and dry under his poncho, twirling the gun indolently around his finger and watching me pull myself up the slope. Then he got up and gave me a hand and yanked me to my foot. I leaned against a tree, resting.

"Git shut o' that," he said, pointing his gun at the ruin in my slacks.

It had to be done, but I would sooner have clawed up a thousand mountainsides than obey him. He understood why I hesitated. He *knew*. He wanted to *see*. His eyes burned again with that insane glitter. His firm thin lips were parted in anticipation of a wonderful treat. My hands refused to move.

"Git on with it," he snarled. "I ain't got all day."

So I had to drop my slacks and take off the pelvic band that held up so much expensive plastic and steel. But this was smashed into the fabric, and I couldn't pull it out without at least removing the shoe in which the Seattle foot fitted so perfectly. I tried to bend, lost my balance, fell. Pat made no move to help.

The cold wet bit through my briefs as I worked the ruined apparatus free. The cotton socks on my stump came with it, and I sat helpless and humiliated beyond anything I had ever endured while rain fell on the lump of red swollen flesh and Ault squatted to look.

God, he was so close, so close, his face not two feet from mine. I wanted to throw myself on him, him and that gun of his, and end it. He might not be ready yet, but I was.

I hadn't purchase enough for a good spring. On the other hand I didn't have far to go, and the gun wasn't cocked. So I mustered my forces and sprang, hitting him solidly in the chest with my head and both hands. I knocked him flat, and heard the gun land in the brush.

"Get it! Pat, the gun! Get it!" I yelled.

Ault's powerful arms squeezed me tight and he rolled me over onto my back, grinning at me in enormous pleasure, aware that his weight was grinding my stump into the dirt. I howled in pain. Holding me down easily with one hand, he raised the other and—

When I came to, he was standing a few feet away, pointing the gun at me again, his face a neutral mask, and Pat was kneeling at my side, crying softly and cradling her cheek in her hand.

I tremblingly felt my jaw. Not broken but hugely swollen and bloody from the carnelian ring that Ault had taken off his dead half brother. With a reluctance that couldn't have escaped him or failed to please him, I sat up and assessed the dirty damage to my stump. There was a lot of it, and all I could do was cover it with the wet dirty cotton socks. I rolled from side to side, hitching up my slacks. Buckled my belt over the empty pant leg. Tried getting up. Couldn't. Felt the prosthesis under my hand and casually tossed it off the path, thinking, If René and Jean were anywhere around, they'd find it as they'd found me fifteen years ago, but someone will see it and make inquiries. The shoe I ignored. As if he'd read my mind, Ault gave me an ironic glance, retrieved both, and buried them under a rotting log.

Again he yanked me up and helped me settle my pack. "Now git goin'."

I hopped once, and fell to hands and knee, hopelessly unbalanced. I began to laugh. Ault kicked me. This time I went all the way down, onto my swollen jaw. I laughed again because it hurt so much and because suddenly everything was really very funny.

"Git up!" he shouted, and fired off a bullet that whizzed past my ear.

The forest rang with the explosion, and I shrieked with laughter. "What am I supposed to do, you lunatic? Fly?" I smelled the cordite, and laughed and laughed.

He brought me upright by the hair and whispered almost lovingly in my ear, "Find y'se'f a crutch stick, boy. Git goin' 'n' find y'se'f a crutch stick. He'p 'm, gal. *Ah said he'p 'm!*"

Pat moved to my side, stupid and sluggish, the marks of his fingers red on her cheek, and he let go of me. I slipped an arm around her shoulders, under her pack, and looked about for a forked branch like the one I had dropped down the hill. Nothing. We would have to find another along the way. Pity, when the good one I'd had was not very far down the hill. I started to say this, and Ault gave me a rude shove. So we started up the narrow path, which was pretty clean in the middle but rough with broken encroaching brush along the sides, and with each hop Pat caved in a little more.

Impossible to continue like this even if we were perfectly matched, perfectly fit, perfectly shod. Another hop was beyond us both. I let go of her and sank to the ground, bending over under the weight of my pack.

"You'll have to think of something better, Ault," I said, and noticed how quiet with surprise he was, and how deep the quiet was, how still the mountain, how soundless the falling rain, how my anger and bitterness were seeping out of me into the earth drop by drop along with my strength. I didn't care anymore. My anger and bitterness were done, and I was done.

"It could have been good, you know, walking the clouds together," I said, meaning it, meaning a time when I had been innocent and uninfected and he could still have saved himself. "But you ballsed it up, Ault, you, who had more than most people. How much more did you have to have to make it?"

Talking hurt. I closed my eyes. What did I care what his answer was? Anyway, I knew what it was. I'd heard it before.

He said hoarsely, "I wanted what you had," and I could hear him pull out his gun. He was just about ready now. He was as close to ready as he would ever be.

"Sure," I said, ignoring Pat's gasp and her clutching hand. "Sure. A father who loved you. Now neither of us has one, or the chance of one. Whose fault is it, Ault? Tell me that. Who're you going to blame? What you want, most people never get, haven't the remotest chance of getting, or hadn't you heard?"

It was like so many fifty-minute hours I'd sat through, on either side of the desk, when shrink asks simple question, client plays dumb, and silence spreads.

Into this tremendous loaded quiet came the sound of voices descending the path. Ault pocketed the gun and looked over my shoulder. I turned and looked too.

Funny. I had imagined this moment, had seen myself leaping for joy on my beautiful new foot when somebody — anybody — arrived to save Pat and Meiklejohn and me. Now I was too tired to be saved.

There were three hikers, all soaked and filthy below their ponchos.

One said, "Hey, you guys got trouble? What's the matter? Can we help? You look all in, fella. What in hell happened to your face!"

I said, suddenly competent, "I fell. Broke my crutch. Say, you wouldn't happen to have any cocoa on you, would you?"

"Sure do," the spokesman said. "Come on down to the shelter with us, we'll make some for you. 'Cording to the book, it isn't far. You look like you could all do with a little of the hiker's friend. We sure can."

Ault's hand went into the pocket where the gun was.

I couldn't take a chance. I said, "We're going the other way, thanks all the same." I couldn't move, and Ault and Pat didn't, so, looking at us uncertainly, they walked around us and back onto the path.

One of them murmured something to the spokesman. He said, "Yeah, right!" and turned around to us. "Hey, you guys hear a couple or three gunshots just minutes ago? Sounded like they came from below us. Somewhere around here."

I saw Ault's hand come a little way out of the pocket with the gun in it.

I said, "We heard them too. I can't tell you where they came from, but there's a big fellow somewhere between here and the shelter who may be hurt. Could have been from one of those shots." Now it was Ault who gasped and froze. "Well, see you around."

"Yeah . . . Hey, listen, maybe it's none of my business, but you sure you're doing the right thing in your condition? The path's not all that well cleared in some spots. Where you heading?"

Ault said, "Gregory Bald trail."

"The— With *him*? Look, maybe I'm talking out of turn, but I happen to know that trail, and it's more a manway than anything else at this point. People don't use it all that much, see. You'll never make it," talking directly to me now, "not even if it was flat from here to there."

He took out a battered little blue guide and flipped the pages authoritatively. "Look," he said, "we're almost to the base of Greer Knob right here where we're standing. And you better believe it's a steep climb up—we just slid down it on our asses, so we know. The trail's like greased, this weather, and not all that well cleared, in case you hadn't noticed. And to get to Gregory Bald trail you got to skirt Greer Knob and then get up to Doe Knob, and that's even higher up at least two miles on, before you make that side trail. Assuming you even see the blaze. I'll tell you right now, we didn't, and we were looking for it too. Sure you know what you're doing?"

Ault nodded and I said no and Pat just stood there.

We looked, all six of us, like a diorama in a natural-history exhibit. Walkers Meet, I thought, and began to laugh again, idiotically, helplessly. "Ault," I sputtered, "don't you see? He's right. It's over," and collapsed onto my side, giggling like a silly kid.

He bent over me and whispered, "Git up 'n' git movin', or Ah'll kill 'em all," pressing so hard on a spot on my arm that it went numb and my fingertips tingled. With a show of solicitude he lifted me up and draped the now useless arm around Pat's shoulders.

His threat was like a blow under the ribs. The breath burst out of me in a grunt, and my fear for Pat and the three strangers, instead of lending me wings and power, drove me into the ground. I sank down again for the last time. One of them ran to help me, and Ault pulled out his gun.

"No," he shouted, and the safety catch went *snick*. "Git away. He's mine. We-uns is goin' on."

"Here, you bastard!" came a voice from somewhere, weak and strained but recognizable. Meiklejohn. "Down here! Want to try again?"

Mist and fog hid him from us — even on a clear day we couldn't have seen him — and played games with his voice. Ault whirled, pointing the gun here, there. No one else moved.

On the downslope shrubs crackled and snapped, wet though they were. Ault fired once, twice, and slipped out of his pack straps.

As the waves of sound rolled away into the trees, a familiar laugh rolled back like the returning tide, not so shattering as usual but reassuringly vigorous. "Missed, Ault! By a mile! Y'aren't going to make it, you fool! Gonna tie a *poem* 'round *your* neck —"

His face contorted with rage, Ault took a step into the brush and fired again, and the spokesman, with a feral howl, sprang onto Ault's back and bore him down.

They lay there as in another diorama — Trouble on the Trail. The stranger rolled off Ault and got up. Ault's legs twitched. His hand moved vaguely toward his neck or face. Then he was still.

Something was happening that I found I didn't want, after all. I crawled off the path to the prone body, shaking off the hindering hands, swearing at them, feeling nothing of my own pain, and reached Ault's head. His eyes dulled fast even as he recognized me, and his mobile lips twitched as if he were trying to tell me one last thing.

"Ault," I said, "Ault, wait, I'll help you. I'll help."

181

His eyes closed, seemed to close deliberately, as if to tell me why that wasn't possible. And he was right. I could see now that a slender brown stem was buried in his throat, the *stob* of a young shrub or tree that had been broken off by a walker's boot or the great paw of a bear going about some business of its own. And I could see his bright life spurting out of him, slower and slower, with each lagging beat of his angry heart.

And then he was gone.